Mercy of St. Jude

A Novel

Mercy of St. Jude

A Novel

Wilhelmina Fitzpatrick

St. John's, Newfoundland and Labrador
2011

Canadä

We gratefully acknowledge the financial support of the Canada Council for the Arts, the Government of Canada through the Canada Book Fund (CBF), and the Government of Newfoundland and Labrador through the Department of Tourism, Culture and Recreation for our publishing program.

Cover design by Maurice Fitzgerald
Layout by Amy Fitzpatrick
Printed on acid-free paper

Published by
CREATIVE PUBLISHERS
an imprint of CREATIVE BOOK PUBLISHING
a Transcontinental Inc. associated company
P.O. Box 8660, Stn. A
St. John's, Newfoundland and Labrador A1B 3T7

Printed in Canada by:
TRANSCONTINENTAL INC.

Library and Archives Canada Cataloguing in Publication

Fitzpatrick, Wilhelmina, 1958-
Mercy of St. Jude / Wilhelmina Fitzpatrick.

ISBN 978-1-897174-75-3

I. Title.

PS8611.I895M47 2011 C813'.6 C2011-901879-9

Dedication

For the men in my life - Keith, Ian and Michael.
In memory of my Aunt Beth.

PART ONE

1

1999

The coffin is mirrored in the night-black window. A gust of wind batters the pane, exploding the image. Within moments it settles back into place.

Annie Byrne looks past the reflection, shifting her focus to the houses of their neighbours, the patches of lawn struggling to survive on the rocky hillside. Several old tires filled with dirt line the side of her parents' yard, her mother's attempt to nurture a few flowers if the sun ever shines again.

Down the street a car pulls up. The door opens, closes. Annie stares intently at the dark sedan. No one gets out. She gives her head a shake; of course it's not him.

She turns away from the window. Against the opposite wall, the open casket rests on its bier, overwhelming the small room. The faded couch and worn wingback chairs have been shoved together in the corner to make space for it. Above the coffin, a crucifix. Pictures of saints line the walls, and on the wood veneer coffee table, surrounded by holy candles, sits a statue of the Virgin Mary, baby Jesus in her arms. The television is covered with a dark throw. The usual knick-knacks and doilies are gone; Annie's mother has put them away at this solemn time.

Annie does not feel solemn. She feels angry. And guilty, of course. What she wouldn't give for one last chance to confront Mercedes, to ask her what had made her so miserable that she couldn't bear to see anyone else enjoying life, especially Annie. But it's too late for that.

There is a clatter of dishes from the kitchen. "I said I'll wash up later, Mom," she calls down the hall.

"That's okay," Lucinda calls back. "Stay put and catch up with your cousins."

Annie still regrets having let her mother talk her into coming home. Two days earlier in Calgary, she'd been jarred awake by the phone, her heart racing with the panic of a call before dawn. The news did nothing to slow it down - Mercedes Hann was dead. Annie had held the phone tight, trying to stifle her resentment and her tears. The contradiction was not unusual where her great-aunt was concerned.

As she'd listened to the sadness in her mother's voice, she pictured her on the other end of the line, gently rounded with the years but still attractive at fifty.

"Never mind what trouble there was between you," Lucinda had insisted.

Annie had been adamant. "I'm not coming, Mom." *And I'm not sad she's dead.*

"Just for a couple of days. It's the least you can do."

"No, the least I can do is stay here."

"Always with that mouth. Bad as Mercedes herself, you are."

"Well, thanks for that." As a child, Annie had been flattered when her mother compared her to Mercedes, until she began to realize that it wasn't necessarily meant as a compliment. As an adult, Annie never took it as such.

"I don't know when you got so hard."

"I am not hard," Annie protested. She lowered her voice. "I'm just tired, Mom."

"Think of the family. I don't ask you for much, Annie, the Lord knows I don't."

"Yeah, yeah, I know. Look, it's five-thirty in the morning here. Let me wake up, will you?" Annie took a slow breath and lied. "I don't think I can get away from work." As a junior geologist in a large oil company she'd hardly be missed.

"Annie, the woman is dead—"

"See? She won't even notice."

"And before she died," Lucinda continued as if she hadn't heard, "she said you had to be here."

"What the hell for?"

"I don't know but your grandfather promised her you would be. So if you won't do it for her, do it for him. She was his sister and he's right torn up about it." She paused for effect. "Did you know the doctor's worried about his prostate again?"

Good one, Mom - Annie almost said it out loud. If anything happened to Callum Hann, Annie would be heartbroken, which Lucinda well knew. From her earliest memories of drifting off to sleep in his overstuffed rocker, to the winter evenings curled up by the fire, listening to the stories her sisters never cared for, her grandfather had given Annie a sense of her history and herself that she could not have gotten elsewhere, especially from her mother, and certainly not from Mercedes who, when it came to family history, was a closed book.

"Fine, all right, enough with the frigging guilt trip." The words were no sooner out than Annie regretted them. Why did their conversations so often end in argument, with her mother indignant and Annie remorseful? "I'll do it, okay?"

Now here she is, staring at the crucifix on the wall. Below it, nestled in a bed of white satin, a set of rosary beads winding through her interwoven fingers, rests Herself, the Great Mercedes Hann, whose dying wish had been to spend her final days being waked in Lucinda and Dermot's living room.

Across from the coffin Annie's father smiles in his sleep. Annie sits beside him and smoothes back his grey hair. It's thinner than she remembers. He's aged the last few years; his cheeks are more hollow, his forehead more lined. He yawns, his false teeth clacking as they ease out of position. Realigning them with his tongue, he smacks his lips together and opens his eyes. He smiles at her and gestures toward her cousins, Pat and Aiden Hann. "Just like the old days, you three sitting here."

Annie smiles back. At the end of the day, maybe her mother was right. It is good to be here with them all. She and Pat and

Aiden were born within a thirteen-month span of each other. They'd gone through school together too, as a result of Pat being held back in Grade One. Growing up, they were always up to something, from hopping the spring ice pans when they were little and forbidden to go near the water, to skipping Saturday night Mass so they could smoke cigarettes and drink beer with their friends in high school. Thanks to "the boys" as Lucinda calls them, Annie had gotten into trouble far more often than her sisters.

They hear the front door open and close, followed by footsteps padding down the carpeted hallway to the kitchen.

"Looks like we're not done yet," says Dermot, easing himself upright and reaching for the bottle on the table. He's already had a few, yet his hand is steady as he pours. He passes Annie a dram of his special stash, reserved for weddings and funerals. He'd cracked it open earlier that evening when Father James stopped by. The heady aroma of incense lingers in the room.

Annie takes it gratefully. "Thanks, Dad."

His hand touches her cheek. She reaches up and holds it there an extra moment.

Dermot pours two more. He gives one to Aiden and holds the other out to Pat. "Don't suppose you'd care for a drink?"

"I'm not here for the company." Pat takes a quick swallow.

Dermot starts to sit down then changes direction to turn off the larger lamp and light the candles. The mustard-coloured walls take on a golden hue. He leans against the coffin and nods. "That's better."

His Newfoundland brogue thickens with every sip of whiskey. Annie has heard her own voice grow flatter and faster since arriving home. In Calgary, she speaks more slowly and with clearer diction, a consequence of too many patronising remarks about her quaint accent.

Pat springs to his feet. "What the Christ are we going to do all night, sit and look at her?" His right hand, sporting a tattoo of a Celtic cross, runs through his overgrown dirty blond mane and matching scruffy beard, so unlike his brother, whose fine dark hair is always neatly trimmed, his face always clean shaven.

"Be one of the more peaceful nights you ever spent with her," says Annie.

"No more than you." He takes a sizeable drink then frowns at the small amount remaining in his glass. "She wouldn't even want me here." His voice is sullen.

"I thought I was finally shed of her, too," Aiden says. In recent years he'd been a frequent driver for Mercedes, running errands and generally being at her beck and call. It was the least he could do, she'd preached, after she'd helped him get an early parole.

"Now, now, sure you knows it's bad luck to be leaving a dead body unattended," Dermot reminds them. "Besides, she'll be six feet under this time tomorrow."

A draught blows in through the open window. Annie inhales the salt air coming up off the bay. A five-minute scramble down the hill behind her parents' house would have her feet in the Atlantic. As a girl she liked to watch out the kitchen window on a stormy day, snug by the wood stove, cocoa in hand. When the wind died down, she'd spend hours scouring the rocks, looking for treasure the raging sea might have flung up onto the beach. On calmer days she'd scale the cliffs along the shore. Hugging the layered rock face, she'd scan the waves, imagining what it would be like to be caught up in that great big ocean, unprotected by family, far away from everyone she knew.

The breeze makes the candles flicker. Their shadows dance on the wall and the coffin, leaving Annie with the unnerving impression that the corpse itself has moved. A shiver runs down her back. "Good Lord, I could have sworn Mercedes was about to rise up from the box."

Pat hurries to shut the window. "That's nothing to joke about, Annie."

"Always thought she had unfinished business with you, Pat."

Aiden leans back in his chair, his stocky limbs stretching out in all directions like a contented cat. His stutter is barely perceptible these days, thanks to countless hours talking to himself in the mirror. It still shows up occasionally when he's drinking.

"Frig off, Aiden. You're just tempting Satan with that kind of talk."

Pat turns abruptly as the living room door opens. Sadie Griffin pokes her head in.

"Speak of the devil," he whispers, sitting down next to Annie.

Sadie clip-clops in as if she owns the place, talking non-stop and charging the room with her unique aroma of yesterday's sweat and cheap perfume. In Annie's memory, Sadie has never changed. She's always been a little, grey-haired busybody.

"My dear Dermot, I just finished setting out Father James's brekkie and I thought I had to drop in to see our Mercedes..."

Annie groans under her breath. "Just what I frigging need."

Pat nods sympathetically. More than anyone, he knows that Sadie Griffin is the last person Annie would want to see. "She's here twice a day." He leans closer, his voice low. "Old bag thinks she's family or something."

In fact, the families are connected on several fronts. Mercedes' mother and Sadie's father were brother and sister. And Sadie's husband, Angus, was the son of their stepsister, Nell, who was also Dermot's mother by a different father. It's an incestuous muddle that does not sit well with Annie's family, although it doesn't seem to bother the Griffins.

On top of that, fifty years earlier Angus's father, Paddy, also known as the town pervert, convinced Mercedes' senile father, Farley, to go to Toronto with him. The two men were never seen again. The Hanns have mistrusted the Griffins ever since.

And rightly so, in Annie's opinion. The Griffin lineage is riddled with undesirables, heavy drinking types always on for a fight, loans left unpaid up and down the shore, illegitimate babies scattered from bay to bay. Each generation seems to perpetuate the family's objectionable ancestry more than the last.

"…the poor thing," Sadie is prattling on, "she had her bad days but she was a good soul, never spared when it came to helping at the convent or them youngsters in Africa, sending money when yourselves hardly made ends meet, such a wonderful woman…" She barely pauses for breath, her covetous eyes touching everything and everyone along the way as her kitten-heels clack across the wood floor to where Dermot stands by the coffin, whiskey glass in hand. "…hard to let go isn't it, Derm, though Lord knows you weren't that lovey-dovey when she was alive but you got to leave her in peace." Sadie's voice rises in pained, cheerful admiration. "Some lovely in that black dress, my, it does become her with them silvery tresses, imagine never needing a dye job, never looked better." She dabs her dry eyes and takes Dermot's empty glass and plunks it down on the coffee table. "Now, Derm, leave her be so she can go with the Lord, and come back out to the kitchen and we'll get a cup of tea into you before I heads out the road, it'll fix you right up…" Still nattering, she tucks her arm into his and hustles him out of the room.

Pat waits until the door shuts behind them. He nudges Annie. "Remember that night we wrote on her sidewalk?"

"Christ, don't remind me. 'ANGUS IS GAY, SO THEY SAY,' in red spray paint. Sadie scrubbed at that for days. Finally had to cover it over with black shoe polish."

"He was still a goddamn fag, no matter what colour you paint it," says Aiden.

"And you're still a homophobe." Annie wags a finger at him. "Better be careful, Aiden. A gay friend of mine in Calgary says there's a little bit of queer in all of us."

Pat holds out his palms as if weighing the options. "Gay or Sadie? I'd pick gay."

"Redneck Calgary?" Aiden looks doubtful. "Didn't think they had queers out there."

"I'd rather be one there than here, with small-minded gossips like Sadie running the place." Annie sighs. "Poor Mom, just what she needs tonight, Sadie in there shaking her tail feathers at Dad."

They all nod knowingly, for therein lies another point of contention between the two families. Years before, Dermot and Sadie had been going around together, but once he laid eyes on Lucinda, Sadie was salt. And who would blame him? Except Sadie, who was more likely to blame Lucinda anyway.

"I'm telling you, Annie, that one still got the hots for your father," Aiden says. "He'll be lucky to make it down that dark hallway in one piece."

"Don't be so foolish, Aiden," Pat scoffs. "They're all too old for that nonsense."

"Mom'll be getting rid of her some fast."

Sure enough, within the minute they hear the front door open, followed by Sadie's voice. "We'll be seeing you tomorrow, Lucinda, and now go get some rest, you're looking that dragged out you are and call me if you needs anything, what's family for now, Lucinda dear, just call anytime."

There is a mumble, presumably from Lucinda. The door shuts extra firmly.

"Did you hear her going on? 'Some lovely in that black dress.'" Aiden's imitation of Sadie is bang on. "'Silvery tresses' my arse."

"'Never looked better,'" adds Pat. "What a stupid thing to say."

As Annie listens, images of Mercedes drift through her mind, unsmiling, serious, alone. Mercedes had only ever seemed to thaw when she was with Callum or Lucinda, or Gerry Griffin, of course. Once upon a time she was like that with Annie too, but that was before the day they faced each other down. "You'll be a nothing in a nothing town," had been her aunt's parting shot. Annie, her heart filled with hurt, had fired back, "Fuck you, Mercedes."

So why now does she feel this strange compassion? Because Mercedes died a spinster? Because she never enjoyed the routine contentment of sharing her bed with someone who loved her, of finding a warm, wanted body next to hers in the black of night? At least Mercedes had made that decision herself.

She hadn't allowed Annie the choice. For that Annie would never forgive her.

The cool June wind whips up off the waves, over the break-water and onto Water Street. An empty chip bag flies up off the ground. It soars for a moment, then drops. Every now and then, a whiff of decaying seaweed, of dead fish perhaps, rushes up from the shore. Sadie Griffin is small against the wind, in-significant against the force of the ocean. Still, she moves for-ward, her path almost straight. Sadie barely notices the cold. Indignation keeps her warm.

Goddamn Hanns. Frigging Lucinda. Fed up with the lot of them.

Sadie's hand catches at the thin scarf around her neck. The wind has loosened it so that one end has come free and is whip-ping about high in the air. She pulls it down, tucks it into her coat and forges onward.

Door practically hit me on the arse she shut it so hard. Pity poor Derm, stuck with that one forever. And them two brothers, not a decent brain between the pair of them. To think they used to make fun of my Gerard. Well, look at them all now. Gerard showed them, he did. And that Annie. I knows all about her, I do. Too chicken to lift her head up in the parlour there. Could-n't even look me in the eye. Thank God I got Gerard away from that little tramp. Imagine messing around with one of them Hanns. Hah! One Hann less now Mercedes bit the biscuit.

Sadie looks up only when she passes the priest's house.

Lights off. Good, I didn't forget. Wonder what Father will have to say tomorrow. Father James, now there's a good one. Wouldn't mind cleaning his house. Fine looking man. Fine arse on him, too. Nothing better than a priest.

Sadie looks at her watch. She picks up speed, elbows bent, fists into the wind.

Gerard be here soon. Home to his mother. Ah, Gerard. My Gerard.

Gerry Griffin eases up on the accelerator. He turns off the highway and onto the road leading into St. Jude. He rolls down the window and listens, trying to distinguish the ocean from the noise of the engine and the wind flying past the car. Before he hears it, he sees it, the white tips dancing on a sea of black. It's one of the few things he misses.

He takes the first right up a street of middle-class houses, some well kept, others not, all in better shape than the one he grew up in. Two doors down from her house, he pulls over. He draws a long, deep breath. The instant he opens the car door he sees her. He pulls the door shut. She stands in the window, her face more clear to him than is possible at this distance, the fair skin framed by almost-black hair, shorter now but still thick, the distinct line of her nose that comes to a small sharp point above her lips, her mouth, soft and full. And her eyes. He has pictured her face every day for five years; always he stops at her eyes, one moment green and warm as late-summer grass, the next, so vulnerable, so wounded. Always he is left with that memory.

She moves away from the window. He is about to open the door again when he realizes that his face is wet with tears. This is not how he wants her to see him.

He drives on, down Main Street, past the Trade School, the town hall, the gas station. Near the centre of town is Burke's store, where old Mona Burke started selling groceries to make ends meet after her husband failed to return from a fishing trip. Over the years, extensions, including a motel wing, were added haphazardly; little of the charm of the original red barn remains. Burke's sells everything now, from groceries and fishing tackle to furniture and appliances. His mother shops there every day.

He parks in front of a small clapboard house at the other end of town. The lampshade by the door is still missing, leaving a bare bulb to illuminate the broken top step. The paint is still peeling. He wonders if his brothers drank away the money he left for repairs. This time he'll hire someone to do the job.

He's not long in the house before Sadie rushes in.

"Gerard, you're here!"

She looks windblown but otherwise much the same as when he was home six months earlier. Her dark eyes are only slightly faded and, except for the two deeply pitted frown lines on her forehead, her face is oddly smooth for a woman near sixty. On top of her head are waves of grey, her old-woman-do, he calls it. She can afford to have it coloured and styled but, even though it makes her look older, she refuses to change it. His monthly supplements would allow her to quit working if she wanted, to stop cleaning house for others and put her own feet up for a change. But she says no, she'll just grow old and die if she sits idle. She says nothing about the tidbits of gossip she picks up along the way, but Gerry knows that gossip keeps her young.

He holds out his arms. No matter what anyone else thinks about his mother, and despite the grief she has caused him, he loves her, and he knows that she loves him, more than she loves anybody, including her other three children. This is not something he is particularly comfortable with; it's a simple truth he's come to accept after twenty-five years, as have his sister and brothers.

With two strides he stands in front of her. He lifts her slight body off the floor as he hugs her, and feels her fierce strength as her short arms squeeze him tight. There is a smell of fresh peppermint and, behind that, something musty. She's been drinking.

"What you doing here so soon?" she asks when he sets her down. "Weren't expecting you till after midnight."

"I got an early flight, then rented a car and hit the highway."

"I'd known that, I'd come straight home. Wish you'd called."

Gerry takes her coat and hangs it on a nail. "Didn't get a

chance." In truth, he needed time once he got here, time to see Annie. He couldn't tell his mother that.

"Well, I'm happy you're here is all I knows." She looks him over. He knows what's coming next. "You're after losing weight. Too skinny by far. Not eating right up in that Toronto, are you? You needs a good boil-up."

"A cup of tea would be great."

"I got fish cakes and cod tongues, a turkey, fresh buns, beans in the oven." She studies his face. "Why your eyes so puffy? And stop that frowning. You'll end up with holes in your head like me."

Her hand comes up to smooth the two vertical furrows above his nose. Smiling, he does the same to her. It occurs to him how odd it would look to anyone passing by the window, both of them standing there, rubbing a spot of skin between each other's eyes. "Crazy Griffins," they'd probably say. It would not be the worst thing they'd ever said about his family.

"So, how are you, Ma? Keeping out of trouble?"

"Don't look for trouble, it won't look for you. You're sniffling. You got a cold?"

"Just the plane. I'll be fine tomorrow. You said something about fish cakes?"

The mention of food launches his mother into action, like a holy woman on a mission from God. She slices a few rashers of fatback pork and throws them into the frying pan. Bustling to the fridge, she hauls out potato salad, mustard pickles and beets. All the while she chatters on about people he knows: Millie O'Shea's new hip, Barber Manning's failing eyesight, the ongoing fight between the Smiths and the Powers over the berry patch dividing their two properties.

Surprisingly, she hasn't yet mentioned the Hanns. Gerry is thankful for that. He does not want to discuss Mercedes. He knows how his mother feels about her, even when she pretends otherwise. And that's fine; she has her reasons for disliking Mercedes, just as Gerry has his for feeling the opposite. Their relationship was something he could never explain to his mother, ever since that September morning in Grade One when Mercedes asked him to read from the catechism. When he'd finished, she smiled directly at him. "Here is a gentleman who can read already," she said to the entire class. From that moment on, Mercedes had treated him as a person distinct unto himself, no preconceived notions or forgone conclusions. No last name.

Out of the blue, a profound sadness washes over him. Mercedes is gone. He will never again sit with her over tea and discuss politics or work or, as in later years, family. They will never again share the pleasure of a new old book, the careful opening of the front cover, the search for written notes or autographs. The first time he was in her house he'd been mesmerized by the wall of shelves overflowing with books - some new, some old, some, even to his young and untrained eye, precious. He hadn't touched them. He'd been content to study the spines and breathe in the odour of old leather and dusty paper. He hadn't known a person could own so many books.

"There, now that's a scoff in the making." Sadie wipes her hands on her apron. "Bet you haven't had a good feed since you were home last, what?"

Looking at the satisfied smile on his mother's face, Gerry wishes he were hungry. All he really wants is a cup of good strong tea and a moment's peace. But there's little chance of getting that now, not if he wants to keep his mother happy. And that's a job he's spent a lifetime doing.

2

1999

With Sadie safely out the door, Annie heads to the kitchen for a cup of tea. A tray of Lucinda's sweet buns waits on the counter, ready for the oven come breakfast time. The cinnamon scent reminds Annie of watching cartoons with her older sisters on snowy Saturday mornings, the kitchen warm from the heat of the wood stove, the windows etched with ice. After licking every last bit of icing from their plates and fingers, she and Beth and Sara would swap pyjamas for snowsuits then head to the graveyard with their sled. Cemetery road had the steepest incline in St. Jude. Fortunately, it was also the least travelled by car. With all three of them piled on one sled, they would gain speed quickly. On a good day, they'd have to jump off before they reached bottom or risk crossing the road and ending up under the wheels of a car, or worse, over the cliff and into the ocean. Beth would swear Annie to secrecy, warning her that if Lucinda found out, she'd take away the sled for good. Beth and Sara are married now and live nearby. Annie sees them when she's home, but they're busy with their own families. She doesn't want to interfere. Her two younger sisters, Mary and Karen, are only ten and seven and have been sent to bed. Annie would like to feel closer to them but, having lived away for five years, she hasn't been around them enough to make a meaningful connection.

Annie is surprised to see her uncle, who's just home from New York for his sister's funeral, sitting at the kitchen table. "Uncle Joe, what are you doing here?"

He takes a small glass of brandy from Lucinda. "There's my little Annie."

"I thought you were tying one on with Jack Griffin tonight?"

"I was that, but Jack went and got right maudlin on me, carrying on about Dad and Paddy like he always does, talking to Paddy like his ghost was there in the room. Old fool finally passed out." Joe empties the glass and laughs. "Talked to myself for a bit but I was no better company than Jack. So I come here to say goodbye to my baby sister." His face turns pensive. "She was a grand girl when she was little, sweet one minute, saucy the next."

"I can't imagine her ever being a child," says Annie. And never having met the child, she finds it hard to grieve for the woman she became.

"What makes a person go hard like that, do you know?" Joe asks.

"Maybe she couldn't help it," Annie says, glancing at her mother.

"Life can make you hard." Lucinda's voice is heavy and her eyes are full.

Annie realizes how tough this day has been for Lucinda. She feels an urge to comfort her, but as she reaches out, Lucinda picks up Joe's glass and moves to the sink. Annie pulls back, unsure why she made the gesture. Displays of affection between her and her mother are generally restricted to homecomings and leavings.

"Best let bygones be bygones," Lucinda says over her shoulder.

Annie would love to do that, to let go of the hurt and move past it, but even with her aunt dead in the coffin, the pain lives on. She simply does not have her mother's ability to forgive and forget, especially when it comes to Mercedes.

1991

Mercedes had been furious when she found out that Lucinda was pregnant again at forty-two. As usual, she didn't hesitate to make her opinion known.

"Look at all the miscarriages, and the four babies who died. Good God, Dermot, don't you know any better? She's too old to be at this anymore." She gestured to Annie's grandfather, who sat quietly at the table. "You're her father, Callum. You know what can happen. Tell her. Tell them."

Before Callum had a chance to say anything, Dermot put his hand on her arm. "Now Mercedes—"

She shook him off. "Don't 'now Mercedes' me, you stupid man."

"Don't you dare call him stupid!" Although Lucinda had always tolerated Mercedes' interference - even when she quietly ignored it - she drew the line at any criticism of Dermot. "It's time you mind your own darn business."

"I would if either one of you had any sense," Mercedes retorted.

The two women stood there, each growing angrier by the second. Callum, always the peacemaker where Mercedes and Lucinda were concerned, hurried Mercedes from the house before harsher words were spoken.

Lucinda and Dermot had not set out to have another child. Like the rest of St. Jude, the Byrnes were Catholic. They used the rhythm method - the Pope said that was acceptable. Annie and Beth and Sara used to joke that their parents had too much rhythm. Wrapped in the innocent insensitivity of youth, they didn't stop to consider the significance of their small family, or the silent toll it took on their mother.

When Karen arrived, it was a huge relief to Lucinda and Dermot that she was normal and healthy, even if temporarily battered from a forceps delivery. On Lucinda's first day home from the hospital, Mercedes came by early to have a look, dressed as usual in her signature style. Except for the salt-and-pepper hair in its perfectly coiffed bun and the faint whiff of lavender, Mercedes lived in shades of brown, from her camel coats, taupe skirts, and beige pants and blouses, to her solid wood floors and furniture and her neutral wallpaper and parchment-coloured curtains. She presented an inconspicuous backdrop, a subtle blend of light and dark merging one into another. Her tan loafers made no sound as she crossed the floor to stand behind Annie who was studying at the kitchen table. She laid her hand on Annie's shoulder, then placed an old geology text next to her books. "I found this at the second-hand store."

Annie looked up. "Thanks, Aunt Mercedes." Her aunt often bought her books. She used to buy them for Annie's sisters, and for Pat and Aiden, until she realized that Annie was the only one who read them.

"A taste of university, perhaps?" Mercedes smiled then moved on to Lucinda.

The sun, an infrequent visitor to St. Jude, shone through the spring frost glazing the window. Basking in its warmth, Lucinda seemed prepared to forget the hostility that had simmered between her and Mercedes during her pregnancy. She told Dermot to take Mercedes in to see the baby.

Always the proud father, Dermot led the way into the living room where Karen slept in a well-worn bassinet. He slid back the cover that shaded his new daughter's lightly bruised face and disfigured head.

Mercedes let out a small chuckle. "Well, Dermot, let's hope she has brains."

There was a sharp intake of breath behind them. "How dare you find fault with that child!" Everyone froze as Lucinda's words, undoubtedly fuelled by postnatal hormones, ricocheted off the flowered wallpaper. "Just because you never had one of your own, just because no man would have anything to do with you, you have to spread unhappiness everywhere you go. Well, may God forgive you and your meanness."

Scooping the baby up in her arms, Lucinda stormed out. Mercedes stood rigid in the middle of the room. Then, without another word, she left the house.

Mercedes, presumably, had meant the comment as a joke. The problem was that her sense of humour was so rarely encountered that it went unrecognized, at least by Lucinda. As Dermot remarked to Callum, "A perpetually sour person should not go trying to be funny without giving us all a bit of warning."

Callum and Dermot tried to convince Lucinda that no harm had been intended but she refused to back down. As for Mercedes, that afternoon she set out for her summer cabin in Bay D'Esprits with only Rufus, her huge black Lab pup, for company.

Two days passed with no sign of Mercedes and no hint of compromise from Lucinda. On the third morning, Callum came by and insisted on taking Lucinda and the baby for a drive to Mercedes' cabin. When they arrived home that evening, Lucinda was in a sombre mood and spent the night secluded in her bedroom.

The next day Callum returned, a nervous-looking Mercedes behind him. He sent Annie and Sara off to the store with a hastily written list of groceries and told them not to come back for an hour.

Sara made repeated attempts to find out what had happened. Lucinda would say nothing, even when Sara enlisted Beth in the effort. As for Callum, it was one of the few times he told Annie that she should not ask questions, that some things were better left in God's hands. And even though Annie stopped asking, she never stopped wondering, because after that day, Lucinda and Mercedes' relationship changed. Where once Mercedes' presence on their doorstep might be met with a silent groan, she was suddenly invited to stay longer. Where once her advice was unsolicited, it came to be accepted, even encouraged. And where once she and Lucinda were merely of the same family, from that day forward they began to develop a deep and lasting connection.

The Most Merciful Virgin Church was the only church in St. Jude. Non-Catholic visitors, for only visitors were non-Catholic, worshipped elsewhere. With its oversized stained glass windows and four-storey-high crucifix, the Most Merciful Virgin was the most impressive and most beautiful building in town. A stone's throw from Burke's store, the church sat at the junction of the two main roads, one of which originated at the far end of St. Jude where the Hanns and the Byrnes lived. The other led to Sadie Griffin's house. Like most good Catholics, Sadie would not pass a church without blessing herself.

Good Christ, she's finally out of bed.

Sadie hurried on towards the church, her fingers already swishing up and down and across her face, her eyes intent on the old blue truck parked in front of Burke's. She watched as Lucinda descended from the driver's side to plant her feet gingerly onto the gravel.

Some frigging lazy. Driving to the store instead of walking. Slackarse.

"Father have mercy on us," Sadie recited, trotting as fast as her legs would carry her from the church to Burke's. She stopped only to catch her wind before going inside. "Lucinda, my dear, what a lovely surprise!" she exclaimed, hand on her throat. "But what are you doing out and about so soon after having another one?"

Christ, she's the size of a house still.

"Afternoon, Sadie," said Lucinda, choosing a loaf of bread. She did not look up.

"I sees you're driving today. Can't say I blames you, barely a week out of the hospital."

Looks like it too. Crying shame, Derm rolling over to that in the morning.

Lucinda put the bread next to a box of cereal and some instant coffee on the counter. She passed Phyllis Burke a ten-dollar bill.

"See you been to church already, too," said Sadie. "I don't think God would mind if you took a break, you know."

"I'm sure he wouldn't, but I feel fine."

"Well, that's a relief."

Some gut on her. Never know she already had it.

Lucinda took her change and turned to leave. Bessie Foley, who had been standing nearby squeezing an orange, dropped it back into the bin and raised an eyebrow at Sadie, who nodded purposefully.

"By the by," Sadie called out, "where was our Mercedes rushing off to the other day with such a heavy foot?"

Almost run me over in the road. Driving like a maniac with that goddamn dog, barking and frothing at the mouth. Got the rabies, that thing.

Lucinda seemed not to have heard. With a wave of her hand over her shoulder, she kept on walking out the door.

Phyllis waited until she was sure the door had closed. "Car was gone three days. Where'd she get to?"

"I said as much when I saw Mercedes at the post office yesterday." Bessie's lips scrunched in frustration. "Not a word, my dear, not one blessed word. Just one of them nods she gives, you know, with that haughty face of hers."

"I don't know why she's so closed-mouthed. I mean, we all only wants to help sure, to be good neighbours." Phyllis glanced at Sadie. "Your Gerry's pretty tight with her. What do he say?"

"Now Phyllis, you knows I'm not one to gossip, especially about family."

Lot of good Gerard is. Time he spends at that house, all he talks about is odes and sonnets. Stupid poetry. History is what I wants. There's dirt back there somewhere, I knows it.

"That Lucinda now. She's not looking like herself, is she, though?" said Phyllis.

Bessie grunted. "What can you expect, having a youngster at her age?"

"True. Least she did the right thing though," said Phyllis.

"Not like some," Bessie tutted, "getting rid of it and all."

Sadie raised her eyes heavenward, hands together. Phyllis

and Bessie blessed themselves. All three muttered prayers under their breath.

"You seen the new one, Sadie?" said Phyllis.

"Not yet." Sadie had dropped by Lucinda and Dermot's each of the last two afternoons. Both times, Lucinda and the baby had been in bed. "I should stop in, I suppose, being family and all."

Phyllis eyed Sadie through the thick bottom of her eyeglasses. "Surprised you haven't already."

Sadie placed a loaf of bread on the counter. "You know me, I don't like to intrude."

"Some sight, they say," said Phyllis. "Bruises and gouges all over the place."

"Sure it's just the forceps," said Bessie. "They'll work theirself out in no time."

Sadie's hand went to her heart. "Pray it do for the poor thing."

Maybe it will. Maybe it won't. I seen where it stayed that way forever. Serve them right.

"Imagine Lucinda and Derm going at it at their age." Phyllis shook her head.

Sadie rubbed her nose and scratched her ear. She rummaged in her purse for her wallet and a tissue. She blew her nose hard. She did not want that picture in her mind.

"They don't stop, they'll end up with a bunch of retards," Phyllis added.

Bessie nodded. "Look at poor Mavis MacDonald, sure, with three of them thick as bricks."

Sadie leaned in and whispered, "Mavis should have looked beyond the MacDonalds."

"And Doris and Donny Whittle." Bessie lowered her voice. "Doris claims her maiden name was White, but I got it on good authority that she was born a Whittle up in Green Harbour. It's not right, I tell you."

"God'll be having none of that," said Phyllis. "Never mind them gene things."

Sadie sighed. "Some youngsters better off not born at all."

"And who'd know better than you, what, having to bury two of your own?" said Phyllis with an exaggerated note of pain in her voice.

Sadie glanced at her friend, but Phyllis was looking down her nose at the jar of jam Sadie had placed next to the bread and her five dollars.

Phyllis punched a few keys on the register. "What's Derm want with a baby? He's too old for that."

"Derm's still a fine figure of a man." Sadie's voice had risen.

Phyllis laughed. "Always with an eye for the fellows, eh Sadie?"

Bessie poked Sadie. "Especially him, what?"

"Don't be silly, Bessie. Sure he's a married man, Derm is."

Wife's a Yankee cow, mind you.

Phyllis squinted at the five-dollar bill. "Don't stop a person looking, especially handsome as him." A sly look passed between Bessie and Phyllis, who added, "Pity Lucinda caught him first, eh, Sadie?"

"Pity about that poor youngster is more like it."

And a pity I got to listen to you two old biddies.

Phyllis passed Sadie her change. Bessie coughed a little too loudly and covered her mouth with her hand.

Sadie picked up her groceries and left.

1999

Gerry lifts the lid off the pot of beans. The sweet, smoky aroma of molasses and bacon fills the room. "My God, that smells good. But you've got enough for an army, Ma."

"Well now, I knows you don't be eating right up there in that Toronto. Sin City, that place. Got to get some good grub in you whiles you're here."

"I'll have to buy an extra seat on the plane. Better get Gus and Kevin on it." He glances around. "Where are they, anyway? And where's Debra?"

"At the bar. Dance there tonight. Won't be back till all hours."

He puts the lid back on the beans. "Who's taking care of Mark?"

"He's sleeping over at Connie's. They does that, Debra and her, saves paying for babysitting."

"And leaves Debra more money for partying. How is our Mark, anyway?"

"Talking about you ever since you were home last, Uncle Gerry this and Uncle Gerry that. Be different he had a father, I suppose."

"Let's not go there, Ma."

Any discussion of Mark's parentage inevitably leads to a tirade against the Hann clan. When rumour spread that Aiden Hann was to blame, Aiden not only denied it, he went so far as to say it could be any number of boys, or men. Sadie had nagged at Debra for ages to make the father, whoever he was, "pay for his sins." Debra remained defiant. Sadie insisted that Gerry, as her older brother, have a talk with her, but when Debra told him it had nothing to do with him and he should just mind his own business, he found himself agreeing. Knowing that Aiden might have been responsible and, if so, was shirking that responsibility, did not make Gerry like him any better, but he suspected that Aiden wasn't far off regarding Debra's reputation, leaving Gerry to wonder if she wouldn't point a finger because she didn't know where to point. For that, and other reasons, he was more than willing to leave the subject alone.

Sadie flips a fish cake in the frying pan. "I'm just saying—"

"I know. Just let it be." Gerry changes the subject. "Did Mark get that speech thing looked after yet?"

"I don't know. Hard to get much out of that Debra. She gets right contrary soon's you mentions anything. Get on her about it, would you?"

"Not like she'll listen to me, but I'll talk to her. It'll get worse if it's not seen to. I'd hate to have the other kids making fun of him."

Sadie tutts. "Debra has a hard enough time looking after herself, let alone a young one."

"Yeah, well maybe some people shouldn't have children in the first place."

"Come off it, Gerard, she does her best."

"I'd hate to see her worst." He takes two teabags from the canister.

"Debra never had your brains. Always was a bit slow, unless she's getting her drawers off."

"Ma!" Gerry laughs nonetheless. His mother still shocks him sometimes.

"I'm only saying she's lucky she only got the one youngster."

"Debra's problem is she thinks the world owes her a living."

Sadie nods. "That's the Griffins for you. And Debra's a Griffin all right."

"I'm a Griffin too. Don't see me waiting for the world to bring me breakfast."

Sadie smiles and nudges a cod tongue to see if it's done. "You're more like my side of the family. The Duffies were always smarter than the Griffins."

"Anyway, I don't want to argue about Debra. I only got two days here—"

"Two days?" Sadie whirls around, slightly off-balance. "How come that's all?"

"Because I've got all my vacation time spoken for." He keeps his voice calm.

"Why? You were only home the one week."

"I know, but I'm going to Europe next month."

"What the frig's in Europe? French frogs slugging back the wine."

"Now Ma, I'm always coming home." He watches her fuss and fidget at the counter, moving food around for no apparent reason. "Besides, I'm going on business anyway so it makes sense to make a holiday of it."

She grunts and marches into the back pantry. A few minutes later she returns, empty-handed but calmer. "So how did you get time off now if you got none left?"

"I told them my aunt died. They're pretty understanding when it's family."

The words simmer around them, "my aunt" and "family" echoing in the stillness. He wishes he could sweep the air and make them disappear.

Sadie's cheeks are red blotches. "Your what? Aunt? Aunt, my arse."

Gerry rubs his face vigorously with both hands. Despite himself, he feels a ridiculous grin on his face. If his mother sees that, she'll have a fit. Bad enough he called Mercedes his aunt, but if Sadie catches him smiling about it, even if he has no clue as to why he's smiling except that he's exhausted and obviously beginning to lose his mind a little, she'll disown him altogether. "Now Ma, it's just a word. Boy, but I'm starving," he lies.

"Not just a word, Gerard, you—"

"Stop!" He says it louder than he intends, but the guilty truth of it is that he has long thought of Mercedes as family. Sitting at her table on cold winter evenings, reading aloud from Keats or Wordsworth, or perhaps from one of Mercedes' favourites, like Dickinson or Bishop, Gerry had sometimes found himself imagining that this was his home, that his mother wasn't the town gossip whose tongue everyone feared, that his father hadn't run off with another man. Later, at home, he would try extra hard to be good to his mother. "I'm sorry," he says now, "but I've been on the go all day. I had a presentation this morning then I was running to catch planes. I never had a decent bite. Let's just eat. Please?" He puts on his most innocent face, one he knows she can't resist. "Speaking of work, why were you at it so late? You should slow down."

"Had to help with the Lady's Guild earlier, set up for bingo tomorrow." She puts one of the teabags back into the canister. "Besides, work gives me a chance to visit."

Gerry knows that his mother doesn't get many invitations

out. Her work is her social life. "Do any of them even ask how you are, Ma? Do they even care?"

"Hah, some of that lot don't know you're alive once you're done with the scrub brush. I swear to Lucifer, door shuts on you and you're good as dead till you're due back with the mop." She smiles coyly. "Then again, they're not all bad. Like that young Father James. He was just asking after you this evening. Wanted to know did you go to church up in Toronto, and make the sacraments and all."

Gerry rolls his eyes inwardly at the priest's supposed concern. He does not go to church in Toronto. He goes only when he's home. It's easier to spend the hour at Mass than to argue with his mother about not going. He takes communion with her as well, but he draws the line at the Stations of the Cross. All that genuflecting and mumbling and crossing himself, the Father, Son and Holy Spirit, over and over again all around the church, it's more than even he can fake.

Sadie's head is cocked to one side. She has an odd smile on her face, sort of sly, secretive even. Gerry watches her a moment, curious as always about what goes on behind his mother's eyes, what thoughts bring that certain lift to her chin. But as much as he has learned how to deal with her over the years, and as necessary to his mental health as that has been, he still can't figure her out. For such a simple woman, she really can be quite complex.

"Yes, indeed," she nods, "lovely man, Father is."

"Tell Father James I'm doing just fine," he says noncommittally.

And he is fine. Fine without the church interfering in his life. Fine without some religious know-it-all telling him what's right and what's wrong, who he should love and who he shouldn't.

He hasn't listened to a priest in five years. He's not about to start again now.

3

1999

There is a large round hooked rug on the kitchen floor. The centre, the ocean, is filled with fish and dories, and all around the border are brightly dressed men and women holding hands. Annie was surprised when she'd learned that Mercedes had hooked it. The rug is warm and bright and evokes images of people celebrating, dancing round and round on a summer day.

"It's not always that easy to let bygones be gone," Joe is saying to Lucinda.

"I know. I'm just not sure what takes more energy, forgiving or not forgiving." There's a regretful edge to Lucinda's voice and her concentration seems far away.

"What bygones are you talking about there, Mom?" Annie, as usual, wishes she had some clue as to what went on in her mother's head. Her sisters have always been able to talk to Lucinda, about their boyfriends and husbands, their jobs or lack of, their kids. But Annie so often says the wrong thing, a wisecrack, something sarcastic or off-colour, which, although it might get a chuckle from Dermot, seldom amuses her mother. As an adult Annie has tried to be more careful about what she says around Lucinda, but they still seem unable to find a place where they can relax in each other's company.

Lucinda shakes her head as if to clear it. "Now, Annie, you know your Aunt Mercedes didn't always watch what came out of her mouth," she says evasively.

Annie rolls her eyes. "Fine, don't tell me. You have to wonder though, is that why she never had a boyfriend?"

Joe looks startled. "Oh, but she did. After she left New York and was learning to be a teacher in Nova Scotia. Callum was so excited you'd have thought she was his own daughter getting hitched."

"Go on! Aunt Merce was going to get married?" Annie is surprised her grandfather never mentioned it. "Who was this fellow?"

"He was from some well-to-do family in St. John's. Apparently he was heading for the priesthood till he met Mercie, so his family wasn't too happy about it."

"Is that why they broke up?" she asks.

"I don't know. All of a sudden it was over and no one wanted to talk about it anymore. Callum only said she was moving back here to teach."

"Mom? Did she ever say anything to you about it?"

"She was never one to talk about days gone by, was she now?"

Annie's can't disagree with that. In fact, Mercedes would often simply leave the room if someone seemed intent on dredging up old stories. Still, there's something about her mother's quick tight smile that makes Annie wonder if she knows more than she's letting on. But it's useless to push Lucinda, who can be as tight-lipped as Mercedes when it suits her. "So, Uncle Joe, tell me what was she like when she was little? What did she like to do? Did you all get along?"

Annie realizes that she really does want to know. What made the child, Mercie, happy? What did she talk about when she sat down to drink her morning tea with her father and brothers? Did they love each other dearly and talk as only family can? Who was this matriarch whom Annie has feared and even hated at times, yet whom she feels such an urge to understand despite everything that happened?

"The older boys were all gone by then, fishing or working the mines. Dad was there but he wasn't much good to us. So it was really just me and her and Cal." He chuckles. "You know how I remembers her best? In our old clothes. We never threw out a darn thing, you couldn't afford to ever do that. Mercie would take our old shirts, roll up the sleeves, sometimes cut the bottom off. She was only five or six, I suppose. Never complained, just got on with it, wandered around the house singing, or sat with Callum at the table practising her letters and stuff."

Lucinda leans in close and pats Joe's hand. The need in her eyes tugs at Annie, and her heart fills at the sight of these two good people attempting to recall the warmth that long ago existed in Mercedes Hann.

Annie slips into the chair next to her mother. "She must have been a sight in those big clothes, hey," she prompts Joe before he loses his train of thought, "so small next to you two big galoots?" She is rewarded with an appreciative glance from Lucinda.

"Indeed she was, but at least she was warm. You should have seen us. On really cold days when you could never get yourself warm for nothing, me and her and Cal would haul our chairs to the stove and pull down the oven door. Then we'd lay a pillow there and put our feet on it." He laughs a beautiful young laugh. "Mercie called it our fireplace. We'd warm bricks in there too, wrap them in towels to take to bed with us."

"Must be why she put in the two fireplaces over there," says Lucinda. "Her and Dad always had the heat raging."

"She sure did a fine job fixing the old place up," says Joe.

Annie is struggling to fix the child in her mind, but all she comes up with is an unsatisfactory composite of her two younger sisters. "What did she look like, Uncle Joe? I have a hard time getting a face in my head."

"Well, my Annie, that's a good one, because she looked like you. That dark hair, and them lively eyes like you got there," Joe says, pointing, "even your colour, kind of pale, but healthy all the same. When she was little, I used to worry she was so white, but she was never sick so I let it be. Thing is, it's not only the looks. I'd say you're like her under the skin too." A frown darkens his face and he looks at Lucinda. "Let's hope she ends up happier, hey Luce?"

Annie pretends not to see her mother's worried nod, the disappointed sigh. "Too bad we don't have a picture from back then."

"My, but sure we never had no camera. I remembers once, some bigwig from St. John's was out our way taking photographs for a book or something. I don't know what became of them. People didn't have money for stuff like that."

"Shame."

"'Tis indeed. Pretty as a picture she was, the very image of an Irish lassie. When she was young, she always put me in mind of something." He pauses, then continues in a soft, low voice. "She looked to me like a Sheilagh."

Annie hears Lucinda's quick intake of breath. She glances at her mother, then back at Joe. "What's that, like a female leprechaun or something?"

"No, my Annie, a Sheilagh is a child of God." His tone is lilting, serene. "A dark-haired Irish angel with fiery eyes and pure white skin, a vision of heaven, she is."

"Sheilagh was Joe's daughter," Lucinda says in a hushed tone. She wraps Joe's bony hand in her two plump, warm ones. "I know what a Sheilagh is, Joey. Our Mercie knew too, more than anyone ever imagined. There's been too many Sheilaghs in this family. Boy or girl, doesn't matter. Just ask our Beth." She inhales a trembling breath, then gives Annie the saddest smile that Annie has ever seen.

For the life of her, Annie cannot look away. Fear grips her. Dear Jesus in heaven, she prays, please let her only be talking about our poor Beth.

1989

The year Annie turned fifteen, Beth, who had been going out with Luke Ennis since Grade Nine, found herself "in trouble". In a good Catholic family such as theirs this was certainly a sin, but a forgivable one as long as everyone behaved appropriately. Abortion was not to be mentioned, especially in Lucinda's house.

The good news was that there would be a wedding, Dermot's favourite reason to celebrate. "A good wedding beats an Irish wake any day," he told Lucinda when they had recovered from the news of their daughter's premarital activities. "No matter if the bride be six months pregnant or a blushing virgin."

Poor as Lucinda and Dermot were, they didn't hesitate to pay their share for the reception and the standard meal prepared by the Lady's Guild - a scoop each of Sadie Griffin's potato salad and Ellen McGrath's coleslaw, a slice each of roast beef, turkey and ham, two sweet mustard pickles, two baby beets, a leaf of iceberg lettuce topped with a wedge of tomato, and a white dinner bun with a pat of butter. Individual plates were prepared before the Mass, spaced out along the white paper tablecloths, then covered with a bit of plastic wrap. The fact that no one contracted food poisoning from the mayonnaise in the potato salad was a wonder never discussed. Then again, any subsequent illness would likely have been blamed on the whiskey or the rum.

After struggling with the guest list for weeks, Lucinda and Beth ended up inviting far more people than they could rightly afford to feed. Besides being concerned that they might hurt someone's feelings, they also knew that they would run into everyone they hadn't invited in the weeks ahead, at the post office, at Burke's grocery store, at Sunday Mass. The list grew longer; more potatoes would have to be peeled.

An hour before the ceremony, all were shocked when Callum phoned Lucinda to say that Mercedes was sick. Illness rarely stopped Mercedes Hann. Lucinda insisted on going up to have a look at her. "I told you Dad, it's no bother," she said into the phone. A puzzled frown settled on her face. "What?" Her voice rose just enough to cause everyone in the kitchen to stop and listen. "Fine. So be it." Lucinda slammed the receiver onto the hook and turned her attention to Beth, who stood large and flushed in the silent room. "All right, then. Let's get you married."

Sadie Griffin did not attend the wedding, either. Then again, Sadie hadn't been invited.

Beth and Luke were young but, except for the oversight regarding birth control, they were sensible. Deciding it would be prudent to save towards a house, they moved in with Lucinda and Dermot. Beth had quit Trades School and gotten on at the fish plant - a dirty job, but a scarce one - and Luke had been hired on at Burke's, stacking shelves, moving furniture, and whatever else was required, while training to be a meat-cutter. Still, savings from their minimum wage jobs were slow to accumulate.

Everyone knew that Mercedes Hann had money. Decades earlier, after teaching for several years, Mercedes had hired Mr. Crosbie Cunningham, a well-known financial advisor from St. John's, to guide her investments. Mr. Cunningham's name had caught her attention for several reasons, not least of which was his ability to make money for his clients. In the years that followed, Mercedes became quite a wealthy woman. She had given loans before, to her brother's widow after he was killed in the Springhill mines, to her nephew Frank Jr. when he was starting out as a fisherman, and to other family members as well. She charged negligible interest but the debtor did have to put up with her advice, which she offered freely, as if she'd acquired that right by granting the loan. She gave generously to charity as well, and not just the church. Her favourite cause was Meade House, a private home near St. John's for unmarried girls and their babies. It seemed an odd choice, considering that Mercedes was quite vocal in her opinion of premarital sex. Besides which, the girls who went there were even choosing to keep their fatherless children. To top it off, Meade House was run by Margaret Meade, an ex-nun, a woman who had forsaken the convent, perhaps even Catholicism itself. Despite it all, Mercedes never wavered in her support.

When Beth and Luke approached her, they expected to get a lecture and the loan.

"We only needs a thousand dollars," Beth explained, her cheeks rosy in Mercedes' overheated kitchen. "But I don't think I should work much longer at the plant. I'm always tired lately, and we don't want to take a chance with the baby, right Luke?"

"Uh-huh," he said and stuck his thumbnail back in his mouth. Luke, like so many others, had always been intimidated by Mercedes Hann.

"Well, anyway, Aunt Mercedes," Beth said, "if we don't buy the house we'll be stuck in with Mom and Dad for ages. We'd never see a lick of privacy."

Mercedes glanced at Beth's belly, which was huge even for seven months, then back to her swollen face. "What example do you think this is setting for your sisters?"

Beth stammered something incoherent.

"They look up to you, Elizabeth," Mercedes continued. "As the oldest, you had a responsibility. And look what you've gone and done. Eighteen years old, unmarried, getting pregnant. For God's sake, what were the two of you thinking?"

Beth and Luke sat there mute and uncomfortable but still hopeful.

Mercedes stood up. "I certainly do feel for you, really I do. But I cannot allow your sisters to think that I approve of what you've done. I'm afraid I have to say no."

Mercedes' refusal made Beth even more determined to buy a house. Despite her size and persistent nausea, she decided to keep working at the plant.

A few days before her due date, she sensed a lessening of movement in her belly. Lucinda and Luke took her to the hospital, where she was immediately sent to St. John's in an ambulance.

Lucinda, frantic, called for a taxi to take her home. When it pulled up, Sadie Griffin got out of the front seat.

"Whatever is the matter, girl? You looks awful," said Sadie, standing in such a way that Lucinda could not get past her. "Bad news from the doctor?"

"Please, Sadie..."

"It's not Dermot?"

"Derm? No, he's fine."

"Your father? Mercedes?"

Lucinda blew out a sharp breath. "Beth's gone to town in an ambulance."

She pushed her way past Sadie and into the car. Still, Sadie held the door open.

Lucinda yanked the door from Sadie's hands and told the driver to hurry. He sped off, leaving a spray of gravel behind him, along with Sadie clutching her bag on the curb.

Once home, Lucinda jumped into the truck. It wouldn't start, just as it hadn't that morning, and Dermot wasn't around to coax it back to life. Lucinda flung the keys out the window and across the yard.

Annie, who had been watching from the doorway, came out. "What's up?"

"It's Beth. She's in trouble."

Annie shrugged, at fifteen more brazen than ever. "So what else is new?"

Lucinda turned on her. "Don't you care your sister's baby might be dead? She's gone to St. John's in an ambulance and all you can do is mouth off." She glared at Annie. "You're worse than Mercedes, God help you."

Annie couldn't move. She couldn't think past the fact that Beth really was in trouble and her mother thought she didn't care. "I'm sorry. I didn't mean it."

"I just don't know how to stop it from happening." Lucinda made a strange sound, somewhere between a moan and a cry. "I got to go after her."

Annie remembered Lucinda's pregnancy two years before, how sad her mother had been when she'd returned from the hospital empty-handed. She wished her father was home but he'd left two days earlier on one of Murphy's boats and would be away at least a week. And Callum had gone to St. John's with Mercedes the day before.

"Maybe we can borrow Uncle Frank's car?" Annie suggested. "I'll go with you."

Frank Hann was a miserly sort, but there must have been something in Lucinda's voice when she called him. Within minutes, he was there with the car.

Lucinda drove off, her foot heavy on the gas. Annie watched through the passenger window as the jagged landscape whipped by, the tough evergreens interspersed with rocky outcroppings and barren patches of land. In the distance, a dense fog hid the horizon. Annie hugged her coat closer against the fall air whistling through the crannies of her uncle's old car.

As she walked into the hospital, Annie thought she understood why Mercedes refused to enter one. The waiting room smelled of body fluids and antiseptic, of sickness and death. She tried not to breathe too deeply.

She watched her mother's fingers flying over her black rosary beads, her lips whispering feverishly. Annie had knelt through hundreds of rosaries, pretending to pray, angry with her mother for making her do something Annie professed to be a waste of time. Now, she put her hands together.

Finally, Luke was walking towards them, his face drenched with tears.

"Oh, dear God. Luke, what happened?" The fear jumping out of Lucinda's voice terrified Annie. "How's Beth? How's the baby?"

Luke stared numbly at her. "Beth is okay, but the baby…he's gone." Then he whispered in a voice that didn't quite believe what it was saying, "He's dead."

Annie's skin shot up with goose bumps. Beth's baby would not have been baptized and so would not be free of original sin. Annie envisioned an endless line of tiny souls drifting within a vast empty space, stuck in Limbo, hanging around with no place to go, no home, no fluffy clouds, no Jesus to belong to.

Lucinda sat Luke next to Annie. "Stay with him, okay. I've got to go see Beth."

Lucinda wasn't gone long when Annie heard a noise down the corridor. When she looked up, she was surprised to see Mercedes hurrying towards them.

"How is everything?" Mercedes' voice was rushed and anxious. "How's Beth?"

Annie tried to speak but instead started to cry. Mercedes touched her cheek and gestured for her to move over. Then she put her arms around Luke and held him.

Annie imagined Lucinda holding Beth and comforting her just as Mercedes did Luke. Annie could not remember the last time she'd felt her mother's arms around her.

There was a whispering sound next to her. She glanced over.

"Dear God, forgive me," her aunt prayed. "I am so sorry, so very sorry."

In that moment Annie forgot her own misery. Never before had she seen such a picture of pure grief.

The hospital that serviced St. Jude was located in Harbourville. Many citizens of St. Jude, Sadie Griffin included, felt the facility should have been located in their town, which, at almost four thousand people, was the largest in the area. They resented having to travel four miles for medical attention. Sadie, who had never driven a car, did not like having to spend three dollars on a taxi to have a doctor examine her feet.

Witch! God, I'm some sick of her. Sick to the death.

Sadie slammed her purse onto the chair.

Frigging Lucinda. Practically knocked me over yanking that car door shut. I hadn't grabbed that fence post, I'd been face down in the dirt.

She flung her coat on top of her purse. "Make you sick."

"What's wrong?"

Sadie spun around. Gerard was studying at the kitchen table.

"Frigging Hanns."

What's he doing home?

"Oh Ma, they're okay."

"Okay? How can you say that, the way them brothers acts? Picking on you all the time, calling you names. Especially that no-good Aiden."

Little prick, shouting at my boy, "Queery Gerry, your father's a fairy." And then hurling rocks at him. Gerard got the mark on his lip to this day.

"Sure Ma, that's years ago. I don't pay him any mind nowadays."

"Like to pay him a piece of mine. Just like I did that Frank with his hand in the collection plate. I told Father, indeed I did, but he said there wasn't much he could do, my word against Frank's."

A Griffin's word against a Hann's more like it, I felt like saying. But sure it weren't Father's fault, I knows that.

"Ah, what odds about them," Sadie said. "Why you home, anyway? Thought you had work to do for Herself while she's away."

Sadie knew it would annoy him to hear her refer to Mercedes as Herself. She didn't care. She'd had quite enough of the Hanns for one day.

"She left me a note saying I better study for my test instead. She paid me anyway, said it was a bonus or something. She's really good to me, you know, Ma."

"A right martyr."

If he starts in about what a saint Mercedes is, I'll throw up. I'll lose that lovely piece of meatloaf I had for lunch before that frigging Lucinda tried to rip the hand off me. It'll go right down the toilet. It really will, I swear to God.

"... don't think I should take that money, though," Gerard was saying.

"That one got lots of it, she won't be missing a few dollars."

"I don't know how she even knew about the test."

"Must have been that Annie told her. You're in the same grade, sure."

"Yeah, maybe," Gerard said, looking down at his books.

What's he gone so red in the face for?

Sadie laid her hand on his forehead. "You okay?"

"Just hungry." He shifted so that his head moved from under her hand. "Where were you?"

"Over at the hospital getting them bunions looked at."

"Can they fix them?"

"Huh? Oh, the bunions. Never mind them. They were just after taking that Beth Hann off in an ambulance. That young Annie might not get to be a aunt after all."

Hope he's not coming down with something. Can't always tell with the forehead.

He brushed the hair out of his eyes. "Why were you so mad when you came in?"

Sadie remembered Lucinda's pinched face and how she'd pulled the door from Sadie's hand. "Nothing important. Let me get you something to eat and a cup of tea."

He smiled at her. "Thanks, Ma."

Look at that face. Them lovely white teeth, them big brown eyes. Most handsomest smile I ever did see. Hit the jackpot with him, I did.

"That'd be great," he said. "I'm starving."

Sadie smoothed his hair, letting her hand linger on the back of his head. He didn't pull away this time.

To hell with the Hanns.

1999

Gerry looks at his watch. It's only ten thirty. He puts the lone teabag into the pot and pours boiling water over it. As he reaches for the cups, he feels his mother's hand catch his arm as she staggers slightly on her way from the bathroom.

"Steady on there, Ma," he says, putting his arm around her.

She squints up at him, then pokes at his lip, as if the action might make the scar disappear. She'd been furious when she'd first seen the cut. Gerry hadn't told her that Aiden Hann was responsible; Sadie, as always, had her own sources. He hadn't told her it was partly his own fault either, even though he suspected she would have been proud of him. It was the morning before the Halloween party at school, and Aiden, who made a habit of picking on anyone he deemed beneath him in the pecking order, started in - was Gerry dressing up as a fairy, how many costumes did he have in his closet, did he want a mop so he could come as his mother - calling Sadie a fishwife and a charwoman and getting increasingly revved up as people started to pay attention. Gerry usually ignored the taunts and left wherever he was as fast as he could, but that day he'd had enough. He stopped, turned around and smiled directly at Aiden. "Better than being a th-th-th-thief," he said. Aiden's face went purple. He bent down, grabbed a rock and whizzed it straight at Gerry's head. Before Gerry could get over the shock of having his lip slit open, Pat stepped in and hauled Aiden away.

"What were we talking about?" Sadie says now, rubbing her chin. "Right, Father James. Yes, indeed, fine man he is. He'll be doing a baptism soon too. That Cathy Green went and had the baby."

Cathy Green is not his mother's favourite person. To start with, she's Annie's best friend; on top of that, she's Violet Green's daughter. But Gerry has always liked Cathy. For a while, she was the only one who knew about him and Annie. Annie. He's finally seen her again. If only it hadn't taken Mercedes' death to make it happen.

"Cathy's life sure has changed," he says. "A year ago she was still going out with Cyril. Now she's a mother and married to someone else."

"Poor son of a bitch, he is," says Sadie. "Didn't take that Cathy long to get knocked up. Probably afraid he'd get away too. Cyril's the lucky one there, I tell you."

"Come on, Ma, don't. Anyway, everything go okay?"

"Baby's still in hospital." She wrestles with the lid on the beets.

"What happened? Did you talk to Mrs. Green?"

"You knows that Violet. Thinks her daughter's the first ever gave birth—"

"Ma!" He takes the jar from her and opens it. "What's wrong with the baby?"

"Ah, nothing. Low blood, bad blood, something like that. Out soon, I'm sure."

"I hope it's okay. That'd be awful if anything happened."

"Yes, awful. Unless it's soft in the head. Or retarded."

"I mean, how do you ever get over it when something happens to your baby?"

"Go on, they're usually fine, sure. Unless you're a Hann." She proceeds to cut thick slices from a fresh loaf of bread. "Dead babies all over the place. Hanns thinks only Griffins deserves dead babies, or retarded ones."

Gerry notices that she has managed, as she so often does, to twist the conversation around to the Hanns. And he, as he so often does, ignores it. "Mrs. Green must be some worried about them."

Sadie grunts. "I was there the other day and that Violet was on the phone for ages, talking to the nurse and the doctor and heaven only knows who, probably the priest and the nuns, God himself even. Swear no one else ever had a problem. Yapping away while I scrubbed her dirt. Blathering on about that Cathy. Thought she'd never shut up. I said nothing, kept my head down the toilet and did my job. Let her rattle on. Don't know for hard times, that one don't."

"Don't be like that, Ma." His mother can really act the bitch when she's in the mood, or when she has a few drinks in. And even though he knows she's a good person deep down, she can be hard to take when he's so tired.

"Like what?" Sadie throws out her hands in righteous innocence, still holding the oversized bread knife. "I'm only just saying what's the truth. That crowd don't think of nobody but theirself."

They're only words, no sticks, no stones, just words, he tells himself. Close your mind and eat something and go to bed out of it just like always. But he can't. Does it have to do with seeing Annie again, he wonders, with being reminded of his mother's role in what happened? Is that why he is suddenly so attuned to, and irritated, by her, despite the fact that he has long forgiven her that role?

"They're good people, Ma. You might not like them, but that's no reason to go around slagging them all the time."

"Hah, good people my arse."

"Please, would you just—"

Her free hand springs up. "Don't be telling me, mister. I knows them way better than you. Been putting up with the likes of them all my frigging life. I got the goods on that lot. Hanns are no better than us."

"Hanns? I thought we were talking about Cathy Green."

"Greens, Hanns, no difference to me. Thinks they're so good, looking down their noses at us. Butter wouldn't melt. Still I don't hold no grudge, no sir, not me. Live and let live is my motto. Do the right thing by your neighbour, the right thing be done back to you. How hard is that? Lucinda, spiteful bitch. Leaving her own family off the invite list. So we're not kissing cousins. No reason to snub her snotty nose at me. No, sir. Keeps on doing it, though, again and again. Bloody Hanns."

Gerry wishes he'd kept his mouth shut. "You're right, Ma. Of course you know them all better than me. You've been around here forever, haven't you, girl?" He yawns again. "Lord, I don't think I'm going to last much longer tonight."

"Right? 'Course I'm right," she says, still sawing the loaf of bread which has begun to crumple under the pressure. "Goes around comes around. We all gets what's coming to us sooner or later. And the Hanns got what was coming to them that time, by the Lord. The whole thing was all for naught, the rushed wedding, getting everybody all worked up, hurt feelings everywhere. That Beth had the wedding so she could have the baby, and Lucinda didn't see fit to add one more person to the guest list. Just one. Me. Didn't have to have the whole kit and caboodle. But no. Had that whole frigging Green clan, youngsters and all. Boiled me. And look what happened - wedding was all for nothing. Hah! Maybe if they weren't so mean, maybe God would have spared that baby. Then again, do the world want more of that lot gracing the earth? Plenty Hanns already. Turning their fat arses away from us. I done the right thing, though. First thing next day I bought a Mass for that dead baby. Lot of good it did him. All the masses in the world wouldn't get him into heaven. Limbo-Larry forever. One less I'll see when I gets there."

His mother's cheeks are rosy under her grey waves. She could easily pass for a sweet little old lady if she didn't open her mouth. It doesn't help that she's been into the booze. It always revs her up to life's injustices, real and imagined.

Out of nowhere, the image strikes. Close up this time. Again, more vivid than is possible. Emerald eyes. Lips like raspberries on fresh snow. Firm chin, the smooth white skin of her neck, her body so close, so out of reach. And those eyes, those eyes...

His mother has a point. Life is full of injustice.

4

1999

"I don't remember her ever going into a hospital before that day. Even when you girls were born, she'd wait till I got home to come see you." Lucinda's sigh is extra long. "We were all heart-broken, especially Beth, but Mercedes blamed herself. And we could never talk sense to her."

"Guilt is a powerful thing," says Annie. "It doesn't always make sense." She feels a pang of remorse run through her, for herself, for her mother and Mercedes, for Beth and her baby, the helpless infant in perpetual limbo. That particular concept no longer worries Annie, however. She has long ceased believ-ing in limbo and purgatory. Hell is another matter.

"Hard to believe she's gone." Joe stands abruptly. "I think I'll go sit with her for a bit. Keep Dermot and the boys company."

Joe has hardly left when Pat and Aiden bounce in, making as much noise as two strapping young men can make after spending an evening pent up with a corpse.

"Thought you were keeping the vigil," Annie says, relieved to see them.

"Uncle Joe wanted to say his goodbyes," says Pat, scratch-ing his unruly head.

Aiden sizes him up. "My brother, the Viking."

"Just call me Leif." Pat looks him up and down. "And by the way, you're no fucking oil painting yourself." He says it low and out of the side of his mouth so Lucinda, who is moving the cups from the drying rack into the cupboard, won't hear.

Aiden pats his neatly combed hair. "Prettier than you. Al-ways have been."

"And me," Annie adds dryly. "Remember when old man Canning caught us raiding his rhubarb patch? He called me and Pat delinquents, while you managed to talk your way into getting paid to harvest the whole frigging crop."

"I never met a person could lie like you." There is admiration in Pat's voice.

"It's a gift from God," says Aiden.

Lucinda shuts the cupboard door hard. "You can leave God out of it."

"What do you say, Aiden?" Pat flops down into a chair. "Time to raise a toast to Great-Auntie Merce."

Lucinda frowns at him. "Like you two got so many fond memories of her."

"I'm fond of anybody gets me out of jail," says Aiden. "Almost drove me nuts after, mind you, nagging day in and day out till I went back to school." His tone is a mix of pride and exasperation. "I still wonder why she showed at that parole hearing."

"I told you, she wanted to get you off my boat and away from me," says Pat.

"Nah. Probably just some latent maternal instinct," says Annie.

Aiden laughs. "Doubtful. But it was good of her to stand up for me."

"I suppose it was," Annie concedes. "Even if she never let you forget it."

Pat's foot is jigging up and down, his body almost vibrating with pent up energy. "Made you her grateful little slave, she did. And you fell for it."

Aiden's mouth tenses. "Kiss my arse, Pat."

Pat jumps to his feet, pushing his chair back so hard it tips over. "Well, you know what I figured out? That run-in with the cops? That was all Mercedes' fault."

"Shut the hell up," says Aiden.

"How could that poor woman be responsible for such a fiasco?" Lucinda asks.

"'Poor woman', my foot." Pat picks up the chair and slams it back into an upright position. "Mercedes Hann called the cops on her very own family."

That shut everyone up.

1997

Annie had lived in Calgary for three years before she returned home for a Christmas visit. She'd been back at other times, of course, but she made a point of avoiding the big occasions. That year, however, Lucinda happened to mention that Sadie was going to Toronto to spend the holidays with Gerry. The coast was clear.

Or so she thought until she bumped into Sadie outside the post office.

"Mrs. Griffin?" Annie looked nervously around. "What are you doing here?"

Sadie frowned. "I lives here, don't I?"

"But you're supposed to be in Toronto."

"Oh, poor Gerard, he ended up in the hospital, he did."

"Hospital?" Annie noticed that her voice was shrill.

"Yes, the hospital." Sadie looked slyly up at her, as if waiting for a response.

One look at Sadie's smug old face and Annie knew there couldn't be much wrong with Gerry, otherwise Sadie would not be standing there baiting her. "Too bad you missed your trip," she said in her most offhand manner and started to walk away.

"His appendix it was." Sadie's voice carried clearly across the short distance. "Will I tell him you were asking after him?"

The bitch. The rotten miserable old bitch. Annie kept walking.

Determined to put Sadie and Gerry out of her mind, she threw herself into all the holiday traditions, carolling in the evening and Midnight Mass on Christmas Eve, early morning presents and turkey dinner on Christmas day, followed by a never ending game of Auction that night. The last tradition was her father's annual Boxing Day party.

People started to trickle in midway through the afternoon. Her Uncle Frank and Aunt Kitty arrived with Pat, who was already in such high spirits that he almost spilled the container of cod tongues he'd brought to fry up for the crowd later on. Aiden was delayed, Pat said, busy fending off some girl from the night before. Mercedes appeared for her obligatory visit early in the evening. Heavy-drinking revelry, off-colour sing-alongs and long-winded recitals were not her cup of tea.

By six o'clock, the place was packed, most of them jammed into the living room where Melva Murphy was singing "Butcher Boy." Not being a fan of the maudlin love song, Annie slipped away to the kitchen for another drink.

Lucinda and Pat were at the stove, discussing how to bump up the pot of turkey soup so they'd have enough to feed the crowd, which was bigger than usual this year. The air was pungent with aromas of roast turkey and Newfoundland savory.

"I'll fry up some onion and sausage. Then we can add some macaroni and a couple of cans of tomatoes," said Pat, taking a long sharp knife and a can opener from the drawer.

Dermot was at the counter, frowning at all the empty bottles.

"Relax, Derm." Lucinda's voice was deadpan. "There's lots of homemade wine."

"God no, Mom," said Annie. "We can't risk people drinking that stuff."

Dermot shuddered. "Yes, that was a right awful batch, wasn't it? Come on, Luce, we has one party a year. Least we can do is put it on right, especially with Annie home."

Lucinda shrugged. "Sure it doesn't matter. It's too late to buy more."

Pat looked up from the can of tomatoes he was opening. "Why don't I run home and get some of Dad's New Year's stash? You can put it back later."

Dermot brightened. “Grand idea, Pat. But you can’t be getting behind the wheel.”

Pat claimed total sobriety, but Dermot would hear nothing of it.

“Fine, Aiden can drive me. He finally got his license and he just got here so he don’t have a sign on him. I’ll finish this and then we’ll go.” Pat slashed the knife back and forth through the tomatoes in the can then dumped them into the soup. He turned, knife in hand, tomato juice dripping to the floor, just as Mercedes walked into the kitchen.

Mercedes stopped, her eyes on the knife. Her normally pale face went white.

“You okay, Aunt Merce?” Pat reached out to her but then noticed the mess he was making and grabbed a tea towel. After wiping the floor he stood back up, dirty knife in one hand, soiled cloth in the other. He dropped them both into the sink.

Mercedes looked startled for a second, then her gaze shifted to Pat’s face and her mouth assumed its usual scowl of displeasure where he was concerned. “A fine mess,” she muttered, although her voice lacked its usual conviction.

For a moment, Pat looked hurt. Then he brushed past her to go find Aiden.

Mercedes buttoned her coat up to her neck and surveyed the counter. “Looks like an early night. Just as well. There’s way too much drinking on God’s birthday anyway.”

Bold with drink and beyond caring, Annie grabbed a jug of water and raised it high. “Jesus have mercy on us and turn this here water into wine. In the name of the Father, the Son and Holy Ghost, Amen.”

Lucinda took the jug from her hand. “Don’t be sacrilegious, Annie.”

“I see they’re teaching you some fine habits out in Alberta,” Mercedes scolded. “What else could you expect in a province led by the likes of that heathen Klein?”

Annie’s urge to spar died a quick death. She and Mercedes

rarely spoke anymore and she had no desire to change that. She went to the stove to stir the soup.

"Now, Mercedes," said Dermot. "Jesus don't mind a little celebration."

"If you run out of liquor, the celebrating will be over whether you like it or not."

"No worry there. We got our Pat on the case." He took Lucinda's arm. "Come on down to the basement and we'll see if there's something hid away."

"Never known that boy to run out of drink, Irish Paddy that he is," Mercedes called after them as they went to the stairs.

At the front door she came face to face with Pat, truck keys in hand. "You've no sense, have you?" she bit into him. "Put those keys away, you loaded sot!"

The combination of booze and resentment made for a long-avoided confrontation.

"Jesus, look who it is, Mother Mary Fucking Mercedes! Leave me alone and mind your own goddamn business. You'd drive Christ himself to the bottle, you would."

Mercedes glared at him. "Driving in your condition! You better watch out, you good-for-nothing fool." She charged from the house, almost bumping into Sadie Griffin who was listening intently on the other side of the door.

Sadie moved to get past Pat, who stepped sideways to stand in her way.

He folded his arms across his chest. "What the hell do you want?"

Sadie pushed an envelope at him. "I found this card to Lucinda among my mail."

"Been no mail for days. What were you doing, you old biddy, steaming it open?"

"How dare you?" Sadie stammered. "If my Gerard was here, he'd—"

"If he was here, I'd knock the face off him." He jabbed the keys in front of her face. "Now get home out of it."

Sadie's mouth opened and closed several times, then she bolted down the lane.

Pat went inside and slammed the door. The room had become uncommonly quiet.

"What the hell are you gawking at?" he shouted at the crowd, his good spirits gone the way of Mercedes and Sadie. "Aiden, come on, let's go."

"Hang on, I'm starving. I barely got a chance to eat since yesterday."

Pat stood impatiently while Aiden made himself a sandwich and a cup of tea. Twenty minutes later, finally finished, he had to go to the bathroom. Pat waited, his body lodged against the door until Aiden sauntered down the stairs tucking his shirt into his jeans. "Hold on to your drawers, Pat. Can't be going off half-cocked now, can we?"

"Christ's sake," Pat muttered, pushing him out the door and towards the truck.

Years before, Farley Hann's house had been the only one on that road, which, back then, was really just a dirt lane up the hill. There would have been little likelihood of meeting another car. As the population increased and more houses were built, Hann's Hill, as it was called, opened up to join the rest of the town. The Hanns gradually acquired a street full of neighbours, including Lucinda and Dermot. On this Boxing Day night, most of these neighbours were either tucked into their own homes or at the Bryne's party. There should still have been little chance of running into anyone.

As Aiden approached the bottom of the hill, a police car moved towards them. Inexperienced with winter driving, Aiden hit the brakes. The truck skidded sideways on the icy road and rammed into the side of the cruiser.

"Mother of Jesus," groaned Pat in the silent aftermath. "You okay?"

Aiden nodded. He was reaching for the handle when, out of nowhere, the doors flew open and they were each hauled out by a uniformed arm.

The policeman holding Aiden was unfamiliar to both of them. He sniffed the air. "So this is Patrick Hann. Driving under the influence, are you?"

The other officer, Bob Turner, shook his head. "You got the wrong one, Maloney. That one's Aiden, the younger brother."

"That doesn't make sense. He's not supposed to be driving."

Maloney shoved Aiden aside and grabbed Pat, twisting his arm behind his back. Pat cried out in pain. Aiden jumped in and dragged Maloney to the ground. Turner rushed to get him off, but not before Aiden managed to pound his ringed fist into Maloney's face, leaving a bloody scratch across his cheek.

Maloney jumped up. "Stupid fucking Newf. Get in the goddamn car."

Stunned, neither Pat nor Aiden moved right away.

"Now!" Maloney screamed, his hand on his holster.

Still shocked but now scared witless as well, they scurried into the back seat.

The end result was that Aiden ended up with a stint in jail. When he came up for parole, things did not appear promising. Punching a cop was a serious matter. Then Mercedes showed up at the hearing. As a well-respected teacher and community leader, her promise to personally oversee Aiden's rehabilitation carried considerable weight.

Anxious to put prison behind him, Aiden, for once, kept his mouth shut.

Snow drifted down in fat airy flakes to settle softly on the frozen white ground. It would have made for a picture-perfect Christmas Eve but that was already three days past. The pot of turkey soup was finally empty. Gifts had been put away; decorations would soon follow. The time had come to prepare for the New Year, to make resolutions. Sadie Griffin, as always, resolved to keep her family safe, her secrets safer. Sadie had been making the same resolution since her oldest son was born.

Them stupid little bastards. Hah!

Sadie snuggled her ear to the phone. She'd been waiting for the call and didn't want to miss a word. "Uh-huh…yes…go on, they didn't…ain't that something…well, not like they didn't have it coming to them…uh-huh…yes, thanks Bessie, be talking to you." She popped the phone back on the hook and went to stand to the side of the living room window, slightly behind the curtain. "You hear about them Hann boys?"

Debra looked up from where she sat on the sofa, the sewing kit open on her lap. "What Hann boys?" she asked, threading a needle.

"Right. Like you don't know."

"Lots of Hanns." Debra pulled the needle through a small white shirt.

"Yeah, sure there are. Too many. Anyway, they got theirselves arrested."

Debra's fingers stopped over a tray of buttons. "What for?"

"Driving into a cop and then beating on him." Sadie pulled the curtain a bit more to the left to better see down the road.

"Really, now?" Debra smiled and picked a button. "The both of them?"

"Uh-huh. Bessie says it was more Aiden that did it, though."

"They in jail?"

"They were till their father bailed them out."

Arsehole Frank Hann. Wonder where he got the money for that.

Debra examined the button, put it back and picked a bigger one.

"Vwoom."

Sadie smiled at four-year-old Mark who was kneeling on the floor with a pile of cars in front of him - police, ambulance, fire trucks - all lined up perfectly straight and from biggest to smallest.

"Vwoom."

Smart boy, our Mark, smarter than poor Debra. Reminds me of Gerard, except when he tries to talk, of course.

"Vwoom, vwoom." Mark's short, stocky body bounced from knee to foot to knee, over and over as he raced a small blue truck across the room.

"Careful there, Mark, don't bang into the coffee table," Debra cautioned.

Sadie folded her arms. "Or that cop car there. No father here to bail you out."

Debra had just inserted the needle into the button and was about to attach it to the shirt. "Give it a frigging rest, would you, Ma."

"Hard to rest with an extra mouth to feed," Sadie said, keeping an eye out the window.

"I told you, I'll get a goddamn job."

"You wouldn't need to still be looking if it weren't for that Beth Ennis."

Debra wiped her nose with the back of her hand. "Despises her, I do."

"Her fault you never got that job. Get on at the post office, you got it made, sure."

"This is the second time that bitch is after screwing me out of a job."

"When it comes to a Griffin or a Hann, the Hann wins every time."

Every frigging time. Fed up, I am.

Debra jabbed the needle through the buttonhole. "Every Jesus time."

Sadie's mouth tightened as a black cat made its way across the yard, leaving little paw holes deep in the pure white ground cover. Sadie didn't like cats.

"It's not fair." Debra's voice was whiny, shrill. "She's no better than me. Just because she got that stupid diploma, thinks she's the smartest thing on two legs."

"Just like her mother. Lucinda always thought she was better than anyone else."

"Don't need no diploma to sort mail. Say your ABC's, you can do that."

"Luck of the Irish. Still, no shamrocks up her arse when she got knocked up."

Youngster died, mind you. Not so lucky there.

"Goddamn Byrnes," Debra grunted. "Sick of them all."

"Then again, she managed to get a husband out of it," Sadie added.

"Christsakes." Debra scratched inside her bra. "Shut up, will you."

"Vwoom, vwoom," said Mark, driving the truck up his mother's leg.

"Come here, you, and give me a hug." Debra swept him up in her arms, tickling his belly and sending him into fits of giggles and shrieks.

"What a racket. Keep it down, you two." Despite her tone, Sadie was smiling.

Arrested. Hah! Talk about a Christmas present.

1999

Gerry sips his tea at the kitchen window, staring out into the black arms of night. A large slanted rock across the street looks over the cliff onto the beach below. As a boy he would lie on that rock, ignoring the smells drifting over from the nearby fish plant, and dream of all the exotic places he'd read about in Mercedes' books. When he was older, he dreamt about Annie Byrne.

Every time he came home, he hoped he'd run into her. The only reason he'd returned for Cathy's wedding was because he figured Annie would have to show up to see her best friend get married. "Annie's not big on weddings, Gerry," Cathy had told him. "I figured you'd know that."

"Gerard?" Sadie's voice is loud.

He turns guiltily to his mother. "Yeah…sorry, Ma. What is it?"

She holds the butcher knife suspended above the cold, wrinkled turkey. "I said you want the white or the dark?"

"Either one's fine."

"Lots here for a plate of sandwiches to bring along tomorrow. Family funeral, after all. Hah! Some family. Should bring something, seeing how much time you spent there with the old bat..." She keeps muttering to herself as she slices the turkey.

His mother generally hides her resentment of his and Mercedes' friendship, unless she's drinking, at which point all Hanns are fair game. Under the influence of one or two, she makes a few digs or snide remarks. More than that and she'll start to rant, calling Lucinda names like "Yank tart" or "man-robber," Mercedes "mercy moneybags" or "dried-up old spinster." The one time Gerry tried to defend Mercedes, who for her part never said a bad word to him about his family, Sadie went into such a rage she scared him. She remembered none of it the next day. He's grateful she only drinks at home.

"...they'll not be saying I don't do things proper, goddamn hypocrites."

"Sandwiches are a good idea, Ma. That's really thoughtful of you."

"Huh? Oh, right, sandwiches," she says, then after a moment, adds innocently, "I suppose they'll all be home for it, eh?"

"White meat sounds good," he says, ignoring the question. "So anyway, what's new with you? How are those bunions?"

"Bunions are bunions." She looks at him. "You're looking some washed out, though. Travelling is hard on the body, especially for a funeral. Wonder who'll be there from away," she says in her most casual voice.

Gerry smiles to himself. "Quite a few, I suspect. People had a lot of respect for Mercedes Hann."

"Yes. Indeed."

"I'm really going to miss her." He'd last seen her when he was back for Cathy's wedding. Just as he'd done in high school, he read to her from one of her newly acquired books. Unlike the old days, however, when she would pretend her eyes hurt so he could read and at the same time earn money for supposedly helping her, this time she truly was not up to the task. Still, she refused to go to a doctor.

"Um-hmm." Sadie's head is lowered over the bird. She carves for a while then turns it around so the breast cavity faces away from her.

"I'm not sure what I would have done if she hadn't been so generous," he adds. Despite himself, he is beginning to feel a slightly sadistic enjoyment in the conversation. He really should go to bed.

Sadie keeps slicing, slowly, methodically. Only a short quick sigh slips out.

"Yes, she was good to a lot of people," he continues, "even helped that frigging Aiden get out of jail that time. Now that's what I call generous."

"Cops should have locked them up and chucked the keys. Good call, that was."

"What do you mean? What call?"

Sadie looks startled. "Nothing. Not a thing." She takes a decisive swipe at the pope's nose and plops it and the knife on the counter. "There. That's that."

Gerry notices that his mother's back is slightly hunched. It occurs to him that she had this same roundness to her shoulders the last time he was home, but he'd forgotten it until this minute. He drains his cup. "How about a fresh pot of tea?"

"Sure, go on. Make you a plate to go with it."

He plugs in the kettle, then hugs Sadie around the shoulders. She glances up at him. Her face looks tired; the colour in her cheeks does not match the pallor around her eyes. Whether he wants to see it or not, his mother is getting old.

"Some scoff here. You must have been cooking for days." He kisses her forehead and hugs her again. "Thanks, Ma. It's good to be home."

5

1999

Pat's hands are fists. His back is rigid. "That cop thought I was behind the wheel. He as much as said so. Now why was that? Huh? Why?"

"Let it go, Pat. Besides, Aiden's better off for it." Lucinda rises unsteadily, one hand on the St. Anne medal around her neck. "I'll go keep Derm and Joe company."

Pat waits until Lucinda is out of earshot. "Mercedes left that party, walked home and phoned the cops. I'd swear to it on a stack of bibles."

"That's a bit hard to swallow, Pat," says Annie. "Even I don't think Mercedes would turn in her own nephew."

Aiden gets up from the table. "Well, we'll never know now." His tone is harsh, angry. "And I, for one, don't give a rat's arse anymore. So drop it."

"What do you want to defend her for?" asks Pat.

"Defend her?" Aiden shouts. "You are such an idiot, Pat!" Turning from his brother, he catches Annie's eye and mutters "fucking fool" under his breath.

Pat obviously hasn't heard the insult. "She did it on purpose and you knows it, too. You just never had the guts to say anything to her."

"Come off it, you two," warns Annie with a glance towards the doorway. "Don't be getting into anything tonight. Mom's got enough on her mind."

Aiden ignores her. "What would you know about guts, Pat?"

"More than you, that's for sure."

Aiden faces him eye to eye. "What the hell does that mean?"

Pat stares him down. "It means I'd face up to responsibility, that's what."

"You don't know the first thing—"

"I knows you were messing around with that poor stupid girl."

Annie looks from one to the other, surprised that a conversation about Mercedes has veered off in this direction. Then again, Mercedes was all about accountability.

Aiden groans. "Don't tell me you're on about that Griffin slut again. Christ!"

"You made your bed."

"Hard not to when she throws herself at you."

"You could have said no."

"Like you would, I suppose?"

Pat crosses his arms. "Like I did."

"Yeah, right."

"It's the truth."

Aiden snickers. "Just proves the bitch would go to bed with anyone."

Annie can't sit silent any longer. "For Christ's sake, Aiden, there's a youngster involved here."

Aiden whirls on her. "Mind your own goddamn business, Annie."

"No, I won't. Pat's right. You should have done the right thing."

"Listen to you," he mocks, "picking up for a Griffin."

"Who happens to be raising a kid without a father."

"Fucking Griffins are all sluts and homos and liars. Just ask Dad – he'll tell you." Frank Hann had nursed a particular disliking for Sadie ever since she'd accused him of stealing from the church. "Like mother like daughter, I swear to God."

"Not like you at all, eh?" Pat jumps back in. "Hand always on the zipper, then not man enough to own up to it when it comes back at you—"

"Shut the fuck up, the two of you. I'm sick of your sanctimonious bullshit. As for you, Pat, I'm glad Aunt Merce got me off your stinking boat. And even if she did what you said," he continues, his voice tight with warning, "you knows it wasn't me she was after. So in the end, whose fault was it?"

Annie hears a noise from down the hall. "Okay, that's enough. The last thing Mom needs is you two going at it."

Aiden walks to the sink and pours a glass of water. He looks at if for a moment then turns and raises the glass high. "To Mercedes. May she finally rest in peace." Only his mouth smiles.

Pat, looking relieved, gives in easily. "Good old Aunt Merce. Dead as a doornail and still pissing off the world."

Lucinda comes in, followed by Joe and Dermot.

"Never known a woman harder to toast than Mercedes," says Dermot. "She's like just-baked bread, she is - keeps getting stuck in the toaster until it finally catches fire."

Lucinda rolls her eyes but she's smiling. "What are you like, Derm? A couple of belts of whiskey and out comes the philosophiser." Her hand clasps his where it rests on her shoulder. "Speaking of bread, I got to get some from the freezer for tomorrow's sandwiches. Wouldn't want you crowd having nothing to soak up the suds."

She bustles off, yelling back for someone to go keep an eye on the coffin.

"I'll be right in, Mercedes," Dermot calls out as he reaches under the sink. "Stay where you're to till I comes where you're at." His hand reappears holding a paper bag. He winks at them all as he heads back to the living room.

Pat and Aiden start to follow when Lucinda calls out from the basement. "Will one of you boys come down and give me a hand? This door is jammed again."

They stop in mid-stride and glance back at Annie. They shrug guiltily, as if they've been caught in the act of doing, or planning to do, something forbidden. Annie is reminded of when they were kids, they with no sisters and her in a family full of girls. A furtive flash here, a quick glance there, always imagining Lucinda or Aunt Kitty looming over their shoulders. Or, God forbid, Mercedes. But how else were they to know what the other half looked like? Her father locked a newspaper over the fly in his pyjamas if he was in the same room with his daughters, and Pat and Aiden only knew their mother's underwear existed because she hung it in the furnace room to dry; Kitty Hann would never hang her brassiere outside on the clothesline. When it came to s-e-x, there wasn't a book to be found until high school, and then it was a beet-faced Sister Angela reading it out to them, tight-lipped, cheeks bursting.

Aiden heads down to help Lucinda. Several minutes later, he returns and places a mickey of rum on the table. Joe's eyes light up.

"You'd find booze in a nursery," says Annie. "Better not let Mom see that."

Pat is nodding. "Remember out in Bay D'Esprits. We'd be raiding the empty cabins to see what was left behind, and himself here never failed to find a few beers."

"Except at Aunt Merce's," says Aiden. "No booze there."

"And the only cabin around locked tight as a jail," Annie adds.

Pat raises the bottle. "To Mercedes, the first in a long line of women who failed to take a shine to yours truly."

"Still no luck with the ladies?" says Annie.

"Same as ever." Pat has always been awkward with women, too often saying the wrong thing in an attempt to be more like Aiden, who attracts the opposite sex with little effort. But Annie knows that Pat can be a girl's best friend when it really matters.

"I'd propose a toast but I can't think of a thing to say." Aiden smiles innocently as Lucinda enters the kitchen laden with frozen buns and loaves of bread. Pat hides the mickey under his sweater.

Annie looks doubtful. "That'd be a first, Aiden Hann without a word in."

Aiden looks straight at her. "Gerry Griffin's home. We'll get him to toast her."

The words hit like a slap in the face. She should have known he'd get her back.

"Who's speechless now, eh?" Aiden smirks.

"You'd have a few things to say to that bastard, wouldn't you, Annie?" says Pat.

She warns him with her eyes to shut up. "So, Mom," she says with forced calm, "what'll we do with these buns?"

Lucinda is glaring at Aiden but when she looks at Annie, her expression softens. "I'm not sure. You want to give me a hand?"

Annie nods, grateful for any excuse to get away.

Joe, who had started to doze off at the table, perks up. "I never understood why Merce took such a shine to that boy."

"I think she felt bad for him," says Lucinda, "growing up without a father like she ended up doing. He certainly brought out the soft side of her, don't you think, Annie?"

Annie says nothing. She does not want to think about Gerry or Mercedes. She doesn't want to remember the last time the three of them were in the same room together. Nothing was ever the same after that. Nothing's been right since.

Joe glances towards Pat. "She liked him better than some of her own, I'd say."

"Gerry was good to her, too." Lucinda rests her hand on Annie's shoulder. "Turned out to be a smart young fellow. I'd say he surprised a lot of people."

"What do you say, Annie? You surprised how smart he was?" Aiden's eyes have that glint of cruelty Annie has noticed before, though it's rarely been directed at her.

She's suddenly had enough of it all. She's fed up with pretending, with feeling like a victim, with saying the right thing. "Hard to find smarter than him or Mercedes," she says, her voice choked with bitterness. "They made a fine fucking pair, they did."

1991

From an early age, it was apparent that Annie was more academically inclined than her sisters or her cousins. By age four, she had taught herself to read. By the time she went to school, she could do basic math. As she grew older, she preferred books, generally on science or nature, for birthday and Christmas presents. While Lucinda and Dermot were pleased that she was so bright, they found her unending questions exhausting. Annie soon learned that Callum and Mercedes' house was a more hospitable environment for her curiosity. And although she found her aunt intimidating, Mercedes always took her seriously, as did her grandfather, both of whom talked about Annie's attendance at university as a foregone conclusion.

Each report card, she and Cathy Green, along with Francis Fowler, would compete for first place. Annie usually came out ahead. Their academic rivalry continued into high school, where the enrolment nearly tripled. While most towns along the shore had their own elementary school, they were each too small to support independent high schools, so students from Royal Cove to Harbourville were bussed to St. Jude. None of the new influx did much to challenge the status quo, however, and Annie, Cathy and Francis continued their three-way contest.

Gerry Griffin was not in the running.

The ultimate prize was a scholarship to Memorial University of Newfoundland, awarded annually to the top student in Grade Twelve. Annie had always assumed, deep within her competitive mind, that it would be hers. When the marks were posted, she was stunned to see that Cathy had won. Not by much, but she'd won.

Even more shocking was the third place winner. Gerry Griffin had beaten Francis Fowler, and he'd come perilously close to overtaking Annie herself.

Gerry wasn't stupid, he was...well, he was a Griffin. He had never shone scholastically, nor was he expected to. Gerry did, however, consistently do better than the Hann brothers, a fact which Mercedes never tired of pointing out. "If you paid as much attention as Gerry," Mercedes would scold, "you'd be able to put two and two together." Being compared unfavourably to a Griffin annoyed Aiden immensely, but he was far too lazy to do anything constructive about it, and instead resorted to calling Gerry names and making snide remarks about the Griffins in general. Unlike his brother, Pat didn't seem nearly so bothered about the negative comparison. Having flunked the first grade, he had fairly low expectations of himself, as did Mercedes.

As for Annie, she had paid little attention to Gerry's academic achievements, which was not to say that he himself had gone undetected. She noticed his eyes, brown and clear, and his hair a few shades lighter than his eyes. She noticed that he didn't smile too often, but when he did, a dimple creased his right cheek. His nose was different too, slightly bony with a rise in the middle, a Roman nose perhaps. And in Grade Nine, when Sister Angela had him stand next to Annie for their class picture, she noticed that his shoulder was finally higher than hers.

Annie and Gerry had rarely played together as children. He was always busy with chores or running errands for Mercedes, and seldom played ball or kick-the-can with Annie and her friends. When he did join in, he seemed to hang near the fringe, not fully participating, as if he felt he didn't belong there. Or maybe he was nervous that his mother might show up and berate him in front of everyone for wasting time when he had work to do. Annie had disliked Sadie more than usual the day she'd done that.

Nor did they hang out as teenagers; Aiden couldn't stand him, and Pat, even though he was older, tended to follow Aiden's lead. As for Annie, she generally tried to ignore him. Occasionally, however, in school or church, or at the store perhaps, Annie caught him looking at her. These random moments always left her with a funny feeling in her stomach, but she'd never stopped to consider if it was funny-good or funny-bad.

Gerry would immediately turn away, as would she - except for that one time in Grade Ten Science lab when she found his dark eyes watching her. In a flash of defiance she stared back, expecting him to blush and look away. He didn't. He smiled. Feeling the heat race up her neck, and furious with herself for instigating the whole stupid exercise, she stuck her tongue out at him, then quickly looked away and laughed loudly at something she pretended Cathy had said. When Cathy asked what was so funny, Annie laughed again. Cathy gave her an odd look but no one else noticed, thankfully. After that, she avoided Gerry in and out of school. If he was at Mercedes' house when Annie was there, she barely acknowledged him, at the most condescending to a nod of her head towards his pimpled puberty-stricken face as she waltzed past him. If anyone had thought to ask, she would have vehemently denied that she knew he existed, let alone felt any attraction to him. After all, he wasn't just a Griffin, he was her cousin, even if her family did wish it otherwise. She'd only found out that they had the same grandmother because Aiden had taunted her with it after she'd beat him once too often at Crazy Eights. When she'd asked her parents about it, Lucinda had sighed an exasperated sigh and told Annie not to be digging up ancient history. Annie had let it go. After all, it made no difference to her.

Despite losing the scholarship, Annie was still determined to go to MUN.

"And how are we going to afford that now?" Lucinda wanted to know.

"I'll get a bigger student loan."

"They only give you so much. It said in the brochure the parents got to help."

"Mom, I'll manage. It's not your problem."

"We don't have money like the Greens, you know." Lucinda carried on sweeping as if she hadn't heard. "Not that Cathy needs it now she got the scholarship."

"Jesus," Annie muttered under her breath, then louder, "I'll be fine, Mom."

"No you won't. I think you best go see your aunt about a loan."

"Right, I can just hear her. 'You should have spent more time studying and less time dreaming on the beach,'" Annie mimicked. "You know what she's like. Your head's not buried in a book, you're wasting time. She's going to blame it all on me."

Lucinda stopped sweeping and stared pointedly at Annie.

That afternoon, Annie stomped off down the wet, grey pavement. The sky was dark. The clouds were heavy. Still, she would have preferred the elements to the overbearing heat of Mercedes Hann's kitchen.

Annie hung up her coat and shook her hair from its wet ponytail, careful not to splatter any raindrops on the always-open bible on the desk. Rufus bounded over to sniff and nuzzle her until Mercedes ordered him away, at which point he immediately flopped down on the rug by the stove. The aroma of hot figgy bread, her aunt's specialty, filled the room. Mercedes' hair was loosely tied and she wore a plaid apron over her brown pants and beige twin set. She was smiling.

"Look at this, Annie." Mercedes turned the page of a slightly tattered book on the flora of the east coast. "Such a rare find. Over a hundred years old."

"Wow!" Annie leaned over to look. She knew better than to touch it; her hands were still damp. "Is Granddad here?" she asked hopefully.

"In the back room. I picked up his new computer in St. John's yesterday and he's been at it since he got up this morning." She poured Annie tea from the big brown pottery teapot. "Here, this will take the chill from your bones."

"So he finally got a computer, did he?"

"Yes. Now, you received your results yesterday. How did you do?" If Mercedes had something to say, out it came – no dawdling, no feigned indifference.

Annie had no such inclination. "Pretty good," she answered.

Her aunt sliced into the raisin-studded bread. Steam rose up as its molassesey goodness sweetened the humid air. "Did you beat them?"

"Ah...I...you know, did pretty good," she stammered, accepting a plate of hot buttered bread.

Mercedes folded her arms and stared at Annie. "Yes, go on."

"I had a really bad cold during exams, and Mom's always over at Beth's helping with her new baby, and I was really tired from the—"

"Ann, did you come first or not?" Mercedes cut in sharply.

"Ann" was a sure sign of displeasure. Annie decided she might as well confess. Playing verbal cat and mouse with her aunt was destined to be a losing battle.

"Cathy beat me by two marks." Mercedes' scowl deepened. Annie rushed to justify herself. "I wonder if her mother told her the questions. She's a teacher, she probably knew them."

"Nonsense!" The single word, issued in Mercedes' cold authoritarian voice, made Annie sit up straight. "Violet Green would no more cheat than I would." Mercedes leaned over and wagged her finger in Annie's face. "If you had one grain of sense in that wasted brain of yours you'd know that."

"They didn't ask the right questions." Her voice had fallen to a plaintive whimper. "There was stuff on there the teachers hadn't even covered. It's not fair."

Mercedes plunked the knife down on the counter. "When you're finished blaming the world, perhaps you can tell me who came in third. I assume it was the Fowler boy?"

Annie seized the opportunity to focus elsewhere. "Francis didn't even make the top three. At least I came in second, and Cathy barely beat me. I'd like to get them marks checked." Sometimes she didn't know when to shut up.

"Enough, Ann. Who came in third?" Each word was a measure in patience.

Annie looked down at her plate, her appetite gone. She pictured Gerry's face, Mercedes' errand boy. The fact that Annie or Pat or Aiden would have been equally capable and in need of earning money had apparently never occurred to Mercedes. And from what Annie had seen, she paid Gerry handsomely, and for the oddest things. She paid him to read, for God's sake. She even let him borrow her precious books.

It had grown quiet in her aunt's kitchen. Mercedes was waiting.

"Gerry Griffin," Annie mumbled, flicking at the handle of her mug of tea.

"Gerry came in third?" A smile lit up her aunt's face as she clapped her hands together. "I told that young man he could do it. I said if he studied hard and let me help him, he could beat out those show-offs who think they know everything."

Annie pushed the tea away. Is that what Mercedes thought of her? A show-off? As she watched her aunt's beaming face, she realized that Mercedes wasn't even aware of the insult. Worse still, she had apparently been helping Gerry all along. Since when did his success become more important than Annie's?

"To think he placed in the top three!" Mercedes continued. "He never made it better than sixth before that. He must have worked so hard, what with all he does to help that mother of his. What a fine lad he's become..."

A fine lad? He'd come in third to Annie's second, yet Mercedes called him a fine lad while at the same time implying that Annie was a failure.

Still Mercedes prattled on. "...always knew he was better than the rest of them..."

Annie looked out the window at the rain lashing the pane. She wished she was out there, away from her aunt's gushing voice. Would the woman never shut up?

"Anyway," Annie cut in, hurt beyond caring if she was rude, "Mom and I wondered if you could lend us some money to supplement the student loan I'll get."

Mercedes focused back on Annie. "That scholarship should have been yours."

"Well it almost was. And it wasn't my fault. If I'd known—"

"Enough excuses. Go home and I'll think about it." She stood up and started to leave the room. "And don't waste that food, we're not made of money."

Annie locked her eyes on the two slices of bread and kept them there until Mercedes was gone. Plump raisin eyes glistening in melted butter stared up at her. Forcing herself to take a bite, she realized she was starving and stuffed the rest in her mouth. She was about to leave and take the second piece with her when she heard Mercedes talking to Callum.

"...her own fault...such a disappointment..."

Annie stopped chewing to better hear what they were saying.

"...first year I taught him, I could see the potential, ragged clothes and all."

There was an indistinguishable mumble, presumably from Callum.

"Yes, I suppose I did." Mercedes' wistful tone made Annie's skin prickle.

There was a shuffle, a chair moving, followed by her grandfather's strong voice. "He's a lucky boy to have you looking out for him, Mercie, that's all I can say. And like I told you a million times, it was never your fault."

"Nor yours. Doesn't stop you from wondering 'what if,' though, does it?"

"Maybe not, but I'm long past feeling guilty for it."

"You're right, I know. You can't just erase guilt from your soul, though, can you? But if I can help young Gerry, maybe God will see fit to forgive us all in the end."

There was a moment of silence. Annie tried not to breathe too loudly.

"I must call and congratulate him. I just hope that wicked witch of a mother of his doesn't answer the phone," Mercedes said.

Under cover of her grandfather's laughter, Annie crept out of the house, carefully closing the squeaky screen door. She deliberately chose not to dwell on what she'd heard. She'd had it with Gerry and Mercedes and had no intention of wasting another minute on either of them. Instead, she thought with regret of the figgy bread she'd forgotten on the table and which Rufus was probably eating that very minute.

Three days later her aunt called her to come over to discuss the loan. Mercedes poured tea, from a pitcher with ice this time. There was no warm bread.

"I've given this a lot of thought, Ann. I don't think you deserve that loan."

Annie could hardly believe it. Mercedes, who had always encouraged her desire to go to university, who had insisted for years that Annie was smart enough to do it, now refused to help her. Why couldn't she support her when she really needed it?

"...rewarding undesirable behaviour," Mercedes was saying. "I've told you that you spend too much time combing the beach, dreaming when you should be studying. You knew you needed that scholarship, and look what you've done. You let everyone down, your grandfather, your mother, most of all yourself. I hope this teaches you the value of hard work. Look at Gerry. If you had half the drive... "

As Mercedes talked on, the hurt turned to anger. What was it with her and Gerry Griffin? Annie thought back to the snippets of conversation she'd overheard on her last visit. What made him a hero and Annie such a disappointment?

She stood up abruptly. "Never mind about the loan. I'll figure it out for myself." Without waiting for a response from Mercedes, she stormed out of the house.

More determined than ever, she put up flyers at Burke's and the post office offering all manner of services, from lawn to child care, but all she got were a few babysitting jobs. There was little extra work in St. Jude, especially for a seventeen-year-old girl.

Just as she was beginning to despair, Callum stopped by the

house complaining that he couldn't figure out his new computer. When Annie volunteered to help, he offered to hire her to set up his documents and teach him how to use it. She told him she would do it for nothing. When he insisted, she let herself be talked into being paid, knowing that her student loan would not be enough to see her through.

With her money problems temporarily sorted, Annie let herself begin to dream about the fall. The future was hers and she intended to grab onto it and fly, leaving Mercedes Hann and Gerry Griffin in the dust of the Trans-Canada Highway.

St. Mary's High was a school divided. The boys, governed by the Brothers, were on one side; the girls, ruled by the Sisters, were on the other. The gymnasium, which also served as the lunchroom, was in the middle. Each day during lunch, the Nuns and the Brothers walked up and down between the tables, making sure there was sufficient distance between individual boys and girls. Each day after lunch Sadie Griffin cleaned up after them all. She didn't like this particular cleaning job. She didn't like the students, and she wasn't fond of the Brothers or the Nuns. She preferred priests. Sadie would clean up after a priest any day.

That hand goes any lower down her arse it'll be coming out the front.

Sadie walked in procession behind Cyril Maher and Cathy Green as they followed the priest out of the gym at the end of the school Mass. Her hands were joined together, her head slightly lowered. Her pious demeanour belied the indignation in her eyes as they focused on the hand caressing the backside in front of her.

I seen them carrying on, during Mass no less. Like he wanted to slide himself under her skirt right then and there. At lunch too, him with his paws everywhere under the table. Disgusting.

Outside the gym doors, Sadie raised her face to the bright sky. Her arthritis had been worse than normal of late and she was relieved to see the approach of spring. Sidling up next to the visiting priest where he waited to greet students and teachers on the school steps, she placed her hand on his arm.

"My word, Father, that glare would blind you but I thank the Lord anyway."

Nice bit of muscle there. Good looking too.

Father Ryan nodded. "Yes, Mrs. Griffin, it's certainly bright."

"You must be starving after that wonderful sermon. I got lunch done up for you at the Priest's House. Cold salmon, potato salad, bit of cheese and bread to go with it."

"Thank you." He removed his arm from under her hand to adjust his robe.

"Sure it's the least I can do after you come all this way."

Especially seeing as they pays me to do it. Still, not like the old days when I got regular work and a steady cheque. Grand job that was. Grand benefits too. Hah!

"That's very kind of you, Mrs. Griffin."

"Might be the church sees fit to save you all that travel some time soon, what?"

Father Ryan smiled and nodded and turned to a group of students.

Sadie carried on down the steps until a sharp familiar voice called her name. She turned. Several steps above her stood Mercedes Hann who, since her retirement from teaching, ran the school library.

"Good day, Mercedes. And how are you?"

Dried up old prune.

"Fine. And you?" Mercedes' tone held an air of forced politeness.

"Well now, I was just thinking how it's nice to see the sun again, get a bit of lube back in the old bones. Such a long winter, sometimes I wonders if I'll ever thaw out—"

"Might I have a word with you?"

A word? Isn't that what they were having?

Mercedes moved ahead, away from the crowd. "A walk?"

"Yes…yes sure." Sadie rushed to catch up.

"Has Gerry spoken to you about our conversation?"

Sadie looked sideways at Mercedes. "Gerard? No…what about?"

Mercedes gave Sadie a wary look. "Perhaps I should wait…"

Spit in her face, I would. That sick of the two of them, all comfy-cozy and secret.

"Something going on, better tell me." Sadie softened her tone. "I am his mother."

Mercedes stopped. "I didn't want to betray Gerry's confidence, especially with so much money involved."

Sadie's head tilted on a distinct angle, like a cat sensing a mouse's presence before it sees the rodent itself.

"Forgive me, Sadie, please," Mercedes said.

Sadie was perfectly willing to forgive, especially with "so much money involved." "That's all right, Mercedes dear. You've always been good to our family."

And a self-righteous pain in the arse.

Mercedes nodded. "I've offered to pay for Gerry's university education."

Sadie's breath caught. "You what?"

"I should have spoken to you first, I suppose." Mercedes started walking again. "I don't want to offend you, really I don't. I know you have your pride."

If there was a hint of insincerity, Sadie ignored it. "What did Gerard say?"

"He said he couldn't let me, that it was too much and that I had my own family."

Christ have mercy! When did he get so stupid?

"Gerard's a proud boy," Sadie managed to say.

Mercedes slowed her stride. "Perhaps you could talk to him?"

I'll talk to him all right. And I'll be getting that money, and I don't care about the why of it. Still...you got to wonder... what's that one hiding?

"Why you doing it?"

Mercedes looked uneasy. "He's a good boy. We both only want what's best for him. Considering that I ask for no repayment, I believe we can leave it at that, and between us?" Mercedes gave Sadie a look that made it clear they understood each other, at least as much as they ever would.

What's she up to? Why's she that determined to look after my Gerard? She got lots of nieces and nephews to fetch and carry for her. Why pay Gerard all these years? Ah, fuck it. Don't matter why. Gerard'll be taking every red cent he can get.

"Debra and the boys be needing help too."

"Hmm, yes, I suppose they will." Mercedes' tone was noncommittal.

"A word down the road, especially from one of their teachers..." Sadie paused.

Mercedes nodded but said nothing.

Ah, what odds. I can't be worrying about that lot, they don't got Gerard's brains.

"I'll talk to him, don't you worry."

"Thank you, Sadie."

"You're welcome, Mercedes."

Mercedes turned and started back towards the gym doors.

Now isn't that just ducky? Mercedes Hann thanking me for taking her money. Darn right I'll take it. Anything for my Gerard.

1999

A crust of congealed milk has collected at the triangular opening of the can of Carnation. Behind it in the fridge is his mother's cocoa-caramel cake, an elaborate treat that takes hours to prepare - further evidence of the time she has invested in welcoming him home. Gerry remembers the chocolates in his suitcase down the hall.

"Back in a minute," he says. Halfway to the bedroom he stops and turns back. If he doesn't say something his mother will pile his plate so high he'll never reach the bottom. As he approaches the kitchen, he sees her sneak a small bottle from the pocket of her apron. She quickly unscrews the top and tips it into one of two cups of tea on the table. He retreats again to get the chocolates.

Back in the kitchen, he holds out the box.

"Maple chocolates, my favourite! Some thoughtful, you are. And tall and handsome. Them women up there must be all over you."

Gerry pretends not to have heard. He has no intention of talking to his mother about his love life. "A cold beer sure would go good with that feast."

"You don't want beer this time of night. Have a cup of tea instead."

She has never liked to see him drink, even though he rarely does around her. He doesn't drink much at other times either, perhaps in reaction to his mother, who has been preaching abstinence and sneaking booze as long as he can remember. He reaches out to take a cup; at the last second, he doesn't know why, he goes for the one she spiked.

"No," she says instantly. "I already put sugar in that one. Take that other cup. It's stronger and hotter. The Lord knows you probably needs it."

"No, no. I like a bit of sugar." He has his finger around the handle.

"Yes, but I already drank from that cup and I got a cold sore coming. See?" She screws up her lip in his direction. "I can feel it, right below the surface it is. Don't want you catching that." Her hand is closing around the cup.

"Darn cold sores. Milk?" he asks, although he already knows the answer. It's either milk and sugar or a tip of the bottle, never both.

"Think I'll have it black for a change." She takes a big noisy slurp.

Gerry winces. "It's still scalding hot, Ma."

"I got one of them asbestos mouths sure. Now drink up and we'll have a yarn while there's no one else here. How's your company?"

His job, "his company," as she calls it, is one of her favourite subjects. He started with an investment firm right out of business school, anxious to help his mother and start paying back Mercedes. The salary is more than decent, and as far as he can tell, he's good at his job. He must be – they keep giving him promotions and raises. He likes it well enough, but the truth is, he gets tired when he thinks about doing it for the rest of his life. His field of study, and his job, have been pragmatic decisions.

"They treat me fine. I can't complain." That's something he never does around his mother. She wouldn't understand that there could be anything to complain about, that he'd rather be in a classroom. On the other hand, he doesn't tell her the good news anymore either. The one time he mentioned a promotion – his first, a small one, nothing to rave about – half the town congratulated him the next time he came home, people coming up to him at church and on the sidewalk, talking about what a good job he had, how the company was lucky to have him, and how proud St. Jude was to have him for a son. For all they knew he'd been made president of the company. He was too embarrassed to say anything. After that, he told only Mercedes about future promotions.

"Well, you deserves it, Gerard. You always did work hard, running around for Mercedes all the time like you did. Don't know why you did it half the time."

Gerry hides his grin. She knows exactly why he did it. They needed the money. She knows the other reason too. He enjoyed Mercedes' company.

"...in school too," Sadie is saying. "Had to work harder than the rest of that lot just to get noticed, so them snooty teachers would even see you in the room."

"Now, Ma, the teachers were fair enough."

"My arse. Goddamn Violet Green and her ilk. Never knew you had a brain, just another stupid Griffin. Lot they knows. We showed them though, especially them Fowlers, always looking down on us. You beat that Francis fair and square." Her voice goes low and bitter. "Wish you'd have beat that frigging Annie Byrne."

Gerry is surprised. She rarely mentions Annie. It's as if by not saying the name out loud, Annie isn't real, and what happened, didn't. He wonders how many nips she's had from her apron pocket. Her eyes have a brightness that wasn't there earlier. "Now, Ma, school wasn't that bad."

"It was too that bad, Gerard." She takes another swig of tea. "They never thought a son of mine could do it, but you did. Had to sit up and take notice then, them frigging Greens and Fowlers, especially them goddamn Hanns. Sick of the lot of them. They knew half the secrets I knows what goes on in this town, they'd fall down with fright."

Gerry groans silently. Now she's going on about secrets. He doesn't doubt that she knows more than a few. He just doesn't want to hear them.

Mercedes had secrets, too, secrets that shaped how she lived her life. "A person must make up for the sins of the past by doing good in the present," she told him once. He'd been surprised; Mercedes rarely spoke of the past except in reference to a history book. Yet Gerry had long sensed that she carried a heavy burden of guilt, even though he could never imagine what she could have done that was so wrong. She was a teacher, a community leader, a staunch Catholic. Why the need for penance? In her living room next to a statue of the Virgin Mary was a small plaque, which read, "Atonement is necessary for the soul to survive." It occurred to him once to wonder if he somehow figured into that atonement. In the end, it was irrelevant. The friendship that developed between them could not have been based on guilt.

The food on his plate is growing far beyond his capacity. "That's enough, okay?"

Sadie places a large bowl of beans next to his fork. "I kept the beans separate so it don't run into the rest. I knows you don't like that. Dig in before they gets cold."

His stomach grumbles, but not with hunger. "Thanks, Ma." He picks up his knife and fork. "It looks delicious."

She smiles at him over the rim of her cup, then drains it and licks her lips.

He could really use a cold beer.

6

1999

Lucinda's hand lifts abruptly from Annie's shoulder. Annie misses the warmth, the contact, but she has only herself to blame. How could she have been that crude, that vulgar, in front of her mother, and about Mercedes on this of all days? Lucinda doesn't ask much of her, a little respect, a little decorum.

Annie looks up, expecting to see her mother's hurt face looking back at her, but it isn't.

"What did Gerry ever do to you, Aiden?" Lucinda's tone is exasperated.

"He did enough. Besides, he's a Griffin, what does it matter?"

"That hardly seems fair."

"Wasn't fair what Sadie did to Dad either."

"Frank's not still harping on about that, is he? That's years ago."

"There's some in this town still looks at him funny even though he never took one red cent from that collection plate. Sadie knows it too. Right, Pat?"

"Give over, Aiden." Pat turns to Annie. "You okay?"

She nods then meets her mother's eyes. "Sorry, Mom."

Lucinda smiles. "Come and help me make sandwiches."

Relieved, Annie pushes back from the table.

Pat stands as well. "I can do that egg and olive spread you likes, Aunt Luce," he offers.

"That'd be lovely, Pat. Best do it in the morning, though. What else, now? I got tuna somewhere. Let's go see what's in the cold room, Annie."

Happy to get away from Aiden, Annie follows Lucinda down the stairs. As she enters the utility room, the close damp familiarity catches at her – the oversized washer bought second-hand some twenty years before, the mismatched dryer that's used only on the worst of winter days. Two fully stocked freezers are crammed into the corner, and the shelves on the wall overflow with cans and jars and boxes. Something is always cooking on the stove upstairs, and there's usually a cake or bread or pan of cookies just in or out of the oven, all in anticipation of some unexpected but welcome company to eat it all up. The fridge bulges with yesterday's leavings, ready for a hearty lunch or waiting to be preserved in the freezer. Annie's father likes to joke that he's afraid he'll end up there himself if he sits still too long.

Unlike Lucinda, Annie keeps a streamlined supply of food in her tiny Calgary apartment. Tins of soup and salmon, sliced meat and cheese for sandwiches, frozen meals ready for the microwave. And eggs, she always has eggs, a perfectly proportioned food for single people such as herself, because, although there have been other men who have eased the loneliness for a few weeks or a month, Annie has been on her own. It's too much work to prepare a big meal just for one. Her friends are as busy as she is and the leftovers stare at her until she throws them out, which makes her feel guilty. She is her mother's daughter, after all.

She feels a tingle behind her eyelids and blinks repeatedly in an attempt to clear what must be fatigue. Her mother's hand grasps her elbow. Alarmed, Annie quickly wipes her eyes and turns around. "What is it, Mom? You okay?"

"I'm fine. But are you, Annie? That Aiden had to open his big mouth about Gerry and I could see it took the good out of you. Did you want to talk about it?"

There's a part of Annie that longs to open up to her mother but she's afraid she'll fall to pieces if she starts talking now. "Don't you worry. It'll take more than a Griffin to get this Byrne down," she says with a gusto she doesn't feel.

"Well if you need to talk, I'm here." Lucinda sounds frustrated, defensive even.

"Sure, but you're right, let bygones be bygones." Annie's face is mercifully buried as she rummages for supplies. "If Mercedes wanted to give money to the Griffins, who are we to say she shouldn't have?" She lifts a box from the back of a shelf. "Look, a whole case of tuna."

"For heaven's sake, who cares about the money? Hardly worth all this fuss when you think about all the other stuff."

"True," Annie agrees cautiously, holding out the tuna.

"Like I say, Annie, I'm here if you need me. Always have been." Lucinda snatches the box from Annie's hands. Her back is stiff as she walks away.

As Annie listens to Lucinda's footsteps tromping up the stairs, she knows that somehow she has let her mother down, but she's not sure how. Without warning, the pace of the last two days slams into Annie so hard her knees tremble. She sits down on an overturned crate and reviews their conversation. Something about it troubles her. "...all the other stuff..." What did her mother mean by that? What else does she know?

Her eyes race to the doorway half expecting to see Lucinda. There's no one there.

Annie is suddenly overcome with sadness, for the death of her own innocence, for the loss of all the joy she started out with. Avoiding this moment has been a constant struggle for five years, but every ounce of fight has finally failed her.

She drops her head in her arms and, finally, lets herself cry.

1991

Annie Byrne escaped St. Jude for MUN, arms flung wide to capture all that university had to offer. She was barely a hundred miles from home. It could have been a million.

This state of contentment lasted through her first year and into the second. Her marks were great and she'd met lots of new friends. She'd even gotten the job as the Resident Assistant for her floor, which, along with her student loan and occasional typing jobs, put an end to her constant money worries. Then, as Joe would have put it, life did that sneaky thing where it slips under the skin of your neck, slithers down your spine and bites you on the arse.

It was the third Thursday in January. As usual, she was in the library transcribing her lecture notes and copying scientific formulas, attempting to disentangle the important from the trivial. More often than not, she recopied just about everything. Who knew what insignificant detail might make the difference between an A and a B on some future exam?

Out of the corner of her eye she saw a young man approach. His overloaded knapsack pulled at his T-shirt, stretching it across a wide chest and flat stomach. Annie grinned, imagining herself on the cover of one of the romance novels she'd read secretly as an adolescent, a hunky guy standing behind her, all muscles and teeth, the manly sensitive type, her own face slightly baffled yet amused.

As the intriguing stranger drew closer, he said, "Hello, Annie." Still half in a daydream, it took a second before she realized that her romantic hero was Gerry Griffin. She hadn't seen him in ages, and then only at a distance. His dark eyes seemed impossibly darker. His bony nose didn't look so beakish since he'd filled out, and his acne had cleared up completely. He was downright handsome.

Just as he stopped next to her carrel, two girls brushed past him, knocking his knapsack onto his arm and sending his contraband coffee spitting in all directions.

"Frig!" he muttered, trying to balance the cup.

A splash of hot coffee hit Annie's arm. She jumped up, knocking her chair over and into Gerry's shin. The rest of the coffee, cup and all, flew from his hand. "Watch out!" he warned too late as it splattered across her desk.

"My geology notes! Shit! I just spent two hours rewriting them."

He gave her an odd look. "What did you say?"

"I said I just finished rewriting my notes and now they're a frigging mess."

He pressed the bottom of his T-shirt onto her papers. "What do you do that for?"

"It's a good way to study. I don't want to get behind."

"Not much chance of that." His eyes creased with the cutest smile.

Feeling her face start to burn, Annie went to find paper towels. When she came back, Gerry was wringing out his coffee-soaked T-shirt into his cup, leaving the lower part of his stomach exposed. It had the kind of toned look she'd imagined on the book cover moments earlier. She immediately looked away.

"Sorry about your notes," he said, taking the towels from her.

"Oh, they're not in too bad a shape really, considering."

He started to clean up the mess. "Going out home tomorrow?"

"No, I'm on residence duty this weekend."

"Oh yeah? Me too, on duty I mean."

"You're an RA too?"

"Yeah, just started. Good excuse not to go home."

"You don't miss St. Jude?"

"God, no." He gathered up the towels, studying the stains like he was reading tea leaves. "You hear about the bash over at Dewey's tonight?"

Dewey's was a popular bar near campus. It was a dive but the beer was cheap.

"Yeah. Me and Cathy were going to go," she answered nonchalantly, "but then Cyril talked her into skipping class tomorrow and heading out home for the weekend."

"That's too bad, should be a great night." He hesitated. "I could ... I mean, if you'd like, we could go together, you know, if you don't have anyone to go with, we could go, the two of us...?" His cheeks had turned a deep pink.

Was this his clumsy way of asking her out, she wondered, or was he just being friendly? Blunt by nature, Annie had never been one to flirt or play mind games, which may have explained why she didn't date very much. Not that she cared.

"Not like a date," he blurted. "Nothing like that. There's a whole pile of us meeting up there later. I just thought you wouldn't want to go over alone."

She felt her face redden, and was about to tell him to take his pity invitation and shove it when he added, "But I hope you come. It'd be nice to catch up."

Since when did she and Gerry Griffin need to catch up, wondered Annie, rearranging her stained notes. Then again, she did want to go to Dewey's and she knew she'd never walk in alone. She shrugged. "Nothing better to do."

"Great," he said eagerly. "I'll be over at nine o'clock."

"Sure, nine o'clock," she repeated. "I'm in 212 at—"

"I know. You're right next door to me," he said, then went red to his roots.

Between the two of them, there was an inordinate amount of heat racing around. If they didn't end this soon, Annie feared one of them would self-combust.

"I've seen you go in and out," he added.

"Oh. Okay."

"Well, see you in a few hours?"

"Yeah," Annie answered, then was annoyed at the quickness of her response.

As he walked away, he glanced back and waved. Embarrassed to be caught still looking, Annie tried to appear busy. Gerry turned back around and bumped into a library cart. She stuck her head down as if she hadn't seen a thing.

For two hours she pretended to study. Was she really going to the bar with Gerry Griffin? What if someone from home saw them? It'd be all over St. Jude in no time.

Finally, she gave up and went back to her room, whether to change her mind or her clothes she didn't know.

She did neither. At nine sharp he was at the door, and in a fresh set of clothes, she noticed. Then again, he'd hardly have shown up in his coffee-stained T-shirt.

Too late now, she decided. She was off to Dewey's on a Friday night with Gerry Griffin. And so what? She was only having a beer with him, for heaven's sake.

The clear night was deceptively cold. Within minutes of leaving residence, her nose and ears were stinging. Gerry made several attempts at small talk, but Annie, head buried in the neck of her coat, was preoccupied with trying to prevent frostbite.

Spotting Dewey's just ahead, Gerry grabbed her mittened hand and started a mad dash down the road. "Come on, it's freezing," he yelled.

Annie had little choice but to hold on tight and try to keep up. Unsure whether the ache in her chest was from running or the feel of her hand clutched in his, she was grateful for the breathless sprint down the hard-packed street. As soon as they reached Dewey's, he let go of her hand to open the door. Inside, the hot smoky air swirled around them. Someone yelled to Gerry from across the room and he and Annie shuffled through the crowd to join a large table filled with Gerry's friends. Annie was glad to see several familiar faces in a nearby booth in case she needed a change of company.

She never gave them a second thought. She had a great night, the most unexpected part of which turned out to be Gerry Griffin himself. There he was with a diverse group of interesting people, confident, self-assured, attractive in a familiar sort of way. Annie found herself studying him at odd moments, his face and his manner. Once, he caught her eye and smiled. This time she smiled back.

The evening was a new experience for Annie. She'd grown through her teens as a medium-sized fish in a very small pond. But that night she sat with an even smaller fish from the same pond, a capelin to her cod, and he was taking the lead. She realized that life's playing field had levelled off, that each person at the table had the chance to become whoever or whatever they wanted. She felt an incredible freedom, a euphoric sensation of liberty and emancipation. Had she only had two beers?

Yes, only two, and Gerry had paid for both. She'd resisted at first, but then she found herself letting him, on some level vaguely aware that by doing so she was allowing the evening to become something more closely resembling a date. A small voice inside her had piped up, "a date with a cousin." She'd shoved it back down.

During a break in the music the others went out for a toke or to visit at other tables. She and Gerry found themselves sitting virtually alone talking about high school.

"Do you think you'll ever move back to St. Jude?" he asked.

"Never really thought much about it. You?"

"Never." He took a sip of beer. "The bigger the city the better."

"I don't mind St. Jude but I know what you mean. Everyone knows everyone."

"Exactly. Here, I'm invisible. No one cares where I came from."

Annie nodded, surprised that he was so open. Maybe that's what happened when you left the small town behind - you left your inhibitions there too. She liked that idea. In fact, she liked it so much that she found herself telling him the whole story of asking Mercedes for a loan, something she'd been too humiliated to tell anyone except Cathy.

"She wouldn't give you anything?" He was suddenly very serious.

"Nothing but a lecture. I wish I'd never asked the old witch in the first place. Thank God I got the RA job. I don't know how I'd do it otherwise."

"Nothing? Nothing at all?"

Annie frowned. "Like I said, nothing. Why?"

He looked uncomfortable. "It's just... it doesn't sound like her."

"I know you think she's this lovely old lady. Well, let me tell you—"

"No, it's not that."

"What then?"

He started to say something, then stopped abruptly and looked away.

Annie could feel the fun draining from the evening. "You know, we were having a fine time till we started talking about her. Can we just drop the subject?"

He was quiet for a moment. Then he smiled. "You're right. Another beer?"

"Sure, but it's my turn to buy."

"No, no, it's on me."

Just like that they were back on track. They laughed and talked and drank more beer, enjoying the music and the people and especially each other. And at the end of the night, Gerry walked her home.

"So. Here we are," he said as they stood outside her residence.

"Yeah. Thanks."

The night was still and silent. He moved closer. "That was fun tonight."

"Yeah, I had fun too."

More silence. She knew she should say good night and go inside, but she didn't.

"Me too," he said, taking the tips of her fingers in his. Then he bent down and gave her the sweetest little kiss, not quite on her lips or cheek, somewhere in between. In a husky voice he whispered, "Good night, my Annie Byrne."

"Good night," she mumbled, barely recognizing the gravelly voice as her own.

Once inside, she stood unmoving, wondering at her own intense disappointment. Her body had this raw ache, and her heart felt full and empty at the same time. As she leaned against the door, it hit her that more than anything in the world she had wanted Gerry Griffin to kiss her, to hold her tight in his arms and really truly kiss her for a good long time. What the hell was happening to her?

She went to bed, her head and heart lightly buzzing, and not entirely from the alcohol. By morning her outlook hadn't changed, except by then it was tinged with a nuance of sweet surprise, as if she had discovered a tiny treasure, one that had been hiding right in front of her. She wanted to hug herself all day.

When Cathy got back on the Sunday, Annie casually let slip what she'd done on the Thursday night. Cathy was full of questions - about what they ate and drank, what she wore, who was there, and in particular, what they talked about. As Cathy was leaving, she hesitated. "Did you and Gerry talk about your aunt at all?"

"Yeah, but it kind of put a damper on things so we changed the subject." Annie eyed her friend. "Something on your mind?"

"Well, it's about Gerry and your aunt."

"Look, I know it used to bug me but that's ages ago. Who cares about that now?"

Cathy shrugged. "Maybe you should."

An uneasy knot tugged at Annie's navel. "What are you going on about, Cath?"

"Look, I'm not meant to be telling you this, but I think I better before you and him get too chummy. Did you know that Mercedes is responsible for him being here?"

"That's baloney. He came in third and earned his place just like the rest of us."

"That's not what I meant. Did you know she's paying his way through?"

Annie paused, hurt that Mercedes would lend Gerry money when she'd gotten nothing but grief. Why hadn't he mentioned it? Was he embarrassed? Whatever the reason, she could hardly blame him for Mercedes' actions. "Look, that's their business if she lent him money. I wish I'd known, but it's not the end of the world."

"It's not a loan, Annie. Mercedes is paying for the whole thing - books, tuition, residence - and he doesn't have to pay back one cent. His very own guardian angel."

Annie felt like she'd been punched. Was her own flesh and blood paying for him but not for her? How miserable could the woman get? And Gerry! To think Annie had confided in him and all the while his pockets were filled with money that should have been hers. From the sounds of it, he only took the RA position to avoid going home, while Annie barely survived on two jobs. Everything but her underwear was a hand-me-down. She even got her sister to cut her hair. And Gerry had insisted on paying for the beer! How generous!

"Who told you this?" she asked, praying it was just an idle rumour.

"Mom, and she heard it from Sadie herself. I'm not supposed to tell anyone."

"The fucking gall of them."

Annie could hardly believe her stupidity.

1993

Violet Green's plush forest-green carpet was lined with the ridges of a fresh vacuuming. Her glass coffee table sparkled with a perfect see-through shine, and, in the kitchen, the upgraded appliances looked as clean and new as the day they were installed. All thanks to Sadie Griffin, who had the art of cleaning down to a science. No one knew dirt better than Sadie.

Jesus have mercy, will she ever shut up.

Sadie blasted the sink with Lysol, then put her head down and scrubbed.

"And like I said to Cathy," Violet was saying as she set her tea cup back in its saucer, "it doesn't matter if Gerry never did well in the earlier grades."

How much frigging longer am I going to hear about that goddamn scholarship? Two years on and she's still bringing it up every chance she gets.

"The last year is what matters most," Violet went on. "And Gerry did just fine."

"That he did." Sadie leaned harder on the scrub brush.

"I suppose you'd call him a late bloomer. Ha-ha."

Sadie turned the water to full blast. Steam filled the air between where she stood and Violet sat drinking tea and eating Jam Jams. Sadie scrubbed harder.

"Not like my Cathy."

Miserable bitch! I been here four hours now, cleaning shitty toilets, changing sweaty sheets, shining fancy silver, and that one gets herself tea and cookies and planks her arse at the table and eats them right in front of me. Boils me.

"And dear Mercedes, what a saint. Imagine paying for Gerry like that, such a good-hearted woman. And no, I never told anyone. I can keep a secret, believe me."

"Thank you, Violet."

Wish I never went and told her about that frigging money.

Violet looked displeased, just as she always did when Sadie used her first name. "Yes. Well…it's too bad, though. Mercedes deserves some credit."

"Indeed she does, Violet."

Damned if I'll be calling her Mrs. Green.

"And like I said to my Cathy, I was so proud of her for winning, but really, there's others not as…well, as well-off, to put it bluntly, but what can you do? Cathy won fair and square, no matter what poor Annie felt about it." Violet took a sip of tea.

Sadie folded the towel and laid it on the counter.

"And poor Francis, getting beat out by Gerry. Must have been a shock."

The nerve of the woman, some days it was too much.

Violet looked up and caught Sadie's eye. "Oh, but like I said, Gerry earned it, yes indeed he did. And don't you let anyone tell you different now, Sadie."

"Don't worry about that, Violet." Sadie picked up her coat and stood waiting, just as she did every week, for her thirty-seven dollars.

Violet took another sip of tea and popped the last piece of cookie into her mouth. She chewed, swallowed, and wiped her mouth with her napkin. Finally, she stood up.

Take your frigging time, why don't you? Not like I got nothing else to do.

Violet took down her purse from the kitchen shelf and, reaching inside, brought out her wallet. She pulled out a twenty, a ten and two fives. Pursing her lips, she put back one of the fives. She opened her coin purse and counted out four dollars in change.

"There you go, Sadie. Plus a little something extra for you."

Sadie shoved the money into her coat pocket. "I'll see you next week, Violet."

Damned if I'll thank the woman, either.

1999

Gerry spots a six-pack at the back of the fridge. As he is opening one up, his mother returns from the bathroom again. This time he can smell the liquor on her. The more she drinks, the more careless she gets about hiding the evidence.

Sadie tutts. "That Kevin, always bringing in darn beer."

"Glad he did. That ham was good and salty." He takes a long swig. As always, the malty aroma of beer reminds him. He sees her, over the rim of his glass, that first night at Dewey's. When she'd smiled at him, her eyes had registered a sense of surprise. In that moment he'd felt they shared a secret, a feeling that had lasted throughout the night, and, in the end, far longer.

"Gerard?" His mother is eyeing him strangely.

"Yeah, Ma?"

"A million miles away again, you were. Anyway, I said Father got his first funeral Mass tomorrow."

"Father?"

"You know, our new young Father James. Who else would I be talking about? I think he's right nervous. He didn't have much chance to get to know her so what's he supposed to say? But I knows he'll do grand. Fine man, smart and educated, not like the bunch around here. Big books all over the house - religion, psychology, all kinds of stuff. Pities him sometimes I do, wasting away in St. Jude..."

If there's one thing his mother likes to talk about more than the neighbours, it's the resident clergy. The difference is that she speaks of the priests with more affection and admiration than she speaks of her children, except for him. This no longer embarrasses Gerry. He cannot control his mother, what she says or does, what she thinks, why she thinks it. Sadie is a force unto herself. He's known that since he knew anything.

"...what can he be saying about Mercedes?" Sadie is still talking. "I'm sure they met, though I don't think she was going to Mass at the end, never saw her there for ages. Not like some, always there, all pious and righteous, likes of that Violet and Dwight Green. The way them two prances around town, Mr. and Mrs. St. Jude they acts like. Too uppity to clean their own dirt. Hires me to scrape the muck off the floor and the shit out of their toilets. Nerve, ordering me around for a few measly bucks. Frigid old bat she is. And him, acting so upstanding. Hah, I knows about him I do. Puny little bugger. Good match, you ask me."

"I imagine he knows enough about her. She had a good reputation."

"Who? Oh, Mercedes. Yeah, sure. Want cake? I done your favourite."

He rubs his stomach. "Sorry, but I'm stuffed. I can't eat another bite."

"And to think I wouldn't let the boys touch it all day. And Mark too, caught him with a finger in the icing, stuck it right in his mouth before I had the chance to stop him. Saucy as a crackie he's getting to be. Debra should take a hand to that boy."

Gerry taps her gently on the nose. "And you'd be the first to stop her if she did."

"Would not."

"You would so. You got a soft spot for our Mark, you know you do."

Sadie shakes her head, but she's smiling. "Anyway, you want cake or not?"

Gerry is so full there's no room for guilt. "I'll have it for breakfast," he teases.

Sadie frowns. "Gerard, not for breakfast—"

"I'm just codding you, girl. We'll have some after the burial, how's that?"

Her face brightens. "Yes, the funeral. Tomorrow be here soon enough."

Gerry smiles despite himself. Leave it to his mother to perk up at the mention of Mercedes Hann's funeral.

7

1999

Annie catches her reflection in the mirror above the laundry sink, the puffy skin, the eyes that have forgotten how to be happy. Is this what she's been reduced to, crying her heart out in a dingy basement storeroom? She presses a damp cloth to her face and holds it there. The cold wetness feels fresh against her skin.

She gives herself a few minutes then heads back upstairs. Her mother is talking on the hall phone. Annie wonders crossly who would call so late. As she nears the kitchen she hears Aiden's voice, still bleating on about the Griffins.

"And you know Sadie. Thinks the sun shines out of her darling Gerry's very arsehole." His voice rises. "There she was on the church steps, bragging about 'Gerard's wonderful job in international investment', like she got a clue what that is, and his car and his fancy apartment. Pitied poor Father James, her paws were all over him."

Joe chuckles. "Sadie loves the priests."

"Then she says, 'Oh, and the women! Dear Father, sure they're always after him, not a lick of pride these days,' and on and on she went. I thought she'd never shut up."

"Sadie's one to be talking about pride. Her own husband had to leave town to get shed of her." Pat lets his wrist go limp. "Not that she was really his type."

Sadie is the last person Annie wants to defend but she can't listen to them slag the wife and excuse the husband. "Like he was any prize," she says as she walks into the room. "Leaving a wife and youngsters to chase gay tail in Montreal. Men!"

"Now Annie, don't be bitter. It makes your face go all scow-ways," Joe teases gently. "You puts me in mind of Mercie her-self when you gets that snarl on you."

"Quick, cheer me up," Annie retorts, reaching for a clean mug from the cupboard.

Lucinda comes in. She waits for a quiet moment. "That was Tom Kennedy on the phone. He wants to see the family back here after the graveyard to read the will."

Annie whirls around. "What do you mean, read the will?"

"That's how she wanted it done, everyone together in the same room."

"Sounds like one of them soap operas on TV," says Pat.

"So that's how you spends your time off the boat." Aiden pushes Pat lightly. "You're a real little woman, aren't you, cook-ing in the kitchen and watching the soaps."

Pat swats at his brother. "Get on, Aiden, I do not."

"Anyway," Lucinda says, raising a hand to her temple, "Tom's been called to Toronto on some emergency and so we have to do it tomorrow, right after the burial."

Joe arches back to look up at her. "Can't we let the dirt set-tle on her first?"

Lucinda shakes her head. "He said Mercedes' exact in-structions were to do it as soon as possible and before anybody left St. Jude. With Tom having to go, it can't wait."

Annie plunks the empty mug down on the counter. "Her and her exact instructions. Bad enough she insisted on a home wake. Who does that in this day and age? Even the poorest bunch in town goes to the funeral home. But no, not Queen Mercedes, she's got to take over the whole house and everyone in it on her way out."

"Annie, if we can't do her one last wish, what's the good of us?"

Annie is ready to argue the point until she notices her mother's eyes. The whites are streaked with red and the skin beneath is dark and wrinkled.

"What the hell's she up to now?" asks Aiden.

Pat tugs at his beard. "Three days dead and soon to be buried, she's still at it."

"Always in control, even under the dirt." Annie waits, expecting someone else to comment. The only sound is the drone of the fridge, amplified by the unusual silence.

"You know what this means," Aiden finally says. "It's probably true."

"What is? Mom, what's he talking about?"

"Well, Annie," Aiden says before Lucinda can answer, "it seems Mercedes may be having the last laugh after all. You see—"

"Aiden Hann, you're just making matters worse with your gossip," Lucinda interrupts. "Listening to the likes of Bessie Foley!"

"Bessie Foley?" Annie sits down next to Joe who gives her hand a gentle squeeze. "She still at Kennedy's office?"

Pat nods. "Just what you wants in a lawyer's office, Sadie Griffin's apprentice."

Annie turns to Aiden. "So what did Bessie say?"

Lucinda raises her hand imperiously. "To make a long story short, Annie, Aiden here has been dating Bessie's niece, although I'm not sure that's the right word for what those two have been doing." She gives Aiden a harsh, disapproving glance. "Never learn, will you? Anyway, Janet, the niece, she said Bessie hinted that the will's going to be a bit of an eye-opener."

"What Janet said Bessie said," Aiden interjects, "and I was there, remember, and in all my glory, I might add, was that some people were in for quite a surprise."

Pat snorts. "Who wants her few lousy bucks anyway?"

Aiden cocks an eyebrow. "Few? How about half a million?"

Lucinda's hand slaps the counter. "The gall of that Bessie Foley. I've a good mind to report her to Tom Kennedy."

Annie eyes her mother. "Yet you're not surprised at the amount."

"Oh, don't mind that one. Besides, it's nobody's business." She pauses. "There is something else, though. Tom let it slip just now that Gerry Griffin is in the will too."

"Wouldn't you know it!" says Aiden. "I always knew he had an ulterior motive."

Pat, who has been tilting his chair back on its rear legs, lets it falls forward with a thump. "What is it with her and that son of a bitch? She'd do anything to spite us, don't matter we never did a thing to her. And he's the biggest bastard I ever met. Well, I've had it with the pair of them." He stands up. "I'll sit with her tonight and then say good riddance, once and for all. Come on, Aiden."

As Aiden follows him out, Lucinda drops into his chair. She seems on the verge of tears, a state Annie has become uncomfortably familiar with since arriving home.

"That bunch never were any good." Joe is suddenly wide awake. "What can you expect the way they carries on, bedding their own kin? God, them Griffins been at that long as anyone can remember. No wonder half the youngsters don't make it. Look at Sadie, sure, burying two of her own."

"Really?" says Annie. "Sadie had two more children?"

Lucinda frowns and shakes her head at Joe. He ignores her and leans in close to Annie. "According to rumour, one was a dwarf and the other was so handicapped they said it was lucky it died." He lowers his voice. "Thing is, no one ever saw them. Home births, they were. And Sadie had them in the ground so fast it'd make your head spin."

"Poor Sadie. I actually feel bad for her."

"It's all in the blood, and Sadie and Angus got the same in their veins."

Annie says nothing. She's not so sure she wants to know any more.

Joe is undeterred. "They were all originally from Little Cove before they moved into here. There was only a few families there, and the brothers and sisters from one family married brothers and sisters from another family, and so they got more related. After that it's the luck of the draw for the youngsters. Some are okay, others not."

"For heaven sakes, Joe," Lucinda pleads, "it's all gossip and hearsay. Don't be talking about stuff like that, not tonight."

"All I knows is that half the Griffins were bad in the head." His lip curls up in distaste. "The worst of the lot was that Paddy though, a sick dirty thing from day one, he was." He slaps the Formica table and the cups and spoons rattle in their saucers. "I should of took care of him when I had the chance. Nothing but a goddamn pervert, that Paddy Griffin."

1943

It was a typical spring night in St. Jude, the ground still frozen, a hint of a thaw in the air. Joe Hann had spent the evening playing darts at the town bar, Patron's Pub. Joe liked his beer and he liked his whiskey. He also liked to spend time with the ladies, unlike his older brother, Callum, who, at twenty-one, found himself tongue-tied around women. Callum had passed the night at home reading, alone except for his father, whom he'd carried upstairs earlier. Through the open window he could hear the shrieks and laughter of children playing hide and seek in a field down the way. His ten-year-old sister was among them. At nine-thirty, he went to call her in. She came right away. Mercedes liked to curl up in bed with a book before sleep.

Joe decided to go home early so he could go fishing the next morning and still get back in time for Mass. He took a shortcut through the woods, past the bog meadow, which would bring him up behind his family's rundown house on the outskirts of town. This route also made it easier to enter through the rear door and avoid the squeaky hinge in the front that Mercedes had been complaining about for weeks and which he kept forgetting to fix.

The sliver of moon that lit his way through the woods gradually withdrew behind a mist of clouds. Rounding the last clump of trees on the final approach to the house, he came upon Paddy Griffin, pants undone, grunting in the darkness.

Paddy was Joe's uncle, sort of, not that Joe had any respect for him. When Paddy was well into his thirties, he had married Joe's mother's stepsister, Nell - she was sixteen at the time - and taken her to Toronto. Nell returned six years later, alone, pregnant, the mother of two girls. She gave birth to Paddy's son, Angus, six months later, by which time she'd taken up with Henry Byrne. Two months after Angus was born, Nell was pregnant again. When she died giving birth, Henry, heartbroken, went out fishing one night and never made it back. With Nell and Henry dead, Henry's parents took on the job of raising the baby. They named him Dermot.

"What the hell are you up to, Griffin?" Joe called out.

Paddy started frantically pulling his clothes together. "Just having a piss. Who the fuck wants to know anyway?"

"It's me, Joe Hann. Christ sakes, piss into the trees at least so I don't walk in it."

Paddy started to stagger and sway all of a sudden, mumbling incoherently.

"Get on home," Joe advised. "Don't want to pass out. Gets awful cold at night."

Paddy spun around and, with a surprisingly sure step, ran off into the darkness.

Heading once again towards the house, Joe's eye was drawn upward to where an oil lamp illuminated his sister's room. Through the window he could see the back of Mercedes' head. Her small hand came up to guide a hairbrush through her long dark hair, past her bare shoulders. Joe immediately dropped his eyes back to the ground.

He wondered why she hadn't pulled the shade. Then he remembered. Weeks ago, maybe even longer, she'd asked him to fix it. It hadn't seemed important at the time.

Swinging back around, he searched the empty darkness. Nothing was visible except the shadows of a late-night wood.

First thing the next morning, he repaired and hung Mercedes' shade. Fishing could wait for another day. The front door's hinge continued to squeak.

One evening after supper, when Mercedes went out to play ball, Joe asked Callum what he knew about Paddy.

"Nothing good. Mona Burke was talking down at the store, said her cousin up in Toronto heard some pretty nasty rumours. Apparently the reason Nell left him was she caught him doing something to one of their little girls, the dirty bugger. Mona hinted Paddy had some kind of disease too, from a whore up north. Not that I believe everything out of Mona's mouth, but there's something about that man makes my skin crawl." Callum reached for Joe's plate. "Why you asking?"

Joe had a queasy feeling in his gut. "Well, I was heading home through the woods last week and I bumped into him taking a leak, at least that's what he said he was doing with his hand on himself. I don't know why he'd be back there at that hour, and it seemed some queer the way he was staring right at the house. After he took off, I saw Merce was up in her bedroom, and I still hadn't gone and fixed that shade yet."

Callum was staring at the ceiling, up in the direction of Mercedes' room. "That filthy disgusting pig." His voice was bruised with rage.

"Now Cal, slow down." Joe laid a calming hand on his brother's arm. "We're not sure what he was up to. Let's just keep an eye on him."

"We better tell Merce so she can stay clear of him."

"Go on, there's no need for that, is there?"

"Sure there is, so she keeps her distance." Callum stood, his hands full of dishes.

"If we goes telling her that stuff, she'll be scared to leave the house. Besides, she's too young to know about what he was doing at himself."

"Joe, if she's old enough for him to be looking at her like that, she's probably old enough to understand what he was doing."

"Lord's sake," Joe whispered, "she's ten years old. Just because he's a dirty bastard don't mean she got to hear about it."

"She got a right to know so she can protect herself."

"Go on, Cal, she don't need to be knowing stuff like that yet." He shifted uncomfortably. "Who's going to tell her, anyway?"

Callum hesitated. "Well, you saw him there, but I can talk to her if you want."

"Look, I probably got the whole thing wrong," Joe backtracked. "I bet he was just having a piss. Yeah, now I thinks on it, that's all it was."

Callum eyed him doubtfully. "If he comes near her..."

"Don't you worry," Joe promised, coming over to help with the washing up. "If he shows his face near here, I'll cut the legs out from under him. All three of them."

As it happened, the problem resolved itself. Model citizen that he was, Paddy had gotten into debt with several local businesses and abruptly left town. Nobody was disappointed. Even his mother at the post office appeared relieved to have him gone.

By the time Callum and Joe decided to try their luck in New York a few years later, their biggest worry was how their sister would manage left in the questionable care of their father. To make life easier for her, Callum had electricity and plumbing installed and arranged for Burke's to extend credit to Mercedes, and Mercedes only, for food and supplies.

They'd forgotten all about Paddy Griffin.

1946

St. Jude was originally a fishing village. As such, it had its share of widows. When the sea took a man, it took his family's livelihood as well, leaving his wife and children to make do. A few ounces of meat would flavour a pot to feed a family of three or six or ten. Hand-me-downs were handed down a few more times. With no man in the house, life was extra hard.

When Sadie Griffin's father drowned, her mother was six months pregnant. Sadie had been making do since the day she was born.

"Big bow wow, Tow-wow-wow…"

Five-year-old Sadie Duffie sang a ditty as she swished the broom across the wood plank floor. Her singing stopped at the sound of someone running across the gravelled yard and up the rickety front steps.

Mabel Duffie's plump body burst into the kitchen. "Ma! Ma!" she yelled, sending the cat scurrying into the neat pile of dirt that Sadie had just swept together.

"Mabel!" Sadie yelled.

"I saw the toilet!" Mabel panted.

Sadie turned to her mother. "Look what she done."

"Weren't me. Stupid cat did it."

"I hates that thing." Sadie smacked at the cat with the broom. "Go away, cat."

Edna Duffie's crooked arthritic fingers placed a small piece of salt beef onto the boiling cabbage. She peered at her older daughter over the steam. "Get on, girl. They really got a toilet?"

"Who? Who got one?" Sadie asked. She'd never seen a real toilet.

"The Hanns. Merce bragged about it all week. Wouldn't shut up for nothing."

"So they don't got to go to a outhouse no more?" Sadie could not imagine that.

Mabel shrugged. "Don't know, but the toilet's right next to her bedroom."

Sadie tried to picture needing to go in the middle of the night and only having to walk to the next room. She couldn't. "Did you go pee on it?"

"No. I wanted to but she didn't say to, and I wasn't going to let on like I cared."

"Why? She's our cousin." Sometimes Mabel didn't make much sense to Sadie.

"Some cousin. Wouldn't even show me the answers on the history test the other day. Thinks she knows everything, that one."

"That's the Hanns for you," said Edna. "Chock full of theirselves. Don't know why Mary ever married that Farley. The death of her, he was."

"That Merce is nothing but a tomboy," said Mabel. "Whenever we plays ball she always wants to be on the boys' team."

"I likes playing ball," said Sadie, sweeping around Mabel's feet.

"So she got a eye for the boys, eh?" Edna eased herself into the rocking chair.

"Nah, don't know they're alive other than to kick the ball. A few of the older fellows were teasing her the other day and she swore at them, right out loud, too. Sister Anne heard her though the window. Got in some trouble, she did. Serves her right."

"Her father falled on the ground by Sullivan's," Sadie offered, trying to be part of the conversation. She put the broom away and found a blanket to cover Edna's legs.

"Farley! Foolish gommel lives at the bootleggers, he do," said her mother.

"What's a gommel?" asked Sadie.

"He's off his rocker, he is," said Mabel, ignoring Sadie. "With a father like that, don't know why they acts so high and mighty."

"What's his rocker?" Sadie asked, looking at her mother in the rocking chair.

"She means he's not all there," said her mother, pointing to her head. "Nuts."

"Yeah," said Mabel, "and the house is some dirty, even if they do got a toilet."

"Who needs a toilet, anyway?" said her mother.

Sadie glanced out the window where the outhouse was

partly hidden behind a row of trees. She'd been putting it off for the last hour. She hated going out there. It was always dirty and it smelled really bad. In the winter it was so cold she had a hard time doing her business once she got there. And in the summer there were flies everywhere, buzzing around the walls and the seat and in the hole. Sadie was always afraid one would fly up her bum. She didn't like to think what would happen then.

Mabel crossed her arms. "I wouldn't use one if I had one."

Sadie looked at her sister like she was crazy. "I would. I'd use it all the time, even if I didn't need to go. I'd sit there and read the catalogue. You're nuts, Mabel."

Sadie put on her coat and her rubber boots. Outside, she picked her way through the tall wet grass until she reached the outhouse. Flies buzzed and flitted around the door.

"I wish we had a toilet," she said.

1999

Gerry puts his plate in the sink and looks out the window. The empty clothesline is a white streak across the yard, cutting the night sky in two. Past a bank of clouds, he sees her again, standing in the window. This new image, his first in five years, has hovered in his mind all evening, entering his consciousness unbidden at random moments. If he closes his eyes, he imagines he can feel her body, warm to the touch of his fingers.

"Come and sit, Gerard." His mother's voice is thick.

Every muscle in his body feels heavy, almost soggy from the mix of tea and beer and beans and turkey. Still, he's in better shape than his mother. Her "come and sit" had sounded like something far less pleasant. "I've been sitting all day," he says as he refills the kettle in hopes of getting another cup of tea into her, unspiked this time.

Gerry pours boiling water into the pot and adds three tea bags. His mother would normally object to such wastefulness – one bag is enough for the both of them in her mind – but she's staring off into space, a spiteful set to her mouth. He opens a new can of Carnation and adds milk and sugar to two clean mugs, then fills them to the top with the strong, dark brew. "Here you go, a nice fresh spot of tea."

Sadie blinks at the mugs. "Why you messing more cups?"

"That last bit of milk tasted funny. I opened a new can."

"Tasted fine to me."

"But you didn't have any?"

"Any what?"

"Milk."

"Milk? 'Course I got milk."

"In your tea, Ma."

"What I said. Just look at it."

"Not this cup." His voice has risen. He deliberately lowers it and speaks slower. "I mean you didn't have any milk in your tea last time, remember?"

She looks uncertainly into the new cup. "Oh…sure…that one."

"I thought a bit of milk would protect your stomach from all that caffeine."

"Sure. Right. Bit of milk won't hurt. Nice to get a bit now and then," she says with an odd cackle.

A burst of noise fills the air, sending his mother's body on a tight little bounce off her chair. She glances around. It's not until the second ring that her eyes light on the phone. Still she sits, a bemused look on her face. Gerry notices that the light on the answering machine he bought her for Christmas is flashing from an earlier message.

Sadie's hand flaps at the air. "That be Gus or Kevin at the bar. Box'll get it."

Sure enough, it's his brother. When Gus has left a message and signed off, Gerry presses the retrieval button to hear the first one.

"Hello, Sadie. Tom Kennedy here," says an authoritative male voice. "I need to see Gerry after the funeral. Have him call me tomorrow. Thank you."

"What's that about?" Gerry asks.

"Mercedes' will."

"What's that got to do with me?" He has an uneasy feeling in his gut.

"Nobody called you up in Toronto to tell you about the will?"

"No. I don't know what you're talking about."

"So if you don't know nothing about the will, then why you home?"

"For the funeral."

Sadie folds her arms and looks pointedly off into the distance. "Didn't jump on a plane when Mabel died. My own sister, that's related. Proud of it too. Not like them Hanns. Too snooty to own up to us. Still you comes to hers. Travels all day, lies at work. Boils me. Poor Mabel dead in the ground."

He waits for Sadie to finish and look at him. "I said why do I have to be there?"

"I just told you. Didn't I? Well…sure, I suppose you're in it."

"Shit!" That's just what Annie needs. "Whatever it is, I'm not taking it." As soon as he says it, he knows he shouldn't have, not in front of his mother.

"Why not?" she yells. "She owes you. All that running around. What's the matter with you? She owes me too, wasn't for me you wouldn't be here. Lots that one don't know, the rest of them too, but I knows, yes by Jesus—"

"Ma, stop," he begs softly. His head feels like it might split in half. He'd like just five minutes alone to remember Mercedes without his mother's interference. As for the will, he can only hope it's a token, a symbolic gesture from one friend to another.

Sadie opens her mouth. She appears ready to rant, then seems to change her mind. "Fine, Gerard. We'll wait and see."

"That's right, Ma. Everything can wait until tomorrow."

Tomorrow he'll see Annie. He's already waited five years for that.

8

1999

Over fifty years have passed since the night Joe caught Paddy spying on Mercedes. Yet by the time he's finished recounting it, his gentle face is spidered with angry red veins.

"The thing is," he continues, his voice bitter, "I knows my father was no saint, but he'd never have gone and left Merce on her own after we went to New York if Paddy Griffin hadn't talked him into it. I should have beat the daylights out of that bastard when I had the chance."

Lucinda, her eyes dark circles of fatigue, is slumped in her chair. She looks sadder than she has all day. There is a sudden commotion from the back steps and she sits up straight. "Who on earth can that be?"

"Let's just not answer it," Annie suggests. "It's almost midnight, too late for visitors now. And you two are exhausted."

"I'd ignore it if it was the front but it's got to be one of our own if they're at the back." Lucinda leaves behind an exhausted sigh as she goes to the door.

Annie hears the clack of the latch, followed by a ruckus as if somebody has fallen into the porch. She pushes back her chair. "Mom?"

"I'm fine," Lucinda calls back to her. "We'll be right in."

Seconds later, Callum Hann makes his way into the kitchen, looking far worse than he had that morning when he'd woken Annie up to welcome her home. There are food stains on his sweater and his previously crisp shirt collar has collapsed and crumpled. The little hair he has left lies in random strands about his head.

"For God's sake, Dad," Lucinda is saying. "The doctor said take it easy. Look at the state you're in. You'd never know you to be the same man from breakfast to now."

Annie takes Callum's arm. "Granddad, what are you doing here at this hour?"

"Well my Annie, I was home looking out the window when young Joe passed by. Never waved or looked in, just went right on by. So, I decided to join him."

"Sorry, Cal," says Joe. "The thought of Mercie laid out in the parlour got me to thinking, and I thought I'd come and stay here. You don't mind, do you?"

"Sounds like just the ticket. I don't think I could sleep out home knowing she was four doors down and gracing this earth for the last time."

"But where am I going to put you?" Lucinda looks utterly worn out.

"They can have the twin beds in my room. I'll take the couch in the basement." Annie lays her arm on her mother's shoulders. She seems shorter and frailer than Annie remembers. A flood of affection rushes through her and she kisses the side of Lucinda's head. "Why don't you head on up, Mom? You've had a long day and it's going to be a longer one tomorrow. The last thing we need is you conking out on us."

Lucinda gives in easily. "Maybe you can get Pat to cook them something?"

"I know he's a better cook than me, but I've had a lot less to drink. Don't worry, I'll get them a mug-up and settle them in." Playing caregiver to her mother is a new role for Annie, yet they both adapt with little effort. "Go. And take Dad with you."

"Thanks, Annie." Lucinda's hand grasps her arm. "I'll see you in the morning."

With her parents off to bed, Annie pokes at the embers in the wood stove and puts the kettle on. The two old men sit, quiet and peaceful, as she cuts a blood pudding into rounds and starts to fry them up.

"Well, Joe, our Mercie is really gone, isn't she?" Callum eventually says.

"Dead as she can be." A note of wonder steals into Joe's voice. "Can you believe we're this old? Sometimes I looks in the mirror and sees the old man looking back at me. 'Who's that old geezer?' I says to myself. To think that our Mercie is but a corpse in the next room and here we sit, two old farts, still alive, still breathing."

"Growing old and ugly beats the alternative," Callum says. "Better to be old than..." He stops.

"Than what?" asks Joe.

Annie turns around.

Callum is staring out into the night beyond the kitchen window. He seems lost in thought or memories, perhaps both. Annie is reminded of summer vacations in Bay D'Esprits. Her grandfather would sit for ages looking, not out to the horizon, but over at the cliffs on the other side. Once when she was about nine or ten, she asked him what he thought about when he looked across that ocean. "I thinks about life, my Annie." He'd paused briefly before adding, his voice almost a whisper. "And I thinks about death."

"I'm not sure Merce would have agreed," he says now.

His tone catches Annie's attention. "You saying she knew she was going to die?"

He nods. "She wasn't scared to talk about it either. She told us what she wanted and who she wanted to be there." He looks at Annie. "That's why your mother badgered you into coming. Merce told us that more than anyone you had to be here. We promised we'd see to it. After that, she called for the lawyer to review her papers. Once she got everything arranged she seemed settled about the whole thing, like she'd made her own decision." He sighs. "I hope I'm that peaceful when my time comes."

Annie spreads butter on several slices of her mother's bread, which is almost, but not quite, as good as Mercedes'. "But I thought she died suddenly."

"In the end she did, I suppose. But that's dying, isn't it? No matter how slow it is in coming, that one moment must be sudden. There's no going back, no undoing it." He pauses, then continues matter-of-factly. "Lucinda spent the afternoon with her, then Sadie Griffin dropped by that evening with communion. Sadie come out and said Merce wasn't looking good, maybe she needed a drop of tea. By the time I made the tea and brought it in, she was gone. Just like that. Sudden. Alone."

"What exactly did she die of, anyway?" asks Annie.

"Hard to say. She'd been poorly for a while. Then old Rufus died. Took the good out of her, that did. Other than that, we don't know. She refused to go to the hospital. And she never went to a doctor in over forty years."

"I always found that odd, an educated woman like her refusing to go to a doctor."

"She used to say she'd rather put her faith in God than some man who thought he was God." Callum's voice is tense with a resentment that he makes no effort to hide.

"They say only the good die young." Joe's voice is angry as well. "You'd think with her disposition she'd have outlived us all."

"Don't talk ill of her, Joe, not tonight. I know she was hard at times, but Merce was a complicated woman. She had a hard complicated life."

Joe rounds on him. "Christ on the cross, Cal, sometimes you don't got the sense God gave a cat. What was so complicated about her and her life? She turned mean, is all, after the old man left her to fend for herself." He folds his arms and looks away. "Worse things could happen to a girl, my Betty could have told you that."

Annie glances swiftly at Callum. He has told her all about Joe's tragic marriage, how Betty committed suicide after their baby died, but she's never heard Joe speak of it.

Callum reaches out to him. "I know Mercie wasn't the easiest person, but she did everything she could for me and Lucinda when we landed on her doorstep."

Joe ignores the gesture. Despite the exhaustion and the liquor, despite the long journey from New York and the reason for coming, despite all that or maybe because of it, he does not back down. "Good? To you and little Lucinda? That must be why she was in such an all-fired rush to get on her own. Lucinda knew better than to get pregnant by Dermot Byrne and you knows it. As far as I'm concerned, she figured it was the best way to get out from under the clutches of her Great Aunt Mercedes."

Callum looks bewildered. "I just don't understand why you're so bitter."

"She's the only one gets to be bitter? Look, me and her got on fine when she was little, but she got too full of herself, or something, I don't know. Ever since that time she went to New York, I could never talk to her after. I wouldn't have minded for me. But what about little Sheilagh? What about Betty?" His voice chokes with years of resentment. "Merce didn't even come when they died. She was in New York and she didn't even show up for their funerals." Joe shuts his mouth firmly then, but his fingers twitch on the table and his leg jigs up and down beneath it.

Not so Callum. Eyes all but closed, he sits in his chair, drained, unmoving.

1959

Three months after his wife died of a brain tumour, Callum and ten-year-old Lucinda returned to St. Jude. Mercedes had barely a week's notice but she assured Callum that it was enough, that it was all she needed, and she welcomed them back home. With all of the renovations she'd done over the years, Callum barely recognized the place.

After Judith's death, Callum had hoped that life in New York might actually improve. This callous honesty was never voiced to one living being; it was barely given definition in his own mind. Yet, after having lived with Judith for more than a decade, the thought was unavoidable. However, except for the barest civility from her sister Ruth, and her father, who was also his boss, the remainder of Judith's family wanted nothing to do with them. Callum didn't care what they thought of him, but he could not expect Lucinda to understand. Having survived ten years with an angry, resentful mother, years of trying, and ultimately failing, to live up to Judith's high society standards, Lucinda did not need further rejection. Quiet and reserved, she had grown into a serious young girl who cautiously watched the life that swirled around her, yet said little about it. When Judith died, Lucinda withdrew even further. She would let no one enter, not even her father. Her slender frame became even thinner as she ate less and less. Finally, hoping for a second chance for himself and his daughter, perhaps for his sister as well, Callum decided to return to St. Jude.

But from the beginning, Lucinda was uncomfortable around her aunt. She said Mercedes was too proper in the way she acted, the way she dressed, the way her hair was never loose around her face. "And she's so bony, she's all bones and knuckles. And her eyes are really weird, like they're too hot or something," she told Callum.

Callum laughed. "Is that all?"

Lucinda hesitated. "She's always watching me." Her voice was low, secretive.

"She's just glad to have you here."

"But, Daddy, she scares me."

"You're still getting used to each other. Merce will stop that soon."

But Mercedes didn't. For long moments, minutes even, she would stare at Lucinda, sometimes with a small smile playing on her face, at other times more sombrely. Lucinda did her best not to be left alone with her.

One early fall morning, Lucinda awoke with a sore throat and stuffy nose. Despite the heat crackling from the wood stove, Callum could see shudders ripple through her. Mercedes offered to stay home with her but Lucinda insisted on going to school.

Callum spent the day repairing his boat, but headed home early to see how she was feeling. As he approached the house, her voice carried to him through the screen door.

"Mother said you were crazy. 'Your father's crazy sister' she called you. She said to watch out for you if Daddy took me back here. She said to call Aunt Ruth in New York if I needed anything." Her voice kept rising. "She said Aunt Ruth knew everything about you and she'd know what to do if you ever tried to take me away."

Callum ran to the door. By the time he reached it, Lucinda was screaming. "Stop it. Stop staring at me. Where's Daddy? Where is he?"

He rushed inside. Mercedes was sitting at the table, so still she could have been glued to the chair. Across from her a wild-eyed Lucinda clasped a soupspoon in her hand like a weapon. The only sound was the sizzle and spit of flaming wood.

"Go to your room, Lucinda. Right now," Callum ordered.

The spoon clattered to the table, but it was Mercedes who stood. "Stay," she said in a shaky voice. "This is my fault. Please, I have to leave." Blind to Callum's hand, she stumbled from the room.

He turned to his daughter. "How could you...?" He stopped, alarmed at the fever in her eyes and the fear and confusion on her small face. "Lucinda? Are you all right?"

Tears rolled down her cheeks. "I...I was afraid you...you wouldn't come back."

Callum knelt down and hugged her until she stopped trembling, then he carried her to the chair by the fire and held her until she fell asleep. Praying only that he was doing the best he could at that single moment in time, and that somehow he would find a way to fix what had happened, Callum eventually drifted off, momentarily at peace within the rhythm of his daughter's constant breathing.

A voice stirred him from sleep. Night had settled over the house, and he looked at Lucinda's face in the near-darkness.

Her lips moved but her eyes were closed. "Please no Mama…sorry Mama…. sorry." For the umpteenth time, he wondered at the control that Judith had insisted upon having over Lucinda, and her equal insistence that he mind his own business. "If you know what's good for you," she'd often added.

Holding Lucinda closer, he tried to reassure her sleeping body but the increased pressure broke her slumber. Sleep-filled eyes peered up at Callum. Within seconds, he watched the fear take over once again.

"I'm here. Shh," he murmured, brushing his hand down her long brown hair.

"Daddy, I'm sorry about Aunt Mercedes. But she frightens me."

"I know. It's okay." He kept smoothing her hair until he sensed that she'd begun to relax. "There's one thing I can tell you. Your aunt wants only the best for you."

"But why does she act that way?"

Callum paused, trying to find the right answer. "I think it's because she'll never have a child to call her own."

Lucinda looked puzzled. "How do you know she won't have any children?"

"I just do, Lucinda. I just do."

Lucinda fingered a lock of hair, pulling the same strands over and over. "Mother used to say your sister was jealous and mean, and that she was an old spinster who hurt little children." She added quickly, "But that I should never tell you she said that."

"Judith said that about Merce?"

"Yes...and other stuff too." The words rushed forth as if she needed to purge them from her conscience. "She said Aunt Mercedes was crazy and selfish. When she got really sick, she told me if it wasn't for Aunt Mercedes, she would have had a different life and this wouldn't have happened to her. What did she mean by that, Daddy?"

Again Callum waited, but this time it was to prevent himself from starting his own tirade against his dead wife. "Lucinda, do you trust me?" he asked.

He could see that this was a tough question for her; he hadn't always been there when she needed him. Judith had been an authoritarian parent. She was not a mother to be trifled with, nor a wife, either. Both Callum and Lucinda had tried to do what was demanded of them for fear of her volatile temper. When Lucinda started to turn more often to Callum, Judith responded by busying the child with social engagements and the charitable causes of her society friends, excluding him wherever possible. As much as he loved Lucinda, it was often a relief to be out of his wife's way, a situation made unavoidable by the increasing demands made upon him at work by Judith's father. Whether the two were in cahoots to keep him occupied was a question he frequently asked himself.

"I think I do, Daddy," she said finally. "More than anybody else, that's for sure."

Callum felt as though his heart would break, so sad was he that his daughter could not believe in him completely.

She must have seen it on his face. Her thin arms clasped him around his neck. "Yes, I trust you. I do, honest."

He hugged her tight, praying for the strength to make things right. "Then there's something I want to tell you, and I need for you to accept it and believe it even though I can't prove it. Can you do that?"

"Yes, I can do that," she rushed to reassure him.

"There are two things. The first is that Judith was a very sick woman, and I don't just mean the headaches and the cancer. She was sick inside her mind too, and sometimes it made her do and say things that were wrong. Those things she said about Merce, they're not true, Lucinda. She hated Mercedes, but she hated lots of other things, too. That was part of her sickness."

Lucinda sat very still. "What was the other thing?"

"Your aunt loves you and wants to help take care of you. She's not used to having a little girl in the house. We got to give her some time. All right?"

Lucinda's forehead creased in concentration. "I'll try, Daddy."

Knowing he couldn't ask for more, Callum carried her to bed and tucked her in for the night. Shortly after, Mercedes came downstairs, her face drawn, her normally perfect bun dishevelled. She was barely twenty-six and already going grey.

"Ah, Mercie. How are you, girl?"

She waved away his concern. "Never mind me. How's our Lucinda?"

"She's so sorry for everything she said. It's been a rough year."

"You don't have to explain." Mercedes sat next to him. "Something she said keeps coming back to me, about how Judith warned her that I'd try to take her away."

"She was crazy at the end, Merce. It's just us and Lucinda now. We can forget about Judith."

She looked at him pityingly. "Callum, you know we can never do that. Judith meant every word, every threat. My God, she wouldn't even let me come to Sheilagh or Betty's funeral. I begged and I cried and it made no difference." Mercedes stared out the window for several moments, then reached into her pocket. She placed a letter on the table and pushed it towards him. "It's from Judith's sister."

Callum didn't pick it up. "Ruth? What did she want?"

"To warn us that she knows everything, and to watch what we said to Lucinda. She said if we ever cast a shadow on her sister's memory, she'll personally seek vengeance upon us all." Mercedes opened the letter and read from it. "'I've got the time and the money, and we both know who would suffer most if that were to happen.'"

"But she's all the way in New York, she can't really hurt us."

"Of course she can. Think about it. She's a spinster with nothing better to do than harbour her dead sister's grudges."

"She's bluffing."

"Read the letter. She's couldn't be more serious. If Ruth

ever made public what she knows it could be the last straw for that little girl, and she's the only one who matters now. Imagine if she ever found out. What would that do to her after all she's been through?"

"But it's all so long ago, no one cares anymore."

"Don't be naïve. The biddies are already circling - just try buying groceries." She pushed back the stray hairs. "No, I won't take chances. I'm just grateful to have you both here with me. We'll let the child get used to us, to the three of us together, and pray to the Lord above that it will all work out. You have to agree with me if this is going to work."

Callum hesitated.

"I mean it. One wrong word and this could all fall apart. For Lucinda's sake, we have to make sure what happened never sees the light of day." Mercedes laid her hands flat on the table. "We say nothing. We do nothing. We leave the past in New York. This is the way it has to be."

Callum knew then that it was useless to argue. The woman who confronted him across the table was one he'd seen often since his return to St. Jude, but this was the first time the strength of her will was directed at him. This woman went about her business of teaching and living in a grim, determined fashion, with no desire or patience for frivolity in any form.

And so, although it was not how he'd pictured their life together, he agreed. And even though they lived in the same house, Lucinda received similar treatment to the rest of her cousins, which was to say she was accorded respect and rewards in direct proportion to the degree in which she earned them. As promised, Mercedes provided a strict Catholic upbringing, and although she may have longed to give Lucinda more, she held herself in check, "for the good of the child," she told Callum.

But Callum knew better. He knew that each night as Lucinda lay sleeping, his sister tiptoed across the wood floor of her bedroom. Mercedes would draw the covers up over the exposed neck, under the vulnerable chin. With silent intensity she would watch a minute longer. And then, if she felt absolutely certain that Lucinda was fully asleep, Mercedes would lean in and tenderly, carefully, kiss her good night.

The 1950's were good years for the citizens of St. Jude. They gained a High School and a Trade School, a fish plant, a motel and a boat builder. The town was booming. New people moved in. More people had more money. Some could even afford household help. Sadie Griffin had never liked school but she'd always been good with a broom. It didn't take her long to figure out that after cleaning someone's house, she came away with a lot more than a few dollars and a bit of dirt under her nails. Twenty bucks was twenty bucks. But a good secret? That was priceless.

Fat-arse Mabel. Don't know how she ever squeezed into this.

Sadie caressed the soft fabric of the yellow silk blouse, enjoying the way it slid so smoothly over her skin. At eighteen years of age, she'd never owned a new blouse, even though she'd been working since she'd left school at thirteen. Her mother's arthritis got worse every year and Sadie was the only one left to look after her. Sadie didn't mind working, especially for the priests. She'd been glad when they got rid of old Father Riley, though. She never did like the way he stood so close to her. His breath smelled bad, too, like rotten cod guts.

"This fish is some salty." Edna Duffie, her mouth scrunched into a wrinkled pout of distaste, sniffed at the food on her plate. "How long did you soak it, girl?"

"Long enough. Cook it yourself next time."

"I don't know how many times I got to tell you. You got to soak..." Edna prattled on, unaware that her daughter had stopped listening.

That new priest now, he's a good one all right. I don't mind if he looks, no, not at all. He can look all he wants. Wouldn't mind a look myself. Have a gander behind that black frock of his—

"I said," her mother's voice was raised, "that Callum got his-self a strange one."

"What? Who?" Sadie chose an extra fine needle from the pincushion.

"Get your head out of the clouds, girl. I said Callum Hann, your cousin."

Sadie glanced up. "What are you talking about, Ma? He got a strange what?"

Edna Duffie crossed her arms over her bony chest, causing the rounded hump on her back to protrude even further. "His girl, that Lucanda."

"Oh, her. Yeah, strange all right. And her name's Lucinda." The blouse had been part of a care package they'd gotten from relatives in St. John's. Mabel had worn it a few times even though it was far too small. It needed only a tuck in the back to hug Sadie's tiny waist. The bustline fit perfectly.

"That's what I said." Edna picked at the fish and brewis in front of her.

"No, Ma, you said Lucanda, with an 'a'. It's Lucinda, with an 'i'."

Mabel be some jealous she sees me in this. Lucky she didn't burst the seams out of it.

"Anyway, she's right queer, that one."

"Not much to her." Sadie pushed the needle carefully into the thin material.

"And she's some quiet, never says boo. Like she's scared of her own shadow. Although they says she's really just scared of Mercedes."

"Can't blame her."

Dermot'll be at the dance tonight. Maybe he'll walk me behind the church again.

"This hard tack's still hard," her mother complained. "How long you say you soaked it? I don't think..."

Sadie imagined Dermot's hands going around her waist, sliding up her back. She pictured him leaning in towards her, his body large and strong against hers, smelling of soap, his lips kissing hers, pressing hard—

"Sadie!" Edna hit the plate with her fork.

Sadie's hand jerked. "Ow!" she yelled as the needle pricked her finger.

"Quit your dreaming, girl." Edna put down her fork and rubbed one gnarled hand with the other. "Hard one to figure out, that Mercedes. Hear much about her?"

"Not a thing. Teaches school, goes to church, walks her dog."

"You keep an ear out at Burke's. Not much gets past that Mona."

Sadie looked doubtful. "I was there the other day and Mrs. Burke was trying to talk to her, saying how she must be glad to have Callum home, and did she like Nova Scotia when she was there, even asking about her father, you know, stuff like that, just trying to be nice to her. Mercedes was having none of it. Just got her groceries and left. Some closed up, I tell you."

"Word is she had a boyfriend once." Edna sounded quite pleased with herself.

"Get on! Her? Where'd you hear that?"

Can't imagine anyone kissing that crooked-arse.

"Aunt Agnes up in Green Harbour. Joe's dead wife, Betty I think her name was, she used to live next door to them before her and her sister run off to New York. Only the sister ever made it back, of course."

Sadie stops sewing. "So the sister would have known the Hanns."

Edna looks confused. "Up in Green Harbour?"

"No, when they were all in New York. If one sister was married to Joe the other one must've been around them all. She'd know what went on, what they got up to."

"Probably did but we'll never know. Poor thing didn't last the winter when she got back." Edna poked around on her plate until she came up with a small scrunchion. She popped the crispy pork rind into her mouth and sat back to enjoy it. "Tuberculosis they said it was."

Another dead end. Some odd, no one knows nothing. I never saw the like.

"Anyway, this boyfriend. He from New York?"

"No, no," said Edna. "That was up in Nova Scotia."

"What happened?" Sadie rubbed the fine silk gently between her fingers.

"Don't know. Something about a doctor." Edna scooped up a forkful of fish and bread all mushed together. "Yeah, that's it, I think they said a doctor."

Sadie pulled the needle through. Her eyes narrowed. "Or she needed a doctor?"

Edna's hand stopped above the plate. "You think?"

"Sure, why not? That one's hiding something, I just knows it."

"Too bad that young Lucanda got to live with her, though."

"Lucinda, Ma. I told you, her name is Lucinda."

No wonder Mabel's a dunce.

"No odds to me." Edna picked a tiny bone from between her teeth.

"Or me. Don't plan on having nothing to do with Lucinda Hann." Sadie paused from her sewing to check out the goings-on outside the window. From where she sat she had a clear view of the whole street.

"Never did like that crowd," said her mother.

"Too stuck up, they are. Swear they were from the King of England."

"That's a good one, what?" Edna chuckled. "Us or the king. Hah!"

"Nothing wrong with the Duffies, Ma. We're good as the Hanns any day."

"Right you are, Sadie. Mary be alive today wasn't for that crackpot Farley."

Sadie's eyes narrowed again. She stuck the needle back in.

1999

Gerry yawns so widely it feels his lips might tear away from each other. Sadie's eyes have begun to droop as well. She doesn't resist when he suggests it's time for bed. Her steps are clumsy as he walks her to her room. Her little nips affect her faster and harder than when he'd first caught her sneaking them twenty years earlier. He's never said anything to her about it. He feels it would be an invasion of her privacy, of which she has so little, and also that perhaps she deserves some comfort, some form of escape, some small measure of a life outside St. Jude, even if it is only in her mind.

He kisses her goodnight and she hugs him tight. She holds him there longer than he would like, but he doesn't try to extricate himself. Finally she looks up into his eyes, smiles a little drunken smile and goes into her room. He shuts the door.

Grateful to be alone at last, Gerry crawls into the single bed he slept in as a boy. He cannot remember when he was ever so exhausted. Every limb and muscle feels weary right down to his fingers and toes. He waits for sleep, craving that blessed blackness to wash over him and sweep away his thoughts, his memories, his regrets. But his mind refuses to give up his ghosts. He opens his eyes and stares at the ceiling, its white backdrop the perfect canvas.

The image slips into place. Annie, her body outlined in the picture window. Annie, staring out into the night, into the black void. Annie. He closes his eyes.

9

1999

Annie leans back against the kitchen counter, the hard edge digging into the curve of her spine. She is thinking about her mother and what Joe, in his anger, has accidentally revealed. Annie hadn't known that Lucinda was pregnant before she was married but, to her surprise, she finds that it doesn't really matter. In the past, she might have held such information close, saving it for a time when she needed something to harbour against her mother. She no longer feels that way and cannot remember why she did. At present, she feels only tenderness for Lucinda, a woman whom she loves without question, yet who remains a mystery.

Still, something doesn't sit right. "Hang on, you two," she says. "Do you mean to tell me that Beth is illegitimate and that Mom and Dad have been celebrating their anniversary from the wrong year to cover it up?"

Callum and Joe, looking guilty, sit up straighter.

"Huh? What are you talking about?" Joe pushes his chair back, as if trying to escape the confines of the cold metal table legs along with Annie's questions.

"Oh, no you don't." She plunks the sausage and bread on the table along with a pot of tea, then sits purposefully down across from them. "Look, we're all adults. I just want to know about my own mother, and the two of you need to fill me in because I can never get a darn thing out of her."

Callum inclines his head and nods, but first he turns to Joe. "I'm sorry, Joey. The last thing I wants is to argue with you this night. Can we let it go?"

Joe's weathered hand pats his brother's even older one. "Indeed we should."

"As for you, Miss Annie," says her grandfather, "I don't suppose there's any harm in telling you about your own parents. Not that there's any great secret, but I knows how you and your mother are. Still, I figured you'd know some of this stuff by now."

"Beth and Sara probably do, but me and Mom, we never did talk much." She can hear the regret in her voice.

Callum touches her cheek briefly, then he begins. "Lucinda met Dermot when she was just sixteen. He was much older than her, a big strapping fisherman ten years on the boats. But Lucinda wasn't your typical teenager. She never had lost that shyness, or sadness, or whatever it was that she brought home with her from the States." He pauses. "Joe, you remember what Judith was like, right?"

"I do. I could never figure how you ended up with her, the rich boss's daughter."

"How did it happen, Granddad? You hardly ever talk about her."

"With good reason." Callum thinks for a minute. "One day I had to go to the main office, her father's office. I was nervous, he being the owner of the company and all. I was standing there getting up the nerve to knock when the door swings open and there she is, the most beautiful woman I ever saw, brown curls all around her face. It was her eyes that got me, though, so blue you could only think of the sky. And that day her eyes were all fired up. She was saying something, not really shouting but in this angry voice, I don't recall what it was about but when she saw me she stopped. I remember her looking me up and down. And then she smiled at me, a big wide smile that softened her face and made it glow. That smile was it for me. Then, when I come out from seeing her father, she was waiting for me."

"Did you ask her out?" Annie says.

"I honestly don't remember." Callum looks mystified.

"There's lots I don't remember from them months. I just recall being bowled over, and trying hard to be the man Judith wanted me to be. I didn't have much experience with girls."

Joe laughs. "I never in my life saw a fellow so shy with the women."

"Sure I never thought I'd have a girlfriend, let alone a wife."

"Some wife." Joe is no longer laughing. "Nothing but a mean, spoiled brat."

"Uncle Joe!"

Callum pats her hand. "He's right. Judith was spoiled like no one I ever knew, the apple of her father's eye. She had a sister but poor Ruth was as homely and dull as the day was long. Never married, never had a date as far as I knew. She idolized Judith, who could do no wrong as far as Ruth was concerned. Same went for their mother. So, when Judith fell for the help at her father's plant - that would be me - well, Judith always got what Judith wanted, and did what she wanted, no matter how mad her father was at her. I got caught hook, line and sinker. But it was just me, so no harm done."

He takes several sips of tea, slowly, as if judging his words.

"When Lucinda came along, Judith had a new purpose, and her and her sister took it upon themselves to mould that little girl into a New York City princess." His old eyes glisten. "Poor Lucinda. She tried to be what they wanted. She did everything they asked her to do, though it was clear from day one that it wasn't in her nature. They just barrelled on, ignoring what she was really like." An angry glint flashes across his eyes. "And where was I in all this? Well, the truth is, I've no excuse good enough. Judith's father always begrudged me taking his daughter and he wasn't about to have no Newfie son-in-law hanging about without earning his keep. That man worked me to the bone, he did, all so I could legitimately pay for the life his daughter was used to. No freebies there, I tell you.

"So Lucinda had to make do as best she could, without me around to interfere or help her. And she did, and she survived.

It wasn't until later that I wondered what she gave up to keep the peace." His mouth tightens and his fist taps the table.

Annie resists the urge to comfort him. She knows he's not finished.

He exhales slowly. "After we moved here, I wondered if she felt cast off from the Macleans, but she never said nothing. Her Aunt Ruth phoned every year, on the date Judith passed away. She always called at our house, even after Lucinda was married and had a house of her own. Merce would take the phone while I ran and fetched Lucinda. I used to wonder what they talked about but Lucinda never said. Neither did Merce. Ruth died of a heart attack last year. We haven't heard from any of them since.

"Anyhow, Lucinda soldiered on. But my Lord, she was so thin and shy and quiet. She'd make your heart ache to look at her sometimes. When Dermot started calling on her, Merce and me were worried that he was so much older than her. But it was the darnedest thing. It struck the both of us in no time flat, and the two of them even earlier I suppose, that this was a match made in heaven. I'm ashamed to say I think it was the first time your mother felt really safe in her whole life." He gives a wry chuckle. "I thought Sadie was going to kill her, mind you. She figured Derm was hers, you see, they'd been going around together a bit. But he was never serious about Sadie. And when Lucinda got in the family way, eighteen or so she was, it didn't matter. Not even back then. It just seemed right natural and they got married. Merce gave them the land this house is on, not next to her place but not too far. Derm and me started building on it right away. It was the only other house on the road back then."

Callum's hands rub across his face briefly before falling to the table. "But the baby died."

Annie leans forward; his voice, normally strong despite his age, has gone hoarse.

"And the next one did too, and then she had a miscarriage

really late. Me and Merce and Derm, we were some worried about her. That was a long hard haul for Lucinda. But it was Dermot got her through, kept her going. He wouldn't let her despair. Finally, along came Beth. Lucinda latched onto that child like her life depended on it, which it probably did. She was the happiest wife and mother, and she looked so healthy, finally had a bit of meat on her bones. I was scared to death something would happen to mess it up. But it was fine, especially with Sarah and yourself coming soon after, healthy as horses. Of course there was other tough times, other babies that never made it. And when Beth lost her first one some years back, Lucinda was awful sad. But like always, she had Derm and they had each other." Callum sits back. "I thank God to this day that Dermot Bryne came into her life."

They sit, the three of them, quietly, at peace with each other. The house hums with the shutdown noises of late night, the muted din of the furnace winding down, the stillness outside, the sighs of old men.

In the tranquility of the kitchen, Annie thinks about her parents, about the deep bond they share. She thinks about her mother and the babies she lost, about how she has kept her sorrow close so many years. Lucinda was never the type to revisit the hardships that life dealt her, nor was she a martyr determined to hoard her pain. Rather, she always said she saw no reason to dwell on hard times, that it made no sense to be making people sad for no good reason. Still, Annie knows her mother would have given anything to spare her daughters the grief that she has known.

For the first time, Annie feels a deep connection with Lucinda, even with Mercedes, a connection that surpasses blood ties yet exists solely because of them. She does not mind that it is probably loneliness that binds them. It makes her feel less alone.

"Annie, Annie!" Pat yells from the other room. "Get in here. Hurry!"

Annie rushes to the parlour, Joe and Callum right behind. The door is shut. When she tries to pull it open, she meets resistance. She pulls harder. It opens.

Annie stops. "For the love of God!"

The coffin is now in the middle of the room. Inside it, Mercedes is propped up with pillows. Her hand, which is tied to a rope attached to the doorknob, has risen with the opening of the door and is reaching out towards them.

Pat and Aiden stand by the coffin, swaying slightly, their faces proud, expectant.

"You're pissed to the gills, the pair of you." She doesn't know whether to laugh or cry. "This is really gross. I hope you know that, you big idiots."

Joe, not completely sober himself, peers nervously at Mercedes. Callum stands quietly by. He is not smiling.

Annie unties the rope from the doorknob then goes to the coffin and removes it from Mercedes' hand. The cold sallow skin sends shivers down her arms. She pushes the rope at Aiden. "Get rid of this right now." She sniffs. The air reeks of incense and scotch. "What the hell did you do?"

Pat leans over the coffin. "Aid spilled it. I told him not to put it there."

"St. Peter won't let her past the gate with that stench on her," Aiden stammers. His speech is slow, some words delayed.

Pat drapes his arm over his brother's shoulder. "You trying to preserve her?"

Holding onto the coffin's railing for support they start to giggle, which soon erupts into hoots of laughter. Annie tries to quiet them but they're too drunk to care, or to notice the sound of footsteps running down the stairs. She grabs the rope from Aiden's hand and shoves it behind the couch.

Lucinda barges in, her flannel housecoat wafting around her. "Enough!" she yells, charging across the room.

Pat and Aiden immediately go silent.

Lucinda stops by the side of the coffin. Her mouth tightens

when she sees the upended bottle lying next to Mercedes. She picks it up by the neck and holds it out towards Pat and Aiden as if she might hit them with it. They both take a step back.

"Have you no respect at all?" she says. "Do you even know the meaning of the word?"

The boys say nothing. They lean in closer to each other.

Lucinda nods. "Right. I didn't think so. Now look at this ungodly mess. Disgusting it is, absolutely disgusting."

Pat tries to stammer out an apology but she thrusts her hand up. "I don't want your sorrys and your excuses. Just clean this up and quit acting like children for once in your frigging lives." Hands on hips, she hones in on Pat. "I'm beginning to think she was right about you. All you had to do was sit up with her on her final night. But no, that was too much to ask. Well, the fun is over for you this night, do you hear me, Patrick Hann?" Not waiting for an answer she shifts her gaze to Aiden. "And you! It's high time you learned to take some responsibility, and not just about this. If you had one lick of decency—" She stops, bunching her lips together in frustration. "Ah, what's the use of talking to you? Just get your arse in gear and fix this, the both of you. I better not smell one whiff of that in the morning. Am I understood?"

"Yes, Aunt Luce," they answer in unison.

"I'm going back to bed. And I don't want to hear another peep out of you two."

The room is silent until they hear the hard clack of Lucinda's bedroom door.

"Which one of you wants to bathe her?" Annie asks with a perfectly straight face.

Pat pulls back. "Jesus, Annie, you're creeping the daylights out of me."

"She's just kidding." Aiden looks cautiously at Annie.

She gestures pointedly to the stained satin lining.

Pat's face is an odd shade of green. "I think I'm going to be sick."

For his sake only, she decides to let them off the hook. "Ah, relax. It's not all that bad. From the looks of you two, you must have drank most of it first."

Joe moves closer to inspect the damage. "What were you doing anyway?"

Aiden starts to titter. "We were giving her a little drinkie-pooh, but she wasn't too interested."

"Not like she ever drank much," Pat adds.

"Might have cheered her up a bit," says Annie, although not with the same degree of bitterness she usually reserves for Mercedes.

The others nod. Except Callum, who turns to go back to the kitchen.

Annie sets Joe and the boys to work, then follows her grandfather out. He is slumped in a chair, his solemn face lost in thought, his gaze far away. She thinks again of Bay D'Esprits. It was the one place she felt she could never reach him. No matter how hard she looked upon that water, at the lonely cliffs on the other side and the hard jutting rocks rising from the Atlantic, she knew that she would never see what he did.

Annie hugs his rounded shoulders and brushes back his limp grey hair. "Sorry, Granddad. Sometimes I don't know when to shut up."

"Oh love, I know she was a trial to put up with all these years. Mercedes long ago gave up trying to please anybody. She wasn't one for making friends."

Annie sits next to him at the table. "I've been around her since the day I was born, but the woman I knew was nothing like the person you keep talking about."

He gives her a mischievous smile, bringing a youthful happiness to his face. "Like I said since you were little, you always put me in mind of Mercie as a girl."

"That's the second time today somebody said I was like her."

"Your mother thought you were like her too, though I think it gave her more worry than pleasure," he adds ruefully. "Guess who else saw it? Mercie. Every time you'd bring home top marks, she'd brag on about it, glowing with pride. Remember how you got straight A's your first semester of university?"

She nods, surprised that he does.

"When Mercie heard about that, she went on and on about how she knew you could do it, knew you could beat anybody in your class. Then she said outright that you reminded her of herself, but she was thankful you had better opportunities."

"I don't get it. Why didn't she ever tell me those things? She acted like she couldn't stand me most of the time."

"Couldn't stand you? Annie, she loved you. She only ever wanted for you to make something of yourself because she knew you could."

"Well, she was no help. Wouldn't even lend me a few measly bucks for school."

Callum looks smug. "She made sure you got the money, though."

"She did not."

"Whose idea was it for you to help me out at the computer, and who do you think insisted on giving me the money to pay you for it?"

Annie leans in, elbows on the table. "You're kidding?"

"She made sure you got what you needed, and it wasn't a loan."

"If she really cared, what could be so wrong with telling a person?" She notices the tremble in her voice, but she doesn't mind it, not now, not here with her grandfather.

"Oh Annie, she forgot how, is all. She said it felt like every time she tried to help she made things worse. Merce was always so nervous for you, afraid something awful would happen and you'd end up like her."

"You mean alone and angry?"

"She wasn't always that way. When she was young she was full of dreams. And she was brazen and saucy, much like yourself." He smiles. "A right card, she was."

"That's what's so amazing." Annie's hits the table lightly with the side of her fist. "I hardly ever heard a funny word come out of her mouth. In all the years I knew her, she was always so serious, forever on the edge of bitterness."

"It's the only way she knew how to be in the end, but that don't mean it's how she really was. A person can only suffer so much before they just let go and give in to it."

Annie leans in close to her grandfather. "So tell me about it."

"Merce was awful private. I don't know…"

"Please, Granddad. I need to know."

He hesitates. "You do, don't you? You more than anyone else, just like Mercie said." He studies her face for a moment, then takes a full long breath. "Something happened a long time ago, something awful. And Merce did what she had to do, and she survived. And when that was done, when she tried to put it behind her and start a new life…" He stops and presses his fingers against his forehead. When he speaks again there are tears in his eyes. "She was after falling in love, you see, in Nova Scotia, where she was an English teacher. She met a young man there from St. John's, Louis Cunningham was his name. They decided to get married." He stops again, and his knuckles rap the table in an angry rush. "But then Louis found something out, something he shouldn't have been told, a thing Merce could hardly believe herself." He peers past her out the window. "Louis Cunningham was her last chance for a regular life and he took that away." After a brief silence he looks back at Annie. "Mercedes suffered more than you can imagine, but she carried on the best she could. Life dealt her some of the cruellest cards and there wasn't one damn thing she could do about it."

There is a raw honesty in his eyes, and his face is filled with torment. Annie longs to ask him to go on, to tell her more about this strange woman that only he knew so well. But it's as if he's no longer present in the room. His eyes seem distant, far away, and Annie can tell that he has drifted back to a time and place that he alone remembers. The only thing she can do to help him is to leave him be, for now at least, to let him rest there with the little sister he loved from the beginning of her life until the sad, lonely end.

Sadie is in a dream. It is not a good dream. She is wearing her favourite blouse, but the silky yellow material is ripped across the front, exposing part of her old, greying brassiere. Lucinda is there. She is holding Dermot's hand. But then Dermot becomes Angus and he is watching Lucinda and Dermot walk away.

The dream shifts so that it no longer feels like a dream. It is happening now. Mercedes Hann stands at her bedside. Sadie knows she is there, somehow she can see her, even though she can't open her eyes. She tries to make her eyelids go up, concentrates as hard as she can, but they're stuck shut.

Mercedes is saying something, talking to somebody. Sadie can't quite make out the words but she can hear the voices. Then a young man rises up to stand beside Mercedes. He puts his hand on her shoulder. There is a smile in his voice as he speaks to her. "Yes, she's dead all right. Dead, dead, dead." He laughs.

Sadie needs to get her eyes open. Her brain pulls at the muscles in her face, hauling and tugging so hard that she loses sight of the two of them. Nothing. No one.

She stops straining. They are there again, but only the back of them walking away. Mercedes Hann and Gerard. On they go, farther and farther, but still she can see them. They keep moving beyond, but never so far as to disappear altogether.

With one final wrench, she opens her eyes. Wide. She stares at the side of the bed. No one. Her heart bounces against her flesh so hard she is afraid it will break through. She takes several long breaths. Keeping her sights on the air beside her, she waits patiently for her heart to settle back into its place inside her chest.

She doesn't blink for a long time.

Goddamn Old Hag. Goddamn Mercedes Hann.

PART TWO

1932-1955

10

If Mary Hann had listened to her doctor, Callum's sister would not have been born.

"In here's our new little girl," his mother told him, patting her belly.

Ten-year-old Callum had always wanted a sister. "Will I be able to hold her?"

"Yes, my Callum." She looked at him so seriously. "And can you promise me that you'll always watch out for her, and help bring her up right and keep her safe?"

Callum nodded, proud of the faith she had in him. He made a promise to himself then, to always protect his sister and his mother.

"We needs a little girl around here, don't matter what Doc Power says."

He touched her stomach protectively. "Why don't he want us to have a girl?"

"Oh, he says I shouldn't have no more babies. But he don't know everything."

Martin Power never claimed to know everything, but as the sole practitioner in the area, he had no time to waste words. When Mary told him of her condition, he was blunt. "You have five healthy boys already, why do you want more youngsters?"

"Now, Dr. Power, it's not up to—"

"You know your history," he cut in, his voice raised. "How much you bled the last time. And those three other baby boys didn't die from nothing. Their lungs don't get enough oxygen once they come out of you, and I can't help them."

"We'll be fine in God's good hands, I'm sure."

"It's not a contest between me and God, Mary. You can't be leaving it all to Him." He studied her face. Just thirty-six, she had the washed-out eyes and pasty skin of a much older woman, and her dark hair had gone almost totally grey.

"Sure it's the will of the Father, you knows that." She rose to leave.

"Well, if a certain father had more willpower you wouldn't be in this state."

She paused at the door and added shyly, "This one will be a girl, wait and see."

"Let's hope so. Just tell Farley to get hold of me at the first sign of trouble."

Unfortunately, when trouble came Farley was not available. A winter storm battered the coast, the snow blowing and swirling so fast and furious you couldn't see your own hand. Your breath froze the second it passed your teeth. In light of such inclemency, Farley had settled in early at Patron's Pub.

This establishment doubled as the town's only restaurant, and the air was pungent with aromas of long-stewed lamb, onions and potatoes. Dr. Power, a bachelor whose balding head was as round as his belly, was also on the premises. He noticed Mary's husband at a nearby table where they were arguing loudly about the Squires government and professing their indignation with the state of the fishery and their dependence on the dole. How they could spend money on liquor when their families were going hungry was a question the doctor often asked himself.

He approached the table. "Hello, Farley. How's Mary?"

Farley twisted around and squinted up at him.

Dr. Power tried again. "How was Mary when you left?"

"Christ sake, Mary be fine. Go on from bothering me, talking nonsense."

"I'm serious, Farley. You need to keep a close eye on her."

"Jesus Christ!" Farley exhaled loudly, clenching his tobacco-stained teeth. "Mary got no need of you yet. Go torment someone else." He turned his back on the doctor and lifted his glass to his lips. "Should mind his own fucking business."

The belligerent words resounded among his suddenly silent friends, who kept their heads down or glanced away. Martin Power returned to his table.

As he sat down to his bowl of stew, Mick Hayes, a local fisherman, rushed in. "Thank God you're here," he shouted when he spied the doctor.

Everyone hushed.

"There's been a awful accident, about ten miles out the road, but the storm got the bridge and nothing can get through from the Port St. Anne side."

Martin Power sprang to his feet, his stew already congealing as the wind's chill swept through the room. "What happened?"

"My Johnny passed it on his way home. A whole carload of people went over the bank and into the water. He come in to get help and then went straight back to see what he can do. If we don't hurry, them people is going to freeze to death this night."

The bar's patrons instantly mobilized, organizing groups to head to the scene and others to gather supplies. Farley Hann sat quietly, his mug of ale in front of him. Several glasses had been abandoned nearby. He nodded and said a few words here and there, his face a mask of sympathy and concern as he drained every drop of beer left on the deserted table.

Farley had not always been such a selfish man. In his younger days, known for his humour and love of a good time, he was liked by all who drank with him. In fact, it was generally agreed upon that the plain, soft-spoken Mary Duffie from Green Harbour had made quite a catch when she'd captured the popular bachelor's heart. But the elder Farley had little in common with his younger self. Some thought this was due to his addiction to the bottle, while others claimed his decline began years before when he was injured in the Nova Scotia mines up in Canada and sent on back to St. Jude.

When he finally staggered home that frigid February night, his daughter had already begun her struggle to enter his world. Unfortunately, Dr. Power was still at the accident, leaving Mary in the care of her sister-in-law, Edna Duffie. Having recently given birth herself, Edna knew the delivery was not proceeding normally and had sent Mary's boys to stay with her own family while she tended to their mother.

The instant Farley stumbled through the door, Edna was on him. "Something's wrong. The baby's coming and it's too early."

"What you barking at, woman?" He came to a stop just inside the kitchen. Half-dry clothes hung from a line over the blazing stove. The walls and ceiling were of rough pine planks, the floor bare boards, swept spotless nonetheless. And on the windows, lace curtains, faded and frayed, but perfectly clean.

"We needs help. You got to go get Dr. Power."

Shoving past her, Farley staggered. He reached out to save himself but the only thing to stop him was the stove. As his blistering hand flew to his mouth, a groan started from the upper floor, gradually escalating until it filled the kitchen with a cry far more piercing than Farley's.

Edna pushed him up the stairs. "Get up there and check on your wife."

She bustled about the kitchen, whispering the rosary as she set water to boil for tea and to sterilize the rags and heavy-duty scissors she'd brought with her. She was about to start the Fourth Glorious Mystery when she heard a grunt, then a body tumbling. Running into the hall, she found Farley in a heap at the bottom of the stairs.

"Heaven help us! Farley, are you all right?" Edna tapped his face. His arm shot up and smacked at her, then he rolled over. She pushed him with her foot. He didn't budge. "Frigging caudler," she muttered, giving him a short kick.

She flung open the front door. The storm had stilled but the frozen air bit into her skin. "Help! Come to Farley Hann's!" she shouted as loud as she could several times into the night. With the house so far from its neighbours, she had no way of knowing if she'd been heard, but soon, Mary's stepsister, Nell, was at the door.

Around midnight, a baby's wail could be heard throughout the house. Farley, awake at last and overcome with emotion, sobbed at his wife's bedside. He swore on Mary's life to take the pledge the next day. Mary whispered to Edna that she'd been given two gifts, her husband and her daughter. Without hesitation she named the child Mercedes, because God had finally had some mercy on her.

When Dr. Power arrived, he could only bow his head as the priest performed the final sacrament on the soul of Mary Hann.

Five years later, fifteen-year-old Callum was the nearest thing to a responsible adult in the Hann household. His older brothers had all left home, either to head out to sea or to the mines in Nova Scotia. As for his father, the pledge hadn't worked.

Right from the start Callum had assumed responsibility for his sister. His Aunt Edna, pregnant again, had been happy to give the infant over to him and, after teaching him the basics, left him to it. Callum was grateful for the chance to fulfill his promise to his mother. When she died, he felt he'd already broken his promise to himself.

Mercedes was a good baby who grew into a happy toddler. What had started for Callum as a sense of duty quickly evolved into an intense protective love, more like that of a parent than a brother. His favourite time of day was when she awoke in the morning. Teeth chattering from the night chill still in the air, Mercedes would crawl onto his lap at the table. He would pull her blanket close around her so that only her face showed, her tiny nose red with the cold, her child's breath sweet against his cheek. Callum felt as though his heart grew larger when she snuggled into him there.

While it was usually Callum who Mercedes turned to when she was hungry or hurt or wanted a bedtime story, she was close to her father as well. When Farley wasn't drinking, he doted on his little girl, buying her treats, playing games like tiddly or peek-a-boo, bouncing her on his knee as they sang silly songs. In fact, it was only in watching the two of them together that Callum caught a glimpse of the father he'd once known, even if it was a childlike version. He felt hope for Farley at those times, hope that his love for his daughter might keep him sober. But, inevitably, Farley would find a bottle, or a bottle would find him, at which point he was useless to anyone.

Fortunately, Callum still had his younger brother to help with Mercedes.

"It's down to you and me now," he said to Joe after their last brother, Frank, left for Nova Scotia. "Just us two to take care of little Mercie here."

They were walking home from Sunday Mass, past the clapboard homes of their neighbours, the houses slapped here and there, some up, some down, some barely a hair from the next one. The cold sea wind whipped through one home and into the next with hardly a pause. Only the Hann house stood alone, its weathered planks grey and ghostly, at the top of a hill at the edge of town.

By the time they reached their doorstep, the three of them were cold and damp from the drizzle of rain that had not let up for days on end. Callum's stomach rumbled. Most of the parishioners would be going home to a hot meal of salt beef and cabbage or chicken and dumplings, or, for the less fortunate, a hash of fish and brewis. Had any of them known the plight of the Hann children, they would undoubtedly have shared their Sunday dinner. But like his mother before him, Callum was proud. Mary Hann had never spoken of the meals they'd gone without; neither would he. Joe, on the other hand, would have told the whole congregation if Callum hadn't been there to stop him.

His sister's red-cheeked face peered up at him. "Is our Daddy gone too?"

Callum turned away from her childish wholesomeness. Farley hadn't been seen since heading out two days earlier in search of a drink. "Might as well be," he muttered.

Joe shot him a warning glance. "He's just codding you, Mercie girl. Dad's over at Sullivan's having a beer, is all. He'll be home any minute now, sure. Right, Cal?"

Callum tried to keep the anger out of his voice. "Any day at all now."

"Don't be minding him, he's just in a bad mood," Joe said, squatting in front of his sister with his palms up, an invitation to patty-cake.

The feisty five-year-old clearly had no intention of being bought off so easily. "I want Daddy and Frank," cried Mercedes, eyes widening as her wailing escalated.

Sticking a smile on his mouth, Callum licked his thumb and rubbed a spot on his sister's chin. "Let's see what we got for dinner, eh, Mercie? I feels like cooking up some of them caplin. Maybe some boiled turnip to go with it. What do you say?" Picking her up, he carried her inside, tickling her wriggling body all the way.

Over his sister's giggles he heard Joe mutter, "Same thing we been eating all week. Wish we had a bit of butter to go on them." Callum didn't bother to answer. Truth be told, his own stomach was starved for a lick of butter as well.

Callum and Joe worked hard to provide a good home for their sister. By the time the war ended, she had developed into a normal, healthy young girl. And although St. Jude changed little during those years, the same did not hold true for the rest of the world.

"Did you hear about all them jobs in New York?" Callum asked his brother one stormy November morning. "They're putting up these huge tall buildings, skyscrapers they're calling them, and from what I hear they needs men like crazy."

Joe swallowed his last spoonful of porridge and washed it down with a gulp of hot milky tea. "New York's supposed to be some kind of place, lots of jobs, people coming from all over the world." He spread a thick layer of bakeapple jam over a piece of toast.

"That's what I read too." Callum was standing at the window looking off toward the ocean. Now in his twenties, he'd become the family patriarch by default as his father had come to drink more and talk less, unless it was to the demons he found in the bottom of the bottle. At times, Farley seemed to lose himself in the past, yet he appeared no happier back there either. Occasionally he would ease off the drink, but more often than not he was as consumed by liquor as it was by him.

Callum looked at Joe. "Would you go there if you had the money?"

"What's keeping me here?"

Their eyes were drawn to the window. Nothing could be seen but squalls of white. Winter had come early. Again.

Footsteps bounded down the stairs. Twelve-year-old Mercedes burst into the room. "Did you see the arithmetic book Miss McCarthy lent me, Joe? It's that fat one with all the numbers on the front. Not that you'd ever look inside the frigging thing." Her green eyes grinned at him, her pointy little nose twitching mischievously.

"Watch that mouth, you saucy brat," Joe replied. Unlike Mercedes and Callum, Joe rarely opened a book.

"Joseph, my duck, you wouldn't know a fraction if it bit you on the arse."

"Mercedes!" Callum turned abruptly from the window. "That's enough."

"Ah, Cal," Joe jumped in, "sure me and Merce are only joking."

"I just think she should be a bit more careful what comes out of her."

"So what? She's the only bit of life in here most days, what with the old man either drunk or hungover and yourself so serious all the time. Leave it alone."

In truth, Callum didn't mind his sister's exuberance. She seemed blissfully unaware of what a boring place St. Jude was, always running in or out, playing ball with her friends, scaling the cliffs or chasing seagulls along the shore.

"Never mind me," she said. "Where's my book? I'll be late if I don't get going."

Callum gestured towards the top of the wood stove. "Up there. Drying off."

She stretched up to retrieve it. "Ugh! Smells like it was soaking in whiskey. What am I going to tell Miss McCarthy?"

"Now, Merce, there was an accident and something got spilled on it."

"Right! And was his nibs in the room? Huh? I suppose he's still sleeping it off."

The innocent five-year-old who had cried for her father had long since abandoned any illusions about him. For the most part, Mercedes ignored Farley, but this time he'd gone too far. Nothing was more serious to Mercedes than school. Always at the top of her class, she had dreams of becoming a teacher herself someday. Callum planned to do everything he could to make that happen.

"You knows he can't see that well anymore, Merce. Leave it and have some tea."

"If he can't see, what's he doing buying a truck?"

"Don't talk to me about that darn truck." Callum's voice was beyond exasperated. "To think of all the things we could have done with that money."

Two months earlier, Farley's only brother had died and left him over four hundred dollars. The next thing they knew, Farley was driving up the lane in Mona Burke's truck, an old Chevy that hadn't been used since her husband died. Callum had tried to make him return it but Farley wouldn't hear of it. Knowing his father would soon drink the remaining money, Callum had taken what was left and set it aside to have plumbing and electricity put in the house. At least they'd get something useful out of it.

"I didn't even know he could drive," said Joe.

"Sure he can't. Have you seen the dents he's after putting in it?" Mercedes shoved her feet into her rubber boots and pushed her hair out of her eyes. "Hand me that toast, will you, it'll do till dinner. And keep him away from my books, okay, Callum?"

He nodded, understanding her frustration. Despite having to quit school to care for Mercedes and then find a job, he did all he could to educate himself. Mercedes gave him any books she got her hands on, which they would discuss when no one else was around. "I will, I promise. Here, put this on."

Ignoring the hat he held out, she stuffed the toast in her mouth, pulled on her mitts and hurried off. Callum watched as she ran down the snow-packed lane, her long dark hair sticking out in tufts and strands as the wind's current worked to force her backwards.

"Hope we can afford to get her out of here when the time comes," said Joe.

"If we went to New York and got jobs we could save enough to send her off to the college to become a teacher like she talks about," answered Callum.

Joe eyed his brother. "I knows I'm not book-smart like the two of you, but I'm no dunce either. So let me get this straight. If we had enough money to get to New York, we could make enough money to get her out of here? That makes no sense, Cal."

Callum watched his sister's retreating back outlined against the choppy sea spitting in the distance. "I got enough money to go," he said.

Joe's mouth fell open. "What? Where? I mean, how did you get it?"

"Well, I'm crewing for Murphy going on eight years now, and I've been putting a little bit away almost every month for the last four of them. I got enough for the two of us to get there and not starve for a bit. Of course, we won't be living in luxury like we are here." Callum scanned the dilapidated kitchen. They did their best to keep it liveable, especially Mercedes, but they weren't miracle workers. "Seriously, Bill Doyle's brother is there and Bill says Don would sponsor us and help us out till we got set up, maybe even point us in the right direction for some work."

"You been mulling this over for a while, haven't you?"

"Started back when Frank left. A couple of years later I asked Charlie Murphy if I could have some pay in real money. He didn't mind once I agreed to take a bit less."

Joe thought a second. "So, was it your money that come up with that new coat for Merce that was supposed to be from the church?"

Callum nodded. "But I couldn't let the old man know. He'd spend every last cent if he thought I had any money stashed away."

"But why didn't you say anything before now?"

Callum had not set out to hide the money from his brother, but Joe had a hard time keeping things quiet. Callum didn't trust that he wouldn't let it slip out in front of Farley. The truth was he worried about Joe, fearing shades of their father in his occasional drinking binges. On the other hand, he knew Joe wasn't mean or lazy, and could just as easily be influenced by good as by bad. Callum hoped that a stable job and a pay-cheque might bring out the best in his younger brother.

"I didn't want to be getting your hopes up till I saved enough for the two of us. And," he added uneasily, "for Merce to get a bit older. I couldn't stand to leave her when she was so little. But she's growing up and can take care of herself now."

Joe nudged Callum. "Imagine the two of us in a great city like that. Lots of pretty women too, I bet."

Callum could feel the blush spreading. He always claimed he was too busy raising Mercedes and running the house to have a girlfriend, but the real reason lay in his irrational fear of women. He went practically mute in the presence of any woman under fifty. It was an insecurity he could not talk himself out of, although the Lord knew he tried, going so far as staring into a mirror and trying the words out on his tongue. But the mere pretence sent him into a cold sweat, and even though he knew people said he was handsome, he also knew any girl in her right mind would not want to be seen with the wild-eyed reflection looking back at him.

Joe was too excited to notice. "New York! Jesus Mary, that'd be something."

"I know. I've been dreaming about it for months. But if we go we should be on the road by spring, maybe get on a construction crew before they got everybody hired."

Joe hesitated. "You sure them two will be all right? Nothing makes her madder than when he starts to crack up from the liquor."

"If he'd just lay off the hard stuff, a few beers don't affect him so bad."

"We'll have a long talk with her before we goes," said Joe.

"And we'll use the last of that money to get the place fixed up," said Callum, "make it more modern."

"I'm sure they'll be fine."

Callum folded his arms. "That's it then. We're going, right?"

A huge grin spread across Joe's face. "I'll be the first one on the boat."

11

Two years after arriving in New York, Callum was heading back to Newfoundland. He hadn't intended to make the trip so soon, especially since he'd recently gotten married, but the last few letters he'd received from Mercedes had made him increasingly anxious. Paddy Griffin had returned to St. Jude. Not only that, he and Farley had become drinking buddies, hanging around Patron's together before ending up at the house where they drank late into the night.

"...he's so creepy," Mercedes wrote. "He sneaks up behind me and tries to tickle me, and then he laughs like it's a game we're both playing..."

Callum had written her immediately and told her to get out, to go to Burke's and ask if she could stay there. He had included money to cover her expenses, money he'd been saving so she could go to school and become a teacher.

He found it odd that she didn't mention the money or Burke's when she wrote back. "...and he's always watching me. He doesn't even look away when I catch him, just keeps staring at me with this weird look on his face. And Dad's getting so blind and so gone in the head that he doesn't know who's who half the time, just keeps talking about going away, moving to Toronto to go to work..."

And then came the last letter, the one that sent Callum's heart racing. "...I told him if he touched me again, I'd cut the paws off him, and I told him to get out and stay out, that if he came back I'd get the police on him. I wish you were here, Callum. I know you can't come all this way but I told Paddy you were coming anyway and he'd better steer clear. He got this awful look in his eyes that kind of scared me..."

Callum was starting to panic. He remembered the rumours about Paddy, his penchant for young girls, even his own daughters apparently. When he tried to call Burke's store to get a message to Mercedes the operator said the telephone lines had been down for a while and she didn't know when they'd be up again. He would have talked to Joe but his brother had just found out that his baby girl had leukemia and he was spending all his time at the hospital with her. And Callum didn't feel comfortable discussing it with his wife. It was too sordid, his father's drinking, a ne'er-do-well staying at the house, his sister caught in the middle. Feeling cut off and desperate, he sent a telegram to Mercedes saying he would be home in a couple of weeks. Judith was not pleased.

The thought of returning to St. Jude left Callum feeling curiously empty. Besides his sister, he had few fond memories of the place. His bones remembered the frigid slush of winter, the throb of muscles that couldn't seem to thaw for days on end, the unrelenting chill of February mornings. He could recall only one season. It was as if he hadn't lived a life there worth remembering. Still, he did not consider New York his home either.

Nevertheless, it was because of his New York connections that Callum was able to get an early start. A cargo ship belonging to one of the company's suppliers was only too happy to accommodate Jim Maclean's son-in-law. The voyage took four nauseating days that had him kissing the ground when they docked. From there, he hitched a ride in the back of a truck headed to Port-aux-Basques, then walked the last few miles. As gust after gust of wet wind whipped into him, he pushed forward toward St. Jude. The foul weather didn't bother him. He was grateful to be off the ship.

A weak light straining through the woods was Callum's first sign of home. Cutting through the footpath at the rear, he came upon his father's truck. Callum wondered if it was still working given Farley's failing eyesight.

Through the warped glass of the bare kitchen window he

saw his father sitting at the table. His face was unshaven, his white hair wild and dirty. He was looking outside but with a stare so vacant Callum couldn't tell if he'd been seen, let alone recognized.

With the storm growing fiercer by the second, Callum hurried to the front door. It squealed as he opened it, then, once he'd stepped inside, was immediately slammed shut by the wind. He looked around the large porch, the back half of which had served as his bedroom most of his life. In the corner was his old daybed. For all its age, he'd always thought it was the most comfortable place to sleep in the house.

"What? Who's that?" he heard Farley shout.

The first thing Callum noticed when he entered the kitchen was the change in his father. Although he'd never been a large man, Farley had become almost skeletal. His body seemed to be shrinking in on itself. The kitchen was in rough shape as well. Crusted dishes and greasy pots covered the counter, and some sort of soup or stew had spilled across the table and onto Farley's lap and the floor.

"Hello, Dad. It's me – Callum."

Farley squinted at him, half blind and fully drunk. His head wavered about, the bloodshot eyes trying to focus. "What's that...that black shit all over your face?"

Callum rubbed his chin, the whiskers starting to soften nicely after five days. "Thought I'd grow a beard, see if you'd recognize me."

His father grunted, which set him off on a great coughing spree, his face swelling so his veins looked ready to rupture. Eventually he hawked a wad of spit into a tin cup next to a near-empty bottle of rum. Wiping his mouth with one hand, Farley picked up the bottle with the other. With shaking hands he poured half of what was left into his glass and slugged it back. Then he poured the rest.

"I think you had enough, Dad."

Farley slammed the bottle onto the table. "You don't be

telling me what to do." He drained the glass. At first it didn't seem to faze him, but then, out of nowhere, his eyes glazed over and he slumped face first across the filthy table.

Callum knew from experience that this was the end of the night for his father. He carried him up to bed and removed his shirt and pants. Farley wore no underwear. Callum tucked a couple of blankets around the withered naked body and went down to the kitchen.

The walls shook as the storm built momentum. He decided he would give his sister half an hour, then he'd head out to find her.

Fifteen minutes later, Mercedes tiptoed in. Her skin seemed abnormally pale in the dimly lit kitchen. When she saw Callum her hand flew to her chest.

"Cal? Is that you? What are you doing here?"

"Is that all the 'how-are-you-good-to-have-you-home' I'm going to get?" he said.

Bolting across the room, she fell into his arms and started to cry.

"Merce, it's okay, it's okay. Everything's going to be all right. I'm home now."

"Oh, Cal, I'm some glad you're here. I've been so scared. And Dad's no help. It's that frigging Paddy Griffin. Even after I kicked him out Dad kept bringing him home. He wouldn't listen to me. I didn't know what to be doing."

"You shouldn't have stayed here, Merce."

"But how? I couldn't just show up on someone's doorstep. Besides, this is my home, not his, even if he acts like he owns the place. He even got the truck running and acts like he owns that too. And all Dad does is send him out for more booze."

He steered her to a chair and sat down next to her. "Did Paddy hurt you?"

"No, not really." She shivered and rubbed her arms with her hands. "It's just...well, he's always watching me and he gets that look on his face, kind of like he's doing stuff in his head, and he gets so close, right up in my face." She shivered again.

"He's been stopping here off and on for months and Dad got him doing all kinds of stuff, getting the mail and buying booze and food and doing all kinds of things like that, just like he's you or Joe. Dad hasn't left the house all week, just sits there drinking till his head hits the table..." She was talking so fast she could barely catch up to herself. "...and he keeps getting worse, it's like there's something wrong with his brain. Paddy feeds him lies and Dad believes him. I'm half afraid to sleep at night."

Forcing himself to remain calm, Callum held her face gently between his palms. "Slow down, Mercie. I'm home now. So what's Paddy telling him?"

"Stuff about how he heard you were making it so big in New York and you must be too big for your boots to come back here and that's why we haven't heard from you. And he says it like the Pope told him and Dad's foolish enough to believe him. Some days he really doesn't seem all there."

"Who, Paddy or Dad?" Callum was only half joking.

"Paddy too, but Dad's really gone. He keeps calling me Mary."

"He thinks you're Mom?"

"I guess so. He looks at me right strange like he's trying to remember who I am. And Paddy plays it up and pretends like Dad is so funny. Then the old man starts yammering at me like I'm really her. I know he's a bit cracked but it's sad."

"I remember Jack Griffin saying how Dad's father went foolish in his old age, but I never put much pass on it. I mean, who's a Griffin to talk about crackpots? Of course, fifty years of boozing and a crack on the noggin down a mine shaft don't help."

"He's even crazier lately. Him and Paddy are always on about going to Toronto. At Dad's age! I hear he's a right laughing stock down at Patron's. Gets all riled up and tells everybody they'll see, he'll go, he's just waiting for the right time."

"The old man wouldn't survive a day in Toronto, especially with that scoundrel Paddy. You did right to kick him out. If he comes back, I'll take care of him."

Mercedes almost smiled. “I was at the mail sending you a letter this afternoon, and I heard someone say he’s gone for good, got run off a few days ago. And they should know. His mother works there. Besides, if he was still around he’d for sure be here drinking Dad’s booze.”

“Speaking of mail, what do you mean you haven’t heard from me? I’ve been writing all the time. I even sent a telegram to let you know I was coming.”

“You did?”

“Yes, but I didn’t think I’d get here this quick. I’m sure glad I did though.”

“I got nothing from you in ages. I was getting worried that something happened.” She winced as a particularly loud roll of thunder rumbled outside.

“What about the money I sent?”

“Like I told you, no letter and certainly no money. And I wrote—” She clamped her hand to her mouth. “Paddy gets the mail. He’s even been helping his mother out at the post office since she got sick. He’d have the run of the place, even the telegraphs.” She stopped. “Surely to God he wouldn’t mess with the mail.”

“He’s been working at the post office? How could anybody trust that good-for-nothing to handle the mail? First thing tomorrow morning we’re going over there.”

“I bet that’s why he left. He knew you were coming.” She clicked her fingers. “Frig! Sure that’s it. He got your money and took off. How much did you send?”

“Enough to get you a place to stay and away from that crook,” he said.

Mercedes smiled. “You’re doing pretty good for yourself, aren’t you?”

“I’m doing okay.” In fact, he was doing better than anyone had expected. The Macleans hadn’t thought it right to have their daughter’s husband working on a regular crew so they’d brought him into the office. He’d caught on quickly – so quickly, in fact, that his father-in-law had begun to leave him in charge when he had to be away. "But I can't stop home too long. Once I take care of things around here I got to get back." His stomach growled; he hadn't eaten since breakfast.

Mercedes jumped up. "I'll make us a scoff while you tell me about New York. First, how's Joe?" She took a log from the woodbin. "His little girl? Is she any better?"

Callum shook his head. "It's not looking good. Leukemia."

"Leukemia! Oh my God, poor Joe." Mercedes put the wood in the stove and stared into the flames. "Is there any hope at all?"

"The doctor said no, but Joe won't believe it. All we can do is pray."

She worked at the wood for a while, jabbing it with the poker, then wiped her eyes on her sleeve. "Tell me about Judith. Is she pretty?"

Callum felt himself blush as he described his wife. Soon, Mercedes was teasing him in a singsong voice, "Ca-lum's in lo-ove, Ca-lum's in lo-ove."

They spent the rest of the night catching up. Around midnight, he took a couple of blankets to the front porch. Outside, thunder and lightening raged. The house shuddered. Mercedes fetched him an extra afghan.

"Some racket." Callum yawned. "I don't expect it'll keep me awake, though."

"Me neither. It'll be the first time in months I won't be hiding a rock under my pillow." Mercedes hugged him tight and went upstairs to bed.

Callum lay in darkness, his sister's words echoing in the night. Maybe he should take her to New York to live with him and Judith. There was little he could do for his father. Callum had a new life now, and although Mercedes might be able to become a part of it, Farley never could.

As the house settled into the night's blackest hours, Callum drifted into an odd restless sleep, half dreams, half memories.

The only reason he was certain he slept at all was because he kept waking up, yet he was never sure when he was truly awake.

Suddenly, his eyes shot open. His gut rocked with alarm but he heard only the hard, exaggerated beating of his heart. He lay still, trying to listen past the storm. There was a springy scratching sound that he thought had been part of a dream. He rushed into the house. The back door was open, sending a frigid breeze across his bare feet and chest and making him grateful he'd kept the bottom half of his long johns on.

He heard a thud above him. He ran to the stairway. The noises were more pronounced - muffled grunts, gagging noises. Callum took the stairs two at a time.

Through the open doorway of Mercedes' bedroom he saw him - Paddy Griffin, naked, his gut hanging out, his arse a sickly white. In one hand he held a bloodied filleting knife, in the other, a switchblade. He was leaning in slightly, talking to someone on the end of the bed that was hidden behind the wall. Callum leapt forward.

Paddy turned. He looked surprised, disoriented. "You? Already—?"

Callum was on him before he could finish. Paddy staggered backwards. His arm swung out hard to the side, goring the knife into the neck of a man sitting naked on the bed. There was a throaty gasping sound as the man pitched sideways on top of Mercedes, who lay gagged, arms tied to the bedpost.

Callum froze. God, no! It couldn't be! But one second of eye contact with his sister told him all he needed to know. As the blood spurted from Farley's neck, Callum yanked at the rope tying Mercedes down, but then she began to moan frantically through the cloth in her mouth. Her head jerked toward the foot of the bed.

Callum spun around. Paddy was stumbling towards the door. Callum hurled himself after him. Catching a leg, he pulled. Paddy fell to the floor but quickly wriggled free and hopped up. He was surprisingly agile.

"Had this all figured out." Paddy spit on the floor. "Now you shows up. Fuck."

They circled each other, closer to the door one moment, closer to Mercedes the next, Callum always with an eye on the switchblade in Paddy's fist.

"She was some good." Paddy cackled. "Fucking virgin, tight and bloody like I likes it. All bloody and smeary now."

Callum assumed Paddy was referring to the blood of first sex, but when he looked past him at Mercedes, he saw that she'd managed to get a hand free and push Farley's body away. Scarlet lines oozed across her stomach. His eyes found Paddy's; they looked inhuman.

"You bastard!" Callum roared. "How could you do that to her?"

Paddy looked over at Mercedes as if to admire his handiwork. Seizing the opportunity, Callum lunged and knocked him to the floor. But Paddy was at least fifty pounds heavier and soon managed to gain the advantage. He knelt on Callum's wrists and pressed the blade to his throat. Callum was afraid to move, yet his mind registered the smell of rotting teeth and stale booze, and the grotesque sight of the man's penis crushed against his chest.

"Three Hanns in one night." Saliva flew from between Paddy's remaining teeth. "I'll get away with it, too..."

Behind him, Callum watched Mercedes rise from the bed. Terrified that Paddy would become aware of what was happening, Callum deliberately kept eye contact with him, yelling and swearing as loud as he dared.

"...they all thinks I'm gone," Paddy gloated, "said goodbye days ago..."

Mercedes pulled the gag from her mouth and reached for the knife.

"...and gone I'll be when I gets done with you." Paddy let out a high-pitched shriek and raised the switchblade.

In one continuous motion, her bloodstained hand yanked the knife from Farley's neck, swung around and swept down to plunge it into Paddy's back.

A look of stupefaction spread over Paddy's blunt, drunk face. The reverberating impact seemed to stun Mercedes as well. But as Paddy tried to get up, she pulled the knife out and thrust it back in. Her eyes were wild, frenzied. In. And out. Again and again, each stab a visceral charge straight from her gut and her heart and her throat. Even after Paddy lay still on top of Callum, she kept stabbing at his back, her arms weak, her mouth open in a silent cry. The feeble jabs barely made contact anymore but she seemed unable to stop, unable to halt the movement, the deathly rhythm of back and forth.

"Merce, stop!" Callum begged. "Let me up. Please Mercedes, stop it!"

Callum struggled to push Paddy away. The dead weight surprised him. He shoved harder and managed to free himself and grab Mercedes' arms. The knife fell to the floor next to the one Paddy had dropped moments before.

Blood was everywhere - on the walls, the bed, the blankets, the floor. The dim ceiling light shone down on the four of them, two still breathing, two forever still. There was no other sound. The storm had died too.

Callum held Mercedes to him, her nakedness no longer relevant. The air seemed to convulse in her throat as she shuddered with each breath. He felt as though she was trying to say something but the words were lost in the spasms that rocked her.

Very gently, he helped her up off the floor and into the tiny bathroom. Together they stared, mesmerised, at the crosshatch of lightly bleeding lines. Mercedes' eyes were riveted on her belly, as if their focal point was permanently fixed there. Seeing the horror on his sister's face, Callum swallowed his own revulsion.

Without warning, she collapsed against him.

"It's all right, Merce," he whispered. "Shh, it's all right now," he said, over and over, smoothing her bloodied tangled hair until at last she stopped shaking.

As her trembling subsided, he felt a peculiar tension come over her. With each deep deliberate breath, she seemed to gain strength. When she finally raised her head, her eyes were crystal hard, and except for the smeared blood, her cheeks were dry.

Callum noticed a small puddle collecting on the floor, then saw the red streaks on her legs. "Merce, you're bleeding…there…"

She looked down. As her hands reached out to cover her nakedness, her face contorted with pain. "It's just…it must be…the monthly…I need a towel."

"Oh. Sorry." Suddenly embarrassed, he found some clean towels and a blanket to cover her. "Merce, we got to get the police and go to the hospital."

She pulled the blanket closer. "No."

"We need to get these cuts looked at."

"No hospital. Just help me clean myself up."

"They could get infected."

"Infected?" Her voice was tight with fury. "That'd be a blessing, a big old gangrene they could just cut out. Wouldn't that be the ticket?"

"We'll get a doctor to come here. The police can bring him."

"Callum, there will be no police or doctor in this house tonight." She said each word slowly as if to a child.

"Don't be crazy. We got two dead men in the other room and you're cut to smithereens there. We got to take care of this now."

"Yes, *we*, you and me, no one else," she declared, as if the indignities she'd endured gave her indisputable authority. And even though she flinched in pain, her voice was strong. "I was the one sliced to bits by that bastard. Well, now I get to decide what to do with him. And I say we keep it just between us."

"But why? It's not like this was your fault. Everyone will understand that."

"My arse they will! If I ever want to show my face in this

town again we got to handle this ourselves. You think people will understand? Like hell! Paddy was living here for months, with no one to keep an eye on things but my crazy drunken father. They'll think he was doing it to me all along, or worse, that I let him." Her eyes, briefly young once again, looked past him towards the bedroom. "But even if we could explain that, and even if they did understand, how do we explain him?"

Callum's eyes followed hers to the blood-splattered room where Farley Hann lay naked and dead, a senile drunk who'd had little dignity in life, even less in death.

Suddenly, the memory of that grey-white body, the blood flooding out as it lay on top of Mercedes, flashed at Callum in all its obscenity. "Merce, I'm so sorry this happened to you. What came over him? Did Dad ever, you know, before, try...?"

"No, never. Paddy dragged him in after he was done with me. I heard him say he had a surprise for him. Dad always passes out with his clothes on, so Paddy must've taken them off him." She paused. "Dad didn't mean it, Callum. I know he didn't mean it." There were tears in her eyes now. "He kept calling me Mary."

Mercedes' stomach wounds were superficial. Paddy had used the tip of the blade to just break the skin, creating razor-thin lines haphazardly across her belly. As Callum swabbed iodine on his sister's cuts, leaving a dark russet trail of tea-coloured paths across her abdomen, he remembered removing his father's clothes when he'd put him to bed. The notion that he might have helped Paddy made the vomit rise in his throat. He forced it back, and then he decided he would do as Mercedes asked.

Two things occurred to him. First off, there was a good chance they hadn't been seen or overheard because of the late hour and the house's isolation. Secondly, no one in St. Jude knew about his visit, and the driver of the truck who gave him a lift was hundreds of miles away and would soon be on the ferry to Nova Scotia. After their night from hell, Callum would take his luck where he could.

"Here's how I see it. Paddy and Dad talked about going away, right?"

Flinching from the sting of the iodine, Mercedes nodded.

"Everyone thinks Paddy already left town, so when someone asks, you say you never saw Paddy or Dad since they drove off a couple of days ago. When it's obvious they're gone, let everyone think they finally went to Toronto like they bragged about. You can act worried or upset or pretend like you don't want to talk about them. People will just think you're angry or embarrassed."

Mercedes winced again. "Do you think we can pull this off, Callum?"

"I hope so, Merce. But we got to get organized before the sun comes up. We can't risk anyone taking any notice of us. And I'm worried about you, if you're up to all the work that's before you. Every move you make seems to bring on more pain."

"If it'll wipe this away I promise I can handle it. Just tell me what to do."

"It's not that simple. Once it's done, we can't take it back, and you'll be here all alone because part of the plan means I was never here in the first place. So I can't come back and help you. I just got to disappear. But I'm worried about those cuts?"

"They'll be fine." She pointed towards the bedroom. "If you can get rid of that, then I'll take care of the rest of it."

He studied her face for signs of weakness. She stared straight back at him.

There was no time to discuss ways or means or what-ifs. Callum rolled his father onto a blanket. As they started to lift, Mercedes shivered. He stopped. She inhaled a sharp breath and lifted again. They carried Farley's corpse to the truck, then repeated the process with Paddy and covered them both with blankets and an old fishing net. There was no room for words; the air was filled already with the fact of what they were doing, their limbs moving automatically, eyes averted from each other and the bodies under the blankets, enclosing them both in a final covenant. It wasn't until they threw Paddy's things into the cab that the spell broke. The suffocating air lifted. The metallic odour lingered on.

By five a.m. Callum was dressed in his father's clothes, ready to go. "You're still sure about this, Merce?"

"Yes. But this is our secret, right? You won't tell your wife?"

Judith was the last person Callum would tell. "What about Joe?" he said.

"God no, not Joe. You know what he's like."

Callum nodded. Joe had never been able to keep a secret, especially when he was drinking. And he'd been drinking a lot since Sheilagh had taken ill.

He gave Mercedes a gentle hug and carried his belongings to the truck along with the jug of water he would wash with later. The Chevy started without hesitation. Whispering a prayer of gratitude, he drove slowly away.

As the town receded behind him, he turned on his headlights and picked up speed, his windows fully open despite the harsh chill of the predawn. Less than an hour later, as the night evaporated into a misty half-light, he pulled onto a side road and drove a quarter of a mile through ruts and overgrown weeds to a bluff overlooking a partially frozen cove. Below, the ocean curved into the rock to form a bay within a bay. Jagged cliffs rose up on three sides. Callum looked across the water to Bay D'Esprits. A lone moose stared back for a moment then lowered its head and retreated into the woods.

Callum searched the area around him for signs of life. Nothing moved. The trees, even the air, seemed eerily still.

He went to the back of the truck. He inhaled deeply, bracing himself, then removed the net and blankets. But nothing could have saved him from the impact of seeing those two dead men. He couldn't swallow. The pain in his head pounded against the back of his eyes. Vomiting and gagging, he staggered to the trees and held on until he finally managed to overcome the awful conviction that it was his life that was coming to an end.

He took slow deliberate breaths until his heartbeat settled. Returning to the truck, he dragged the bodies into the cab and placed their possessions and the knives between them. He wasn't sure what he intended people to think if they were ever found. He was too tired and weary and confused to think the deed all the way through. This was simply the only scenario he could dream up.

Quickly, he washed and changed into his own clothes, tossing those that had belonged to his father in with the bodies. He rolled up the windows and gave the truck one last inspection, then clasped his hands together and looked up to the overcast sky.

"Dear God," he prayed out loud. "I know this isn't right, but for the life of me I don't know what else to do. Please forgive me and take care of Mercedes. In the name of the Father and of the Son and of the Holy Ghost, Amen." He made the sign of the cross over the truck. Then he shifted it into gear and pushed it forward. It rolled easily to the edge. With a final shove, over and down it went.

Callum stared in perverse fascination as it bounced off a large outcropping on the side of the cliff. The impact propelled it out into mid-air so that it broke through the sish some distance from the cliff's face. As he watched it sink below the thinly iced surface, he thought of his father. Not the dead man in the truck, but the other man, the man whom his mother had loved, who had once upon a time tried to be a decent parent, especially to Mercedes. Even when his mind was no longer quite his own, Farley Hann had loved his daughter as best he could. And yes, once upon a time before that, he had done the things that good fathers do. Callum forced himself to remember those times – the family picking blueberries in the back woods, a much younger Farley laughing, carrying a giggling Joe on his shoulders through the thickest parts; Callum and Farley fishing off the dock, just the two of them, alone and quiet. Callum thought about this man who was his flesh and blood, a man he had never known well despite that. That man's blood, along with the blood of Paddy Griffin, would stain him forever.

Rooted to the earth, Callum prayed for the soul of his long ago lost father. He felt water on his face and was surprised that the spray of the crash could reach him at such a great distance. As his mind caught up to the moment, Callum felt the rain kiss his forehead, diluting the salt trickling past his lips. He looked again across the water to the quiet desolate landscape of Bay D'Esprits. He longed to be there, alone, on the other side of that Godforsaken cove.

12

"Callum!" Judith stood in the doorway, her lips pursed in an angry pout.

Callum shoved the envelope aside.

"That's the third time I called out to you." She cupped her palms to stare at her cuticles. "It's like you don't notice I'm here lately."

Callum felt the sweat on his forehead. "I didn't hear you."

"How could you not hear me?" Her eyes skimmed the small sitting room.

The house that Judith's father had bought them for a wedding present was not as big as Judith would have liked. They would buy a larger one when they could afford it themselves, Callum had told her. "Can we at least get a maid?" she'd replied, extending one perfectly manicured hand. "My nails are a disgrace." He'd said no, that he would take over washing the dishes. She'd looked annoyed at first, but then she smiled as only Judith could smile. He reached out and drew her close, still amazed that she was his wife, that he could take her in his arms whenever he wanted. She leaned back to look up at him, her finger tracing his jaw line. "What beautiful children we'll have. A boy, then a girl. She'll play piano and take ballet, and he'll be tall and strong like you." Her hands and eyes caressed him. "He'll study law or medicine, and she'll have the most splendid debutante ball. Can't you just see them?" He could, almost. He could certainly see why he'd fallen for her, with her sky-blue eyes and full red lips, her soft brown curls that nestled just so against her high cheekbones. She was more exciting than any woman he'd ever known. Besides, Judith had a plan, for her and for them, a plan with a family. "You're so different from Daddy, Callum," she told him. "I thought all men were like him until I met you." At moments like those he could ignore the things that bothered him, like her want of a maid and a bigger house, or when she corrected his speech or his table manners or picked out his clothes. She was just trying to help, she insisted, so that they, and, some day, their children, would fit into New York society. Didn't he want that, she asked, pulling him closer still so that the heat from her body against his erased everything else from his mind.

She still had that effect on him.

"I'm sorry. I was...thinking, that's all."

Judith held out her hands. He started to reach up to take them until he realized she was still studying her nails. "I'm going to have to get these done."

"Good idea."

She peered at him over the tops of her fingers. "This from the man who thinks manicures are a waste of money? Maybe now's the time to mention that maid again."

Callum could only nod. He knew he was supposed to laugh, but he wasn't sure what sound might come out of his mouth if he tried.

She eyed him suspiciously. "Callum?"

"Yes?" he said, hoping only to survive the next few moments undetected.

"What did your sister have to say?"

"Not much...except...she's coming to visit. She'll be here next week."

"Next week! But that's not enough time to get ready for a visitor."

"She already got the ticket. Besides, it's Merce. There's nothing to get ready."

"Don't be ridiculous," Judith snapped. "Of course there is. I need to get the guest room in order. And plan some activities for her. And Mummy and Daddy and Ruth are here for dinner with the Wilkinsons week after next. What will we do with a fifteen-year-old during a dinner with the Wilkinsons? We'll talk to your brother—"

"We can't tell Joe," Callum stammered. "It's a surprise. Just me and you know."

"This is rather strange, travelling all this way and keeping it a secret from her own brother." She studied his face. "Can I see the letter?"

He held it out, glad he'd had the instinct to hide the first page right off. There was only one page now, the part that Mercedes had written for public eyes.

"Is everything all right, Callum?" Judith asked, taking the envelope.

He nodded, forcing a smile. Things were far from all right.

Callum had gone to St. Jude an innocent man. He'd come back a murderer. The fact that he hadn't actually killed anyone was irrelevant. He took full responsibility.

Initially, the need to escape the island undetected was enough to keep his mind on constant alert. Back in New York, the subterfuge continued as he concocted answers to polite questions about his family and the trip, creating layers of lies and omissions, all the while consumed by the knowledge of how his life had changed overnight yet trying to act as if nothing had changed at all. Each night he would semi-awaken, gasping for air, clawing at the bedclothes in a sweat of terror, overcome by the sensation of free-falling within an endless abyss and the certainty that if he didn't wake up he would drown in a bottomless black hole.

Each morning he reminded himself that it was over. He'd had three letters from Mercedes, and although they were full of false cheer, they made no mention of trouble. If they could bluff their way through just a little longer, all would be well. Not the same as before. Never that. But they would manage.

Then the fourth letter arrived.

When Mercedes stepped from the train, Callum's heart felt

ready to break with the pressure of trying to smile. She was haggard and drawn, dressed in the heavy brown coat he'd bought her three years before. Too big then, now it was too small.

Once they'd escaped the overcrowded platform, he held out his arms. She immediately broke into tears. His smile disappeared.

They stood in the June dusk holding each other for a long time. People passed by all around them. Aromas of meat and exotic spices rose with the steam from a food vendor's cart. A young boy waving a newspaper shouted to the passers-by jostling their way along the busy sidewalks. Taxi drivers cursed and yelled and honked their horns. Mercedes buried her head in Callum's shoulder, oblivious to it all.

Finally, they walked to a nearby diner. Callum ordered tea and sandwiches.

"You cold, Merce?" Despite the warmth, her coat was buttoned to the neck.

"Not really. I'm just tired. I'm tired of it all, and it's only a couple of months."

"If it's still that early, how can you be sure?"

"I've never been late before, like a clock I am." She closed her eyes for a second. "Besides, I just know. Some things you know even if you wish you didn't."

The waitress brought their order. Callum concentrated on pouring tea. "There are places where you can have it taken care of, you know?"

"There's adoption everywhere, even home there's orphanages—" She stopped abruptly. "Callum! How can you talk of such a thing?"

"Because it's not your fault."

Her voice fell to a tiny whisper. "I killed a man, Callum."

"But you had to—"

"I know, I know I had to. And I'll learn to live with it because I had to. But a baby is different, a poor tiny baby. God could never forgive that."

"There's times when there's exceptions even to God's laws."

She leaned in. "There can't be exceptions to this. What has this place done to you? You never would have said this a few years ago."

The righteousness in her voice triggered something deep within him. "This place, as you call it, opened my eyes, but no more so than our very own little St. Jude. The world is full of bad people, Merce. I may be one of them. That bastard certainly was. But you're one of the good ones. Don't let this ruin your life."

Mercedes reached for his hand. "This baby is the only innocent one in this. If we do something to hurt him, then it's all over for us."

He felt again the gnaw of true powerlessness. She was still a child for all her eyes had seen, as blameless as the baby growing inside her.

"You sound as though you've thought it through, like you know what you want."

She shook her head. "I only know what I can't do. Funny thing is, I didn't know that until you brought it up. But I mean it. Everything else is just so awful, don't mention that again. I can't stand to think about it. Or maybe I'm afraid I'll start to think about it, and then I'm forever the devil's no matter what I do."

The tears started again then. At first she wiped them away, but others just kept rolling down her neck and under her coat collar. She gave up trying to stop them. Still, the waitress dropped the bill onto the table without giving them a second glance.

"Merce, I got to ask you something." He forced himself to meet her eye. "Is there...well, is there any chance the baby could be Dad's?"

If he'd punched her in the face she couldn't have looked more shocked.

"I'm sorry Merce, but if it is, then...for the baby's sake you have to..."

She squeezed his hand so hard it hurt. "No, Dad didn't do anything. Paddy just sort of pushed him onto the bed. I'm not sure he was fully awake even."

Relief surged through Callum. "I'm sorry, I just didn't know what to think. Mainly I tried not to think about it at all. The whole idea was so horrible."

There was a hint of a smile as she nodded. "Until this minute I didn't think anything worse was possible. Something to be grateful for, I suppose."

There was no sarcasm in her tone, no undercurrent of anger. Trying to hide his own, Callum turned his attention to the steady flow of people passing by the diner window. Several glanced in. Did they wonder about the story unfolding just beyond the glass, about the young girl huddled into her ugly winter coat?

Callum placed several bills beneath the untouched sandwiches. "Let's go home, Merce. We got a nice warm bed waiting just for you."

In the car Mercedes sat quietly, eyes downcast, hands in her pockets. She seemed unaware of her surroundings, even though it was like nothing she had seen before. But as they drove onto the Brooklyn Bridge, she sat bolt upright.

"How long does it take?" she asked, one hand on the door, the other on the dash.

Callum smiled. "Don't worry, it's just a few minutes."

Mercedes said nothing else until she had watched the bridge recede behind them out the rear windshield. "Does your wife know yet?" she said then.

"I didn't say anything in case you decided—" He stopped. "Sorry."

"It's the kind of thing a woman should know is going on in her house."

He hit the steering wheel. "Nothing's 'going on.' Stop acting like it is."

She flinched and sank further down into her coat.

"Oh Merce, I'm sorry." He reached over and touched her shoulder. "It's just that it's so wrong. As for Judith, I can tell her right away, or you can, or we can wait."

"Would she think I should do something about it?"

"I don't know. We talked about having a baby. So far we haven't been blessed."

As the irony hit him, so did something else. "Wait a minute. I just had an idea, maybe a solution. Your baby - could it be our baby, mine and Judith's?"

Mercedes' face showed a glimmer of hope. "Could we really do that?" Then her voice wavered. "But would she want to after how it was made?"

"We don't have to tell her about that, do we? We'd have to tell her everything."

They were quiet again. Rows of brownstone townhouses, interspersed with tall brick apartment buildings and lower-level shop fronts, passed by outside the window. Eventually they came to a street lined with newer homes, none of which bore the slightest resemblance to the house they'd grown up in. Callum pulled into the driveway of a white two-story with a covered veranda running across the front.

Mercedes stared at the house. "My God, Callum! Is this yours?"

"It sure is, thanks to Judith's father," he said, trying to hide his resentment. "How about we don't say anything yet? I need to think it through."

"Okay. And thanks, Callum. I don't know what I'd do without you."

"I'm here, Merce, whatever you need."

Inside, Judith bustled toward them, her full skirt swishing to a standstill as she stopped in front of Mercedes. Callum stumbled through the introductions - his dishevelled sister in her too-small coat, his sophisticated wife in satin blouse and pearls.

Under cover of getting the tea ready, he reinvented the lie of their father going to Toronto before quickly moving on to discuss Mercedes' trip, the weather in St. Jude, news of old neighbours, whatever he could think of to fill the silence.

Judith let him ramble on. Finally, she looked across the table at Mercedes. "Why would your father move away without telling you?"

"He was always talking about it so I suppose he just up and went," Callum said.

Judith looked up at him. "You don't seem very concerned."

"He's a grown man."

"But he's old and alone. Don't you worry?"

"He can take care of himself—"

"He's with Paddy—" Mercedes said in the same instant. She looked at Callum.

Judith was watching them closely. "Paddy? Who's Paddy?"

Mercedes looked away. "He was—"

Callum jumped in. "He went to Toronto at the same time and they used to talk about it at the bar so they probably went together." He stood over Judith, teapot poised.

"I need a cup, dear."

Callum's laugh was too loud. "Oh, right. Of course you do."

As he got a cup and filled it, Judith's questions started. How had the men travelled to Toronto, did they have money, what was Paddy like, did he have family? Her eyes rarely left Mercedes, who kept adding more cream and sugar into her cup, noisily stirring and sloshing. Callum answered whenever he could, but he had to be careful. After all, he would hardly be expected to know very much.

Still, there was a limit to how much his sister could take. "You're looking some worn out there, Mercie, girl," he finally interrupted. "Do you want to go to bed soon?"

"Please," she said meekly, so unlike the brassy sister he was used to.

Judith sipped her tea, her eyes peering at Mercedes over the rim of the cup. "This Paddy Griffin doesn't sound like the best character."

"Just a local," Callum said. "How's your tea there, Judith? More sugar?"

She ignored him. "Weren't you afraid without your father?"

"It's a small town," he answered for Mercedes. "Not much happens."

Mercedes' eyes, wide and bright, met his for a moment.

"It must have been a difficult trip," Judith went on.

"I got seasick," Mercedes said, her voice weak.

"Typical Hann you are, my girl," Callum teased. "Can't swim in the water, can't stand to be on it either. Just like myself."

Judith eyed him curiously. "But didn't you work on a boat back there?"

"That I did. Longest days of my life. I was supposed to be catching fish, but I always started out feeding them first. Kind of put me off eating them for a while."

Mercedes pushed her cup away. After a look from Judith, she pulled it back. A thin milky puddle had sloshed into the saucer. Mercedes stood, one hand on the table, the other on the back of her chair. The tip of her tongue slid across her dry lips.

Callum leaned far forward so that Judith had little choice but to look at him and away from Mercedes. "Is everything ready upstairs? She's exhausted."

"Of course it is," Judith muttered, her eyebrows raised.

"Come on, Merce, I'll tuck you in." As they headed up the stairs he called back in a firm voice, "I'll be right down, Judith."

As soon as they were in her bedroom, Mercedes whispered, "I don't think she likes me."

Callum turned on the lamp on the bedside table. "She's just getting to know you, is all. It'll be right as rain by morning. Don't worry about another thing tonight," he added. "You needs a solid sleep so we can handle all the other stuff tomorrow."

"I'll try but it's been hard to sleep." Her voice fell to a frightened whisper. "It's the dreams. Every night it's like they're waiting for me, you know?"

The sound of running water and the rattle of cups and saucers drifted up to them.

"I do." He put his arms around her. "I'm right across the hall. If you need anything, anything at all, just call out to me."

"Thanks, Callum."

"You did the right thing coming to me. Maybe tonight we'll both get a decent sleep." With another hug, he left her to settle in and went back downstairs.

Judith's bright red fingernails drummed the countertop. "Your sister's pretty. She looks tired, though."

"She is." He took a dishtowel from the drawer. They said nothing while he dried the dishes and put them in the cupboard.

Judith reached out to take the dishtowel from him. "I'm sure she'll be her old self again by morning. Not that I know what that is," she added.

"Morning will be here soon enough, too," he said. "I think I'll go to bed."

"How long is she staying?"

"I didn't want to ask when she was leaving on her first night here."

"What took you so long?"

He yawned widely. "When?"

"From the train station." Judith wiped down the perfectly clean table.

"Oh...the train was delayed. One glitch and the whole schedule goes off."

"Did she say anything else about him?"

"What? Who?" Did Judith always jump from subject to subject, Callum wondered, or was his conscience making him uneasy?

"Upstairs. I wondered if she said anything more about your father."

He leaned back into the counter. "No, Judith. Nothing."

"What about that other man, I forget his name."

"No," he said quickly, "nothing there either."

Judith folded the towel, her eyes on his face. "What was his name again?"

"Paddy," he mumbled.

She leaned forward as if she hadn't heard.

"His name is Paddy Griffin," he repeated, forcing himself to be patient.

"Paddy. Of course, Paddy Griffin. Has anybody talked to Paddy's family?"

"I don't know, Judith." Why did she keep saying that name, as if it was a name like any other, like Joe or Frank, benign and harmless? "I'm just glad she's here."

"She seems a bit off to me."

Callum crossed his arms. "How the hell would you know? You just met her."

"Callum! Don't use that tone with me."

"Sorry," he said, and he was.

"I can sense there's something wrong. A woman knows these things."

"Can't we just leave it till morning?"

"Fine." Her nails tapped the counter. "But if there's anything to discuss, we'd best do it before she wakes up."

He really did not want to talk. All he wanted was to go to bed and go to sleep and forget about it all for a few unconscious hours. But he realized that Judith had a point. He sat down. "You're right, Judith. Merce needs our help."

She stopped tapping. "What exactly is going on?"

There was something antagonistic in the timbre of her voice, the haughty way she held her head, but he ignored it. He had a story to invent.

"Well, you see, there was this boy in the next town to ours," he began.

"A boy?" Her mouth curled in a knowing smirk. "Of course, yes, a boy."

"Anyway," Callum continued, "they fell in love - at least Merce did - and he said he wanted to marry her. Then his parents got wind of it and shipped him off to the Brothers to finish high school. I don't think he even knows about Merce's condition."

"Aha! So! Mercedes has a condition."

"Yes, Judith. She's pregnant. That's why she's here."

She threw her hands out. "And what are we supposed to do with her?"

"I'm not sure. But she's my sister and I have to help her. There's no one else."

"Can't we do something with it? You know what I mean, don't you?"

He caught on faster than Mercedes had. "She said that would be the most sinful thing she could do in this whole mess."

Judith rolled her eyes. "Well, she'll have to put it up for adoption. Then she can go home and no one will ever know." She thought a moment. "I might have an idea."

Callum felt an instant relief. Here, finally, was someone who could take charge, who would know what to do. Judith had a mind designed for the intricacies of life. She knew what someone meant even when they said differently, or when something insignificant mattered and when it didn't. He, on the other hand, was not good at figuring out such complexities and preferred to accept life at face value or, since he'd met Judith, take her word on it.

"Up near my uncle's hotel there's a convent, St. Agatha's, that takes in girls in this situation." She waved her hand disdainfully. "One of the Barry girls went there."

"That sounds like a good idea. We'll talk to Merce in the morning." He would save the idea of adopting the baby until then, as if it had occurred to him overnight.

"I'll make some inquiries first thing."

Callum felt suddenly drained, incapable of coherent thought. "How about we sleep on it for tonight?" He took her hand. "Thank you, Judith."

For the first time since the nightmare began, he thought he might actually get a decent sleep.

13

"I know about the boyfriend you made up," Mercedes whispered the next morning when Callum came to her room. "It's really easy to hear what anyone says down in the kitchen." She paused. "But what you said earlier, about adopting?"

Judith hustled in, heels clicking on the wood floor. "Good morning."

Callum gave a discreet shake of his head to Mercedes. "Judith, I was just telling Merce how I filled you in on everything. So now we can figure out what to do."

Judith reached over and lifted Mercedes' chin, her freshly manicured nails pressing into the soft flesh. "I am very disappointed in you." She dropped her hand abruptly. "Come down and we'll discuss what on earth we're going to do with you."

Mercedes' eyes flashed for the briefest moment, then she nodded meekly and followed Judith down the stairs.

In the kitchen, Dinah Shore's "Shoo Fly Pie" filled the silence.

"Well, I don't know about pie, but breakfast sounds good." Callum's voice was louder than he intended.

"I'm not very hungry," Mercedes mumbled, watching Judith slice a loaf of bread.

"There's someone other than yourself to think about now," Judith lectured.

Callum saw the tears in his sister's eyes. "You'll be good and hungry when you sees what Judith can do to a couple of eggs." Breakfast was the one meal she could cook reasonably well. "You like scrambled, right?"

Mercedes went almost impossibly paler. She bolted from the table.

Callum started to follow but the rap of a spoon on the counter, accompanied by a curt shake of Judith's head, stopped him. He cranked up the volume on the radio.

"Go easy on her, would you, Judith?"

She slapped another slice onto a stack of toast. "There's no sense coddling her."

"I know, but she's hardly more than a child."

"A child! A child does not do what she did with that boy."

A jolt of anger shot through him, but just then he heard his sister's heavy footsteps on the stairs. He switched off the radio.

Judith placed a dish of fried eggs and bacon in front of Callum and passed Mercedes some dry toast. "I thought you'd prefer something plainer."

"Thank you," said Mercedes gratefully.

"I suppose we'll have to go see your brother." Judith sounded reluctant.

"Yes," said Callum, "but we won't tell him what's going on. He'll tell Betty and she'll tell her sister and then everyone back in Green Harbour will find out. Besides, they got enough to worry about." He smiled at Mercedes. "It'll do Joe a world of good to see you, though."

Judith put down her fork. "We have work to do first. And the sooner we start the easier this will be on everyone." Her distinctive New York accent barrelled across the breakfast table to where Mercedes sat unmoving, eyes glued to a crust of toast that had fallen beside her plate. "I made some inquiries this morning, discreetly of course, about St. Agatha's. Sister Ignatius is the Mother Superior, and a nosy, bossy woman by the sound of her." Judith's tone was contemptuous. "Full of questions about the girl and the father and the family. I made it clear that was none of her concern."

"We don't want them angry at Merce before she even gets there," said Callum.

"Don't worry. They're quite familiar with this sordid sort of thing. Heaven knows this has happened to better girls than you, Mercedes."

Callum's mouth opened but one look at his wife's face and his anger died. The disturbing truth, he realized, was that Judith had meant no offence.

Judith glanced up from her notes. "Callum? Something wrong?"

There was no point arguing; she had it all figured out. And really, wasn't that what he'd hoped for? "No, nothing. Go on."

"Anyway Mercedes, Sister Ignatius will take you in when your time is closer. Till then you can work in Uncle Harold's hotel as a chambermaid or a cook or something. The people there won't know we're related, of course. You'll be an out-of-towner who came to us through the church..."

As Judith filled in the details, Callum had the unsettling thought that he'd given power over his sister's life to someone Mercedes didn't even know, someone who, really, he didn't know all that well, either. Yes, he'd wanted Judith to take over, and, yes, he was relieved that decisions were being made, but he was beginning to wonder how they had all come to this place in time. How had he and his sister ended up sitting at this table in this house with this woman determining both their futures?

"... and you can go home and start over," Judith finished with a self-satisfied air.

Callum looked at Mercedes. "Mercie, is this what you want?" he asked gently.

"What she wants?" Judith said incredulously. "Want has little to do with it. The bottom line is this is what she gets, and it's as good as it gets."

"Callum, it's fine. I mean, there's no other choice, is there?" Mercedes tried to smile. "I think I'll lie down for a while." She rose unsteadily and left the room.

"Well!" Judith crossed her arms. "A little gratitude might be nice."

"Judith, please. Give her a break."

"Oh, for heaven's sake." She stood up. "I have work to do."

Early in the afternoon Callum went to check on Mercedes.

She was asleep, her face like pale wax. Except for the rise and fall of her chest, her body never stirred.

Supper was a quiet affair. Judith made several stabs at conversation but eventually even she gave up. They picked at their food, the meat tough and overcooked, the potatoes crunchy in the centre.

"Should we go to your brother's tomorrow?" Judith asked when they were done with the pretence of eating. "It's too late to go now, don't you think?"

For once, Mercedes looked Judith in the eye. "Yes, it's far too late now."

The next morning after Mass they drove to the Bronx. As they turned onto Joe's street, they saw an old car raised up on blocks. It had no windshield, no tires. Three shabbily dressed children played on the road, unsupervised. A foul odour, of sewer maybe, wafted into the car. Judith rolled up the window.

Joe's apartment was at the back of a small house, past the garbage bins. Two half-rotted steps led to his door. Judith's gloved hand barely touched the rusted railing for balance.

"Joe? Joe, you home?" Callum called through the open door. Inside, he could see dirty dishes and empty beer bottles on a makeshift table.

Seconds later, Joe appeared. A smile instantly brightened his face, softening the effects of his unshaven chin and the cigarette hanging from his lips. "Cal! What a nice surprise." The cigarette fell from his mouth. "Mercie? Is that you?" he yelled, brushing past Judith to lift a squealing Mercedes off the floor and whirl her into the house.

Callum stepped on the cigarette and followed them in. "Surprised you, didn't we? Merce said you always loved surprises."

"Huh?" Joe looked puzzled as he set Mercedes back on her feet. "No odds. It's some good to see you, girl. Betty," he shouted down the hall. "Bring Sheilagh here."

In all the commotion, Judith hung back, her eyes on the open door.

When Betty came in, she carried a small child whose fine, silky hair was as black as her face was white. She looked to be about six months old, but in fact was about to celebrate her first birthday.

With extraordinary delicacy, Joe took her and snuggled her to his chest. "Sheilagh, this is your Auntie Mercie," he said. "Can you smile for her?"

The child stared listlessly up at him. Even when he held her out for all to see, her gaze didn't shift. Soon, Betty reclaimed her and went back down the hall.

Joe sat next to Mercedes on the sofa. "I think she's better these days. Them doctors don't know everything, no matter what they thinks," he muttered.

"God is keeping an eye out for her, Joey. You just keep saying them prayers." Callum turned to his sister, his voice breaking. "Isn't she beautiful?"

Mercedes nodded and leaned her head against Joe's shoulder. Callum watched the tears slide down her face. She swallowed silently.

It was an awkward visit, filled with erratic bursts of conversation. Joe kept asking about Mercedes' trip, but his questions were half-hearted. He kept coming and going from the room whenever there was the slightest peep from Sheilagh. Betty rejoined them a couple of times but, like Joe, she was constantly alert. When she did sit with them, her nervous fingers fidgeted non-stop.

"So poor old Dad is home on his own," Joe remarked at one point.

Judith, who had been quiet throughout, spoke up. "You didn't know? He's gone to Toronto with Paddy Griffin."

"Paddy Griffin?" Joe looked taken aback. "That son of a bitch. Remember Cal? That time I caught him behind the house?"

"It was nothing, forget it." Callum did not look at Mercedes. "Anyway—"

"Nothing!" cried Joe. "Watching Merce through the window was nothing?"

"That's so long ago." Callum tried to wave him off. "How about a cup of tea?"

"You were fit to be tied. I never seen you so mad." He started to rise. "I'll go put the kettle on."

Mercedes' hand gripped his arm. "What do you mean, 'watching Merce'?"

Callum reached out to her. "Mercie, it was a long time ago—"

She pushed his arm away. "No. Tell me what he's talking about."

Joe threw Callum a questioning glance. Callum nodded.

"Couple of years ago, I came up on him behind the house..." Joe reddened.

"And?" Mercedes demanded. "What was he doing?"

"And...he was rooting at himself, his drawers half down around his ugly fat arse."

"Oh?" Her lips were tight.

"Anyway, I walked up on him and he ran out the woods stuffing himself together. Then I saw you up in your bedroom, and the light was on, and it was pitch black outside." Joe blushed again. "It was before I fixed that shade on your window."

Mercedes glared at Callum. "I should have known. Why didn't you tell me?"

"Merce, I didn't think—"

"Callum was all for telling you," Joe cut in, "but I said you were too young to be hearing that dirt. Then the bastard went away so it didn't matter."

Mercedes stared at Joe as if he was out of his mind. "Didn't matter!" A small, strangled cry escaped her lips. Callum had never seen her look so hopeless.

He noticed Judith watching them. Faking a smile, he made

a show of rubbing his hands together. "Time for the big news, eh Merce?"

They all stared blankly at him, including Mercedes.

"Merce is going to stay and go to work at Judith's uncle's place," he announced.

There was a prolonged moment of silence, a moment when he wasn't sure if he'd said the right thing at all, or if he'd said it loud enough for all to hear. But soon it seemed to register and work as a further distraction. Joe was full of questions again. They fumbled through as best they could until a child's cry interrupted. Joe hurried off. Judith sat rigid in her chair, pushing at the excess skin around her cuticles, her eyes focused on the rusted swing suspended from a branch of the yard's only tree.

Eventually Joe trudged back in and dropped down onto the couch. Mercedes placed her hand on his. They sat for a while, hands together, not speaking.

Callum nodded at Judith, who immediately rose. "I'll wait for you in the car. Goodbye Joe." She pulled on her gloves and hurried down the steps.

Joe hugged Mercedes. Both had tears in their eyes. Callum watched, helpless in the knowledge that there was so little he could do for either of them and nothing they could do for each other. They were all powerless in this great city, incapable of saving themselves or one another from the pain to come.

Just as they reached the car, Mercedes caught hold of Callum's arm to stop him. "If Joe hadn't kept you from telling me, would I be here now?"

He shook his head. "It's not Joe's fault, Merce."

She stared at him for a moment, then got in the car and closed the door.

With plans to leave for the hotel early in the morning, Mercedes went to bed right after supper. Callum would have done the same but Judith insisted on having tea, so they could talk, she said. As the water boiled, he looked around at their impeccable kitchen. The aluminium bread bin shone on the counter. The chrome of their barely used stove reflected off the new refrigerator, the hum of its motor constant in the background. Lace curtains framed the sink's bay window, providing by day a view out into the pretty back garden. At night, the view turned inwards, into their brightly lit, sparkling kitchen. "Good Housekeeping" perfection.

He tried to keep the conversation light, away from provocative subjects like Joe or Mercedes or unplanned pregnancies, but Judith kept niggling away. She seemed determined to burrow down and root out whatever it was he might not be saying. Sure enough, without meaning to, Callum found himself talking about adopting the baby.

Judith's nostrils flared. "Are you insane?"

"It was just a suggestion. I shouldn't have brought it up."

"If you think I'm going to raise that baby you're out of your mind. This is your sister's problem, not ours. I think we're doing a hell of a lot more already than she should expect. She ought to be grateful instead of trying to foist her little bastard on us."

"Judith!" He glanced upwards. "It's just an idea. She don't even know how serious I am."

"Serious? How can you be when we haven't even discussed it?"

Callum couldn't believe he'd been so stupid as to raise the issue. In fact, he didn't fully remember how it had come up. But it was like that with Judith. She somehow managed to get him to say things he was only thinking. Sometimes he was hardly aware he was thinking them. Even when he'd proposed to her, the next day he couldn't remember the words he'd used for the most important question of his life.

"It's just...well, we've been trying for a while and no luck, so I thought maybe this is how we're supposed to be parents. Can't we even talk about it?"

"I hardly think we need to run out and take somebody else's cast-off just yet."

"But we're married going on a year. Surely something would have happened by now if it was going to." He took down the teapot from the shelf by the stove.

"What's the rush to be saddled with children?"

"Saddled with children? But we decided—"

"What did we decide? You said God meant for us to be making babies."

"That's not how it was. You agreed. You said fine, we should have a family."

Judith took a tea bag from the canister. "I didn't mean right this minute, did I?"

"I don't get it. We've been going about it, and you're still not pregnant." Even as he spoke, some insight nagged at him, just beyond his grasp.

Turning her face away, she muttered something about it not being the right time.

There was an escalating ache at the back of his skull. "Every month I wait for the news and nothing happens, and then I feel worse, thinking I can't give you a baby."

"Now, Callum, it's not that simple and you know it. I want children. I do. But we need to get established first. All the good families do it this way."

"Do what? Lie to each other?" Anger had replaced his earlier confusion. "It's not that easy to not get pregnant - just look at my poor sister. How did you do it?"

"I didn't do anything. Neither did you, not when it wasn't the right time."

"Like you got them headaches at the right time, or is it the wrong time?"

Judith busied herself with getting down the cups, avoiding an answer.

"Headaches so bad I couldn't even sleep in my own bed." There was a whistling noise as steam shot up from the kettle.

"My headaches are real. They come and I can't do anything about them."

Callum moved the kettle to another burner. “Then tell me why Ruth said she never knew you to have headaches.”

She whirled on him. “How dare you question my sister!”

Callum replied in as cool a voice as hers had been heated. “I was rubbing a stiff neck one day and Ruth asked what was wrong. I’d slept on the couch after you had one of them nights when you had such a pain in the head you couldn’t stand the bed moving at all. She was right surprised when I told her how often you got the headaches.”

“You bastard! What right—?”

“They’d be hard to hide though, wouldn’t they, sick as they make you?” He rubbed his temple. “I said as much to her, but she said the last time you went to bed sick was after some big party at the Wilkinson’s. And to think I was worried that it might be married life that was causing it, that I was asking too much, or too often.”

“Don’t be crass. So I didn’t want a family right away. What’s wrong with that? Look at your brother. They’re only together because she got pregnant. Well, their daughter is paying the price. That child will never see her second birthday.”

“What’s that got to do with Sheilagh being sick?”

Sweat coated her forehead. Her eyes looked slightly crazed. “Maybe God is punishing them, giving them a weakling for a child.”

“How can you say things like that?”

“With your family? Look at your sister. A little whore to the nearest boy. Well, I won’t have her bastard as my own. She’s not foisting that on me, the little slut.”

Callum’s hand rose. For the first time in his life he was ready to strike a woman.

Mercedes ran into the room. “Stop! Please, stop fighting. I’m causing so much trouble and you’re so good to me.”

Instantly sorry, he lowered his hand. “Merce, come on. You know it’s not your fault. None of this was your doing.”

“Not her fault?” Judith asked, disbelief scorching every syllable. “Whose fault is it if it’s not hers?”

Mercedes had gone white as paper.

"I just mean mistakes happen," Callum stammered. "You know?" he pleaded.

Judith was still full of fight. "I never made this mistake. We had a wedding night, remember? Maybe your sister should have closed her legs and waited her turn."

Her anger was contagious. "What the hell would you know about waiting your turn?" Callum stormed back. "You never had to wait for nothing your whole life with your rich old man always there to hand it to you."

"Yeah, well what about you? You were happy enough to take this house."

"Stop it," Mercedes cried. "I'm going tomorrow, and I'll be having this baby next winter. He'll be going to a family who wants him, where both parents want him."

"Merce, wait. Please, just wait a minute."

"Good night, Callum. And thank you, the both of you." She went back upstairs.

In the suddenly silent kitchen, Callum glared at Judith. "This isn't over." He put the unused teapot back on the shelf. "But I'm going to sleep now and so should you. We got a long day ahead of us."

For the first time in their marriage, he was the one who chose to sleep apart; in fact, he had a vicious headache. Yet as bone-weary as he was, sleep refused him. He was still awake long after the echo of Judith's footsteps up the stairs had faded into the still New York night.

14

Callum watched from the porch as Mercedes curled into a corner of the back seat, her head all but disappearing into the collar of her coat. When he turned around, Judith was holding out his keys. Dark shadows underlined her eyes.

"I'm not going, Callum." Her fingers dug deep into the skin of her brow.

"Judith, please." He took the keys and held onto her hand. "You arranged it all."

She snatched her hand away and took a gold band from her pocket. "Tell her to wear this, see if she can fool anybody. And from now on, you can just leave me out of the whole filthy business. I want nothing more to do with it."

Callum's hand closed around the ring. "Fine. If that's the way you want it."

Without another word he put on his coat and walked to the car, motioning for Mercedes to move to the front. As they drove off, she glanced back at the house.

"She's got a headache." He passed her the ring. "She gave you this."

Mercedes stared at it for a moment, then silently slipped it on her finger.

Gradually, they left the city, and Judith, behind. It was a peaceful drive, a quiet reprieve for which Callum was grateful. Their conversation remained simple - the weather, scenery. Mercedes seemed almost relaxed for the first time since her arrival.

Too soon, they arrived at the hotel, a large white building surrounded by rows of small white cabins nestled in the trees.

Mrs. Waterman, one of the cooks, took charge of Mercedes. From the glances of some of the kitchen staff, Callum sensed that his sister's reason for being there was hardly a secret, despite Judith's wedding band.

Mercedes' room was barely large enough to hold a single bed and chest of drawers, but it was clean and had a good-sized window that looked out over the parking lot and into the woods beyond. With her few belongings, they soon had her settled in.

"I guess I should be going," said Callum. "I'll be back though, soon, and often."

"Thanks, Callum. I'll be okay, really I will."

Mercedes hugged him tight. He held on for an extra few seconds. For the second time in as many months, he felt he was abandoning her, leaving her to deal with the inconceivable reality that her life had become. But they both knew he couldn't stay.

He let her go and stepped back. "If you need anything, you'll call me, right?"

She stood in the doorway trying to smile. "I will. Go on home now."

Callum watched as the door closed behind her. Mercedes was on her own, again.

The best he could do was visit, which he did whenever possible, even if he could only stay an hour. Judith protested that, between work and trips to the hotel, he was hardly ever home. She needed him too, she said. They had to try to get close again, she told him, to get back to where they were before his sister came. Callum agreed but he would not negotiate when it came to seeing Mercedes. To make up for it, he did everything he could to make Judith happy. He brought her flowers regularly, he cooked and cleaned more than he ever had, he attended society events without protest. Judith either noticed the effort he was making or realized the futility of complaining because she soon stopped. In fact, she rarely mentioned his sister's name.

Callum felt an intense need to spend time with Mercedes. He was filled with guilt over what had happened to her. If he hadn't left her in St. Jude, if he'd left someone else in charge, or if he had never left St. Jude in the first place, she would not have been in this position. His mother had died giving birth to his sister. From that moment on, she was his responsibility.

As for Mercedes, she seemed to accept her situation. "I'm fifteen, pregnant and not married," she told him when he worried that she might be lonely. "That's my life. It doesn't matter how it happened. I just have to do my job and earn my keep."

"But are you making any friends, Merce? Is there anyone you can talk to?"

"Everyone is fine, but they're not real friendly. It's like I'm contagious. But I read a lot and Mrs. Waterman is nice to me. She's teaching me how to hook a rug."

Mrs. Waterman had worked at the hotel since it opened. She was kind towards Mercedes, asking after her health and taking meals with her. Mercedes was grateful to share grace and a table with another human being. Mrs. Waterman said little about herself, except that she'd had a daughter who died. She never mentioned a husband.

As time went on, Callum brought larger clothes and supplies as needed, along with regular updates on Joe and his family. Joe apologised for not visiting but Mercedes was actually relieved. "At least I don't have to lie to keep him from coming," she told Callum. "I just wish there was something I could do." But Joe's daughter was dying; there was nothing to be done.

Callum tried to convince Mercedes to spend Christmas with him and Judith. Mercedes claimed the hotel was fully booked and she wasn't allowed to leave, but he knew she couldn't bear the thought of eating in Judith's presence, taking in food to nourish a baby that no one wanted. Callum drove up to spend Christmas morning with her. It was one of the rare times that Judith bothered to object anymore.

January settled cold and dreary upon the nearly empty hotel. The trees were covered in snow and the roads laced with ice, yet Callum still made the trip as often as he could. Mercedes had become more emotional as her due date approached. She spoke often of the past, of St. Jude and Joe, even of their mother whom she'd never known. She seemed to be searching for answers to some unknown question.

One day he found her in tears at her bedroom window.

"Mercie, what is it? What's wrong?"

"It's all going to be over soon." She pressed her forehead against the cold glass.

Callum patted her back. "Yes, it will."

"I sing her a lullaby every night. And I pray for her and dream of holding her."

"Her?" Callum asked lightly. "When did you decide that?"

"Just one day, she wasn't a 'he' anymore. I can't remember when. I can't even remember not being pregnant." Mercedes scraped some frost from the corner of the window. "When do I leave here?"

"You can go to St. Agatha's two weeks before you're due. Won't be long now."

She stared off into the hills. "No, not long at all."

Ten days later he arrived at the hotel for the last time.

Mrs. Waterman saw Mercedes to the door and pressed a card into her hand. "This is a special novena," she whispered. "Say this every day and don't despair. Nothing is hopeless when He is on your side, Mercedes." In a whispered rush of words, she said to Callum, "They'll take good care of her at the convent."

Fighting tears, Mercedes manoeuvred her oversized body into Callum's car, then shut her eyes tight as he drove away.

When he pulled up in front of St. Agatha's, he saw the relief on Mercedes' face. Some months earlier, Callum had offered to bring her for a visit but she'd declined, stating that as she had no other option, it was hardly necessary to arrange a preview.

"Sure it doesn't look that bad at all," she said.

A young nun hurried out to open the passenger door. "Welcome to St. Agatha's. I'm Sister Mary Margaret." She looked to be not much older than Mercedes, yet there was a sense of serenity about her. "Come in and we'll get you straightened away. Will you be staying for tea, Mr. Hann?" Her accent was vaguely familiar.

"Yes, if I could, Sister, just to get her settled."

She led them up the front steps. "I'll go tell Mother Superior," she said.

An oddly comforting aroma met them inside the door. Antiseptic cleanliness mingled with the tang of lemon, while at the same time, the bouquet of baking bread wafted through the entrance hall, good homemade sweetbread aromas that made Callum think of home. Not Farley Hann's home. No, certainly not that. It was more the idea of home, fathers fixing things, mothers baking, children playing, all living happily together.

He was surprised to see tears on his sister's face. "Merce, what is it?"

She sniffed the air. "This place. It reminds me of something. Something good."

Callum passed her his handkerchief. "I know. Me too."

Sister Mary Margaret came back just as Mercedes was wiping her eyes.

"Don't be sad, Mercedes. It will soon be over and everything will go back to normal. Let me show you your room," she said, leading her away.

Callum was just finishing his tea with Sister Ignatius when Mercedes returned. As he watched her shuffle into the warm kitchen, her puffy face still so innocent, the unfairness of it all struck a fresh chord of anger in him.

"Is anything wrong, Callum?" Mercedes asked.

"No, no," he answered quickly. "How are you feeling? Is everything okay?"

"I'm fine. I hope you don't get in trouble taking all this time to cart me around."

"Don't worry about me. Come meet Sister Ignatius."

The Mother Superior was a tall, large-boned woman, her intimidating presence further emphasized by the severe black and white of her uniform. After spending time with her, however, Callum had come to believe that she was the best person to see his sister through the days ahead.

"Welcome to St. Agatha's, Mercedes." Sister Ignatius's voice was firm yet gentle. "What a fine name, full of our Lady's love and goodness."

"Thank you, Sister." Mercedes looked about to curtsey then seemed to stop herself. She turned to Callum instead. "Have you been here before?"

"They needed some family history, and I had to make sure this was a safe place for you - no offence, Sister. You're in good hands here, and there's a hospital close." He glanced at his watch. "I got a crew to check on before the day is done."

As they walked outside, he could feel Mercedes' fingers pressing into his arm.

"Something bothering you, Merce?" he asked once they were out of earshot.

"It's just…well, you never said anything in ages, about maybe adopting?"

The last time they'd talked about it several months earlier, he'd told her that Judith was adamant, that there was no way he could talk her into it. Mercedes hadn't mentioned it since. "Ah Mercie, I'm sorry, but nothing's changed."

Her palm circled her distended belly. "She's become my friend, you know? She's all I had to talk to. We kind of got to know each other."

"Still think it's a she?"

"I know it's silly but I'm sure it's a girl. I think mothers know these things. Oh God," she cried suddenly, her voice a tortured whisper. "I wish she'd never come out now, then I wouldn't have to give her away." She pressed her face against his shoulder.

Callum hugged her gently. "Ah Mercie, don't cry."

"I can't seem to stop anymore," she sobbed. "I'm after crying more in the last nine months than my whole life before it."

"I hate that you got to go through this. But things can't be any different, can they? You can't take care of her. And a baby needs two parents."

She stepped back from him. "I just got no control anymore. My body grows and grows, my baby gets bigger and kicks and hiccups, you and the Sister talk about me like I don't have any say, and I guess I don't. It seems so long since I was me."

"It's almost over. You can go home soon."

"Home?" she cried out. "Where's home? Where will my baby go?"

"Sister says there's a wonderful family waiting to have a new little one."

"Isn't there any hope at all that you can do it?"

"I'm afraid not, love. I didn't know you were still hoping."

She lowered herself onto the convent steps. Her head was down and tucked into her chest, as if she was trying to stop or hide the tears.

He sat beside her and raised her chin. "I'm sorry," he said, looking into the saddest eyes he had ever seen.

"Callum, please, will you just think about it? I can't stand the thought of never knowing what happened to her. She's all I have in the world to hold onto."

"Judith and I are trying to make up to each other for all that meanness of before," he continued in a shaky voice. "I can't ask her to be doing this, not now."

"I'll do whatever you want, Callum. Anything. Just don't let them take her away. Oh God," she pleaded, "help me."

He put his arm around her. "I wish I could, but there's nothing I can do." He heard the tremor in his voice and couldn't hide the tears.

She immediately tried to move away from him. "Callum, no. Please don't cry. You've done everything you can for me. I'm sorry, please, I'm so sorry."

He grabbed her hands. "Mercie, stop! Don't do that." He was beyond trying to stop the tears from coming. "Whatever you do, you can't be feeling sorry for me."

She pulled back and took a long breath. "It was too much to ask for. I'm sorry."

"You'll see, it'll all work out for the best." He wiped his eyes and looked up at the sky. The winter sun was fading fast. "Will you be all right?"

She pushed her hair away from her face. "I'll be fine. I will, I promise."

"I'll be back tomorrow, but I told them to call me if anything happens."

"It could be in the middle of the night. I can't ask you to come then."

"You didn't ask, remember? For any of this. I have to be here with you, Merce."

"Thanks, Callum. I don't know what I'd do without you." She squeezed his hand, then pushed him towards the car.

He started the engine but took a moment to catch his breath. In the rear-view mirror he saw her, eyes closed, hands around her belly, her swollen body rocking lightly back and forth. He wanted only to jump out of the car and hold her again, to stay with her until it was over, or to take her with him and never leave her alone again. But most of all he wanted to do as she asked and promise not to let them take her baby away.

She opened her eyes. He waved goodbye in the mirror.

He came back the next day, and again the day after that, which was her birthday. The Sisters had made a cake. They all sang happy birthday. Mercedes was sixteen.

Even though Callum knew his sister was safe at St. Agatha's, something drew him to her. Their time seemed finite, as if they only had these days, right now, to spend together. The thought, the feeling, the premonition, whatever it was, scared him to death. He tried to reason with himself. She was in good hands. There was a hospital nearby. She'd had a normal pregnancy.

Yet he could not rid himself of the sense that they were losing control. He came every day and stayed as long as he could.

There were no other pregnant girls at St. Agatha's at the time. According to the Mother Superior, theirs wasn't a regular home for unwed mothers. They offered the service only for special families that needed help, like the Macleans. Despite that, Mercedes found a new friend in Sister Mary Margaret. Originally from Newfoundland, Margaret Mead had moved to New York with her father at the age of eight, the only child to survive a house fire that took the lives of her mother and six siblings. Though only five years older than Mercedes, she was infinitely familiar with death and sorrow, yet a determined survivor.

As caring as the Sisters were, they were also pointedly honest about Mercedes' situation. She was pregnant, without a husband or any prospects of one.

"They said I might not even get to see her," she told Callum. "I always pictured myself holding her right after she was born. I tried not to think further than that."

"I'm sure they know what's best for you, Merce."

"Sister Justine said this would be the easiest way. She'd know, right?"

"Well, she was a nurse in the war. I think you can trust her."

Sure in the belief that the Sisters would never willingly hurt her, and without a mother to advise her differently, Mercedes succumbed to the view that this was how things should be. Nevertheless, deep in the night, alone except for the child inside her, it was harder to accept. None of the Sisters had ever been pregnant; none had ever carried a baby for nine of the loneliest months on earth. None would ever know the feeling of a child growing ever so slowly within their own life's body.

On the Saturday morning of her first week at the convent, Callum arrived early, glad to have a whole day to spend with her. Mercedes was making bread, one of her favourite chores. She said it warmed her soul, kneading that great mound of dough, so full in her hands, its warm breath puffing out with each new fold.

Suddenly, she pressed her sticky, floury hands to her stomach. Callum could see the shock in her eyes.

For the rest of the day, he watched helplessly as Mercedes went from ripping pain to mind-numbing relief and back again, each respite increasingly short lived. His hands felt bruised from the pressure of her grasp, yet he was grateful for it.

Early in the evening, she started to vomit. Dry retches overpowered her, the lingering force of one seeming to prompt the next. Then she began to shake. To make matters worse, her stomach continued to heave as her body shook. She no longer had the strength to squeeze his hand. No one had prepared them for this.

Eventually, he was sent from the room. Callum paced the wood floor, listening as his sister's groans increased and decreased in pitch but not in frequency.

Sister Justine came out and led him to the kitchen. She poured him a cup of tea.

"Mr. Hann, things are not going well. Whatever it was that got your mother is probably the same thing that has Mercedes in its grasp. But in her case, the damage from the rape has made it worse."

Callum glanced sharply at her. "You know what happened to Mercie?" He'd told the Mother Superior some of the truth, but he hadn't expected her to tell anyone.

"Sister Ignatius had to tell the doctor in order to explain her condition." She shuddered. "That man did not just cut her on the outside, he went inside as well."

"Inside? You mean, with the knife, he cut her inside..."

"Yes. It's amazing she was able to carry a child after what was done to her."

Callum suddenly remembered it, the blood on the floor at her feet and on her legs. He remembered her embarrassment and his rush to cover her up. "I didn't know. She said it was just...Oh my God, poor Mercie."

"The man who did this, has anyone tried to find him? Perhaps it might cause some change in him if he knew what his crime had wrought."

Callum recalled Paddy Griffin's leering face. This woman could never understand or condone what he and Mercedes had done. He shook his head. He didn't trust his voice.

Intelligent eyes stared into his. Bowing her head, she made the sign of the cross, then looked back up at him. "The doctor is quite concerned. He needs to bring someone in to perform a Caesarean section. It will be expensive, Mr. Hann."

Callum didn't care about the money even though he had none. Judith's parents were good for it. "Whatever she needs. Just take care of her."

Sister Justine placed a hand on his arm. "Your sister is lucky to have you."

He almost laughed. "Lucky? Mercie's the farthest from lucky I ever knew."

The doctor came in and walked straight up to Callum. "We have to get the baby out right away. She went through quite an ordeal, didn't she?"

"The worst fate that can befall a girl."

"We can't move her, not with so much blood lost." He patted Callum's shoulder. "Have faith, Mr. Hann. The good Lord takes care of his children."

Callum said nothing. The Lord had done a rotten job so far.

For two hours he waited. When he wasn't praying like a madman, he wanted to scream like one. Conflicting images drifted through his head – Mercedes laughing and talking like her old self, then her face earlier that night, the dead-eyed defeat, all playing and replaying like non-stop echoes. Finally, Sister Justine and the doctor came out.

"We've done everything we can for now." Sister Justine's voice was not reassuring. "Your sister will stay here, but there's an ambulance on the way for the baby."

"How is she?" Callum asked.

"She's jaundiced and may have pneumonia, and she—" The

doctor stopped abruptly. "Sorry. I thought you meant the baby."

The truth struck Callum then. "Mercie said it was going to be a girl."

The doctor looked grim. "I'm afraid it's the only child she'll ever have."

"She's going to need a lot of care for the next while," Sister Justine added.

"But she will get better?"

"We hope so, given her age and general state of health."

"What about the baby?"

"Again, we're hopeful, although in one so young, it's hard to say. But this could interfere with the adoption. Neonatal care is expensive."

Callum had been so concerned with his sister that he hadn't thought about the baby. This child who Mercedes loved without ever having seen might be abandoned, not just by people unknown to them all, but by her own family as well.

A door opened down the hall. Sister Ignatius appeared, papers in hand.

Callum turned to the frost-framed window. Outside, the pristine white of snow-laden fields dissolved into the night's invisible backdrop. In his mind's eye he saw his sister's face, the wet, black lashes on chalk-white cheeks, ultimately and always alone no matter how much he wanted to help her.

He turned around. "The adoption is off. We're keeping the baby."

15

Callum was almost as surprised by what he'd said as everyone else appeared to be. But he knew immediately that it was the right decision. "I'll…Judith and I will raise her."

Sister Ignatius eyed him warily. "Mrs. Hann was quite clear that the baby should be adopted when we spoke on the phone last summer."

"Yes, I know. But now the baby's here and I'm scared what might happen to her. The baby's real family, Merce's family, we've got to be the best place for her."

Sister Ignatius looked to the doctor. He nodded. She dropped the papers. "If you leave now, you and your wife should have time to discuss the details, get some sleep and be back early tomorrow."

"But I have to be here when Merce wakes up."

"Mr. Hann, I don't think you fully comprehend the situation. There is a family expecting word of their new child, a child who is ill. We need to know who will be responsible. I'd advise you to make haste if you intend for this plan of yours to work."

There seemed to be an emphasis on the word "plan." The Mother Superior was no fool. Neither was Judith. Callum had no idea how he would coerce her into such an unselfish act, but one way or another, he intended to raise his sister's baby.

"Well?" Judith asked, smoothing the last traces of night cream into her face.

"Merce had a girl. The baby's in the hospital but the doctor thinks she'll recover with the proper care." He sat down hard on the bed. "And enough money."

"I see. And your sister?" Judith asked through the dresser mirror.

"There was a lot of damage, on the inside. She can't have any more children."

Judith sat down next to him. "God works in mysterious ways."

Over the past months they had soft-shoed around each other trying to repair their marriage. Even so, his instinct at that moment was to shove her spiteful words down her thin white throat. But he needed her, and her family's money, too much.

"Judith, there's more to what happened to Merce than we told you."

"I always knew that." She folded her arms and waited.

"I can't tell you everything and I got to ask you to accept that, for all our sakes. But I'll try not to lie to you anymore."

She gave a small sideways nod.

He strained to keep his voice even. "The first night I was back in St. Jude, a noise woke me up in the night. When I went upstairs, Mercedes was being raped."

Judith's wide eyes had grown ever larger. "Raped? Oh, Callum, that's terrible. Poor Mercedes." She stopped and thought a second. "It was Paddy Griffin, wasn't it?"

Not for the first time, Callum was amazed at how quickly she figured things out, as if the knowledge was already there, inside her, waiting for the spark that would trigger it into the open. He nodded. There was nothing to gain by denying it.

She stood abruptly. "I knew there was something wrong there, just the way you spoke of him, you and Mercedes. There was something in your voice."

"He was an animal."

Judith's eyes locked on his. "You said 'was'? What does that mean?"

He didn't answer.

"What happened to him? Tell me!"

"He was going to kill her."

She backed away from the bed. "He's dead, isn't he?"

Callum looked at her, unblinking, for several moments.

She sucked in a sharp breath. "Jesus! You killed him!"

"Judith, listen, please." He reached out towards her but she moved farther away. "I did what I had to do."

She stared at him as if she didn't know him. "My husband's a murderer!"

"No. It was self-defence—"

She seemed not to have heard. "Daddy will be furious. Our name will be dragged through the mud. Our reputation, my father, this could ruin us."

Again, Callum reached out. "Nobody knows, Judith. And nobody has to know."

Her hand shot to her mouth. "Where is your father?"

"Judith, there are some things better left—"

"Callum, answer me! Is he dead, too?"

He nodded. He had no capacity left for lying.

A look of horror washed over her. "Was he…did he…? His own daughter?"

"No! Besides, he didn't know, didn't realize, that it was Merce."

"How could he not know?"

"He thought she was my mother. His mind…it wasn't right anymore."

"Great! So he was crazy as well?" Like a caged animal, she began to pace, past the dresser and the window, to the corner and back again. On her third trip, she paused to look outside. "You're certain no one knows?"

"No one even knew I'd been home to St. Jude."

She pulled the curtains shut. "Didn't anyone wonder where two grown men disappeared to?"

"The whole town thinks they drove off to Toronto. They were bragging about going there for months."

She walked to the dresser mirror and peered intently at her reflection. "This is a fine mess you've gotten us into."

"There's one more thing we have to talk about. It's about Merce and the baby."

Her eyes met his in the glass. "Not tonight."

"I'm sorry, Judith, but it can't wait."

"Please. It will hold until morning."

He shook his head. "No, it won't."

She slumped onto the bed beside him.

Callum felt an unusual compassion for her. "I'll put the kettle on. Come down when you're ready." Surprising himself, he kissed the top of her head before he left.

When she came down, he poured her a cup of tea. "There's only one way to say this. I think we should adopt the baby. People will think we did a quiet adoption and hopefully not ask a bunch of questions. No one knew Merce was pregnant so we won't have to explain that."

He waited. The argument didn't come. Feeling hopeful, he described Mercedes' desperation. "She couldn't bear thinking about losing this child to strangers."

Judith frowned. "The baby, it's half the father. If he was the kind of man to do what he did, what will he have passed on? What kind of family was he from?"

Callum noticed she'd already relegated Paddy Griffin to the past. He looked forward to the day they'd never have to refer to him in any tense again. "They're not the smartest crowd in the world, but they're not a bad lot. As for Paddy, he came and went from St. Jude over the years but he always ended up in trouble." He stopped. It was time to leave Paddy Griffin where he belonged. "What are you thinking, Judith? About the baby and us and everything? Let's be honest with each other, okay?"

She blinked back a rare well-up of tears. "I've been trying to get pregnant for months now and I can't. I know we haven't been doing it that much but something should have happened. I wasn't even all that careful before and now I really want to and ... nothing." Actual tears, like rich fat dewdrops, rolled down her cheeks. "Who's being punished now?" She laid her head on her arms and sobbed into the tabletop.

A rush of relief spread through Callum. He caressed her back. "None of us are to blame. You had a right to be mad at me, even at Merce. I'm still not sure we made the best decisions. All I know is we have to keep going, and I really want that baby to be part of us before it's too late."

As suddenly as they'd begun the tears were over. She shrugged his hand off her back and reached for a tissue. "But what's the hurry?"

His rejected hand lay on the table. "They either got to give the baby to the adoptive parents, if they still want her, or to us. I know what I want."

"What about what I want?"

"Somebody has to take on the hospital bills, and I can't see some stranger wanting to do it. We need to head up there first thing in the morning."

Her eyes narrowed into angry slits. "You've already decided, haven't you?"

"There's no other way. Don't you see?" he pleaded.

"No, I don't see at all."

"I have to do this for her."

"For who?"

"For the baby."

"For Mercedes, you mean."

"For God's sake, what's the difference?"

"Can't you tell?" she demanded. "Don't you know?"

"Judith, what are you talking about?"

"I'm talking about you choosing your sister over me."

He stared at her in disbelief. "I'm choosing an innocent child."

"The hell you are!"

And in that single instant, he didn't care anymore. He pushed his tea away and stood up. "With or without you, I'm raising that child."

"And what if I go to the police?"

"I'll have to take that chance." Even as he said it, he knew she'd never do it. And just as suddenly he felt sure she wouldn't leave him either. She would not let her father be right, nor would she allow the family name to be sullied.

On the other hand, if he was wrong, if his marriage did end, Mercedes would be saddled with even more guilt. "We can do this, Judith. We can raise the baby, be a family. Think about it, a helpless baby. We can't give her to strangers. Please, Judith?"

She sat absolutely still, except for her face. The woman had one of the most expressive faces Callum had ever seen. He watched as the anger subsided, the resignation set in, the calculations began.

"I can't believe you've put us in this situation. But we are a family and families should stick together," she said stiffly. "We will have to make the best of it."

"It will all work out, I promise."

"We shall see." She stood abruptly. "For now, let's get some sleep."

The red-tinged sky rose slowly behind them as they drove into daybreak. Callum, still tired after a restless night, glanced over at Judith. Her face was paler than usual. Tiny lines edged the corners of her mouth, lines he'd never noticed before.

Judith broke the silence. "If I am going to do this, I have certain conditions."

Callum missed the brief vulnerability of the night before.

"This needs some getting used to," she said, "taking on a child all of a sudden. Most women get nine months, and what do I get? A day? Less than that even."

"I'm sorry. I wish there was some other way."

She dismissed his apology with a flutter of fingers. "There are issues we need to deal with. For starters, no one is to know where it came from, including your brother."

"But the Sisters at St. Agatha's all know. And your father and your uncle."

"My family will do whatever it takes to keep this quiet. And those damn nuns won't breathe a word if the money's right."

Callum kept his voice as even as possible. "What else?"

"She has to stay away from the child, no contact whatsoever. If I could arrange it she'd never know we adopted it, but I can't figure out a way around that."

He took his eyes from the pavement. "But we're family. She's bound to see her some time even if we do live in different countries."

"Not if you prevent it."

"I can't do that. Besides, Merce is going to need help after all this."

"We'll get her some help. I didn't mean we'd just turn our backs on her."

Callum hesitated. "I thought she could stay with us for a while. We could make up some excuse about why she was sick."

Judith's head turned sharply in his direction. "You're not listening to me. If, and I do mean if, I adopt this baby, I will be her only mother. She must never ever know about Mercedes. Is that clear?"

"Yes, I heard you but how can that happen?"

"I'll tell you how." Her voice had risen. "Mercedes has to agree to every bit of this or it's off. I know you think this wasn't her fault but that hardly matters now. I have to do what I think is best, and as far as I'm concerned she has to stay out of that baby's life. For that to happen she'll have to make sure they never meet." She waited half a minute. "Which means giving you up along with her little bastard."

Callum clenched the wheel. No one besides Paddy Griffin had ever inspired such anger in him. "I can't just send Mercedes home alone after this nightmare. You got to understand I can't do that to her."

"If I know anything at all in this whole mess it's that you love your goddamn sister." Her voice shot up in anger. "But that's the point. It's all her, isn't it? I won't have her in my house, with her brother and her baby, both of whom would be more rightly mine than hers. It will never work."

"But where can she go? She's too sick to go back home, and there's—"

Her hand sliced the air between them. "I wasn't awake half the night for nothing. I'm hoping she can stay at St. Agatha's until she's recovered."

"I thought she was only allowed to stay a week after the baby was born?"

"I'm sure they'll make an exception. We'll pay dearly but they'll agree, especially if it's for the future of that child. It's going to be ringing up a lot of bills."

Callum deliberately kept his focus on the snow-covered road ahead. "She," he said.

"She? She what?" Judith asked impatiently.

"You said 'it.' She's not an 'it,' she's a baby girl."

He could feel her silent antagonism across the seat.

"As for Mercedes," Judith finally said. "We could have her tutored. Some of the best people have their children tutored, and those nuns are more educated than most. Afterwards she could go to university and finally take care of herself."

"And where would we get the money for all this?"

"You know damn well where we'll get the money."

"Dear old Dad keeps on coming through, doesn't he?" The car sped faster.

"Slow down!" In one breath, her voice softened. "Does it matter where the money comes from? If I can convince the Sisters, leave that part to me, okay?"

The temptation to make all of it as right as possible, to take everything he could get for Mercedes, was too great. "She could be a teacher like she always dreamed."

"Only if she agrees completely to do as I say."

He felt a ripple of excitement. Judith could never understand the magnitude of that dream but she was willing to pay for it to make Mercedes go away. It was an easy concession to make with the weight of the Maclean fortune behind her. Funny, he thought, how little money mattered to one for whom it meant so much.

They pulled up in front of St. Agatha's. As he got out of the car he glanced up to the second-floor window where Mercedes lay waiting for whatever fate God, and they, had in store for her. He opened Judith's door.

She didn't move. "Do we have a deal?"

The icy air felt sharp in his lungs, but it did nothing to deaden the pain of what he had to do to his sister. "Yes, and may God have mercy on our souls."

She eyed him coldly, then took his hand and stepped from the car.

"Can I have some time alone with her first?" he asked once they were inside.

Judith looked at her watch. "Five minutes."

Knowing she'd be keeping time, Callum hurried upstairs. Sister Mary Margaret seemed to sense his urgency and immediately left the room.

Callum kissed Mercedes' forehead. Her eyes opened. "Callum, you're here."

"How are you, Mercie? Are you in pain?"

"How's my baby? Is she gone yet? Did they take her away already?"

Callum put his finger to his lips. "I only got a couple of minutes before Judith comes in. Remember what you asked about my adopting the baby. I know I said we couldn't but I worked out a deal with Judith so I can."

Her eyes widened with hope. "Oh, my God, Callum, thank you."

"But you have to agree to what she wants." His voice was rushed.

"I'll do anything if we can keep her."

"She's got conditions. I don't like them and neither will you. Just remember, I'll be the baby's father. Maybe over time Judith will mellow and I'll try to change things. But can you accept them for today? Because I don't know what else to do."

"It's that bad?" The hope in her voice had almost disappeared.

He didn't answer. He couldn't even meet her eyes.

"You told her?"

He squeezed her hand. "Merce, I had to. But she thinks it was me that did him in and we got to keep it that way. She's got too much to lose if it's her own husband."

They could hear footsteps approaching. "I'll do whatever it takes, Callum, even if it does feel like a deal with the devil. As long as I know she's under your roof."

Judith walked in. "Hello, Mercedes. How are you?"

"I'm okay," she answered timidly.

"Callum told me what happened - the truth this time. I am sorry for all you've gone through." Judith raised her arm, palm outstretched, towards Callum. Puzzled, he took her hand. She continued in the same cold, formal tone. "Your brother wants to adopt the baby. I'm willing to comply but you must agree to several provisions."

Mercedes nodded.

Judith let go of Callum's hand. "I'll come straight to the point."

And she did, issuing conditions and ultimatums. There would be no negotiating: it was an all-or-nothing deal.

"Always remember," she said finally. "I know the facts now. If the truth ever came out, if people ever knew what the two of you did that night, it would destroy your brother." Judith levelled her gaze on Mercedes. "You wouldn't want that, would you? Especially after all my husband and I have done for you." She took her leather gloves from her pocket. "One more thing. I'll be leaving a letter with my father's attorney and one with my sister outlining everything that happened to Paddy Griffin." She paused. "And to your father."

Mercedes shrank down into the blankets.

"They'll be instructed what to do should my daughter ever discover who gave birth to her, even after I'm dead. When I say she will never know, I do mean never."

Judith leaned in close to Mercedes. Her words, when they came, were spoken slowly, each syllable clearly articulated. "She will never be your daughter. For your brother's sake, and hers, don't ever forget that."

Callum looked at this woman who was his wife, who would be the mother to Mercedes' only child. And he looked at Mercedes, who had done nothing wrong in her sixteen years but who was at the mercy of that same woman. They both were, he realized. They could never go back now. Judith knew too much. If she ever thought it necessary, if she ever felt threatened, she would not hesitate to ruin both of them. Then who would take care of Mercedes' baby?

That's when he understood. There was no true justice in the world. There was no fair play and certainly no rewards for the likes of him and his sister. Judith would never mellow. No amount of time would ease her barren bitterness.

Callum decided then and there that safeguarding his family was the only thing left to him worth doing. No matter the cost, he would protect Mercedes and her baby.

Mercedes agreed to live by Judith's conditions. In the end, it was a simple decision. She had no choice.

16

Despite everything that had happened to her, Mercedes recovered quickly. And although she would have been happy to stay with the Sisters forever, once she'd completed high school Sister Ignatius told her it was time to go forward with her life. With Callum's encouragement, she moved to Nova Scotia and became a teacher.

Mercedes was not looking for a husband. In her mind, she was as happy as she could rightly expect to be, teaching and studying. Louis Cunningham convinced her otherwise. After all, he said, he was willing to forgo his family's dreams and give up the priesthood. What bigger sacrifice could he make to prove his devotion, his commitment to her? Mercedes, encouraged by Callum yet again, dared to believe him.

In the doctor's office, with Louis by her side, Mercedes received the results of her blood test. She had venereal disease.

It was a shock, of course. At first. But as the doctor continued, his voice bristling with contempt as he discussed causes and symptoms and treatment, Mercedes remembered the recurring rashes, the fatigue, the headaches. She'd ignored them all. Eventually they'd gone away.

When she managed to find her voice again, she tried to explain. Louis Cunningham would not listen. He could barely stay in the room as she told him about the rape. He wouldn't let her finish before he marched out the door. There was no sympathy, no forgiveness, no absolution.

Eventually, Louis became the priest his mother had always wanted him to be.

Mercedes' sole concern was for her daughter. She immediately contacted Sister Ignatius who tried to reassure her that, because of the Caesarean, there was less likelihood that Lucinda would have been infected. Mercedes insisted that Callum follow up with a trip to the doctor. Lucinda was fine.

At the end of that school year, Mercedes returned to St. Jude. It wasn't fondness for the town that brought her back. St. Jude held little appeal beyond familiarity, but at least she knew the demons that would confront her there.

She was hired by the local school board and quickly established herself as a dedicated professional. Her no-nonsense approach ensured her a position of respect within the religious-based education system. She became known as the town spinster. The title pleased her. She had no desire to laugh or be silly, no inclination to amuse herself making girlfriends. Or boyfriends. She had concluded that neither the pain nor the memories would disappear, that time would not heal some wounds, and that she was stuck with her history and the consequences of it. No decent man would ever want her, and she would need no man.

Still, there was one obstacle she couldn't face. It was only when Mona Burke began to question her hesitation that Mercedes knew she had to deal with it.

She chose a cool fall Saturday morning. Rising before the sun, she set off along the back trail; she did not want to meet anyone along the way. Dressed in warm clothes and sensible shoes, she made her way through the low bush at the edge of the woods, gradually heading into denser growth. She'd travelled this route often as a girl, back in the naiveté of childhood when she'd taken her environment, and her life, for granted. Yet somehow it seemed new, the auburn of autumn, the scarlet reds of the falling leaves, the bushes and trees in emerald and jaded greens. Nothing moved except the birds.

The house appeared alone in the distance. She walked resolutely towards it.

The back door was missing and most of the windows were

smashed. Broken glass littered the ground. Garbage had gathered in tight piles in the windswept corners. Mercedes did not care about the exterior. She stepped over the debris and through the door.

For years, against her will, she had pictured the freeze-frames that would slap her in the face if she ever walked into that house again. But nothing happened. Harmless memories drifted through her mind; she and Callum and Joe huddled around the stove to stay warm, Callum helping her with homework, Joe stirring porridge on cold winter mornings. It was nothing like she had dreaded for so long.

The mattress from her father's daybed lay on the floor. Sticking out from under it she saw a nylon stocking and a pair of soiled underwear. The bed on which Farley had sprawled drunkenly so often had been put to other uses during her absence.

At the stairwell she hesitated, unsure if she was ready to take those last steps. She heard a meow. A thin black cat sashayed around her ankles, pressing his raised back into her calves. In fine feline form, the animal started up, his haunches gliding seductively. Each foot forward had a confidence, a certainty of belonging, a grace that only a cat could possess in a stranger's house. She felt compelled to follow.

At the top, the cat stretched and yawned, his tiny mouth opening larger than his whole face had ever seemed. He continued towards her bedroom. So did Mercedes.

Her progress up to that point had been so smooth that she was unprepared for what happened next. She felt an immense pressure pushing against her, as if the walls were caving in, forcing her to the floor, while at the same time, her mind was bombarded with images: the bloody knife, the bloodlust in his eyes, her father's blood, blood everywhere. She smelt again his stinking breath, felt again his body pressing against her, pushing into her, then the knife, the knife cutting.

She clawed at the floor, afraid to open her mouth. She struggled to breathe through her nose, but it was as if no oxygen could permeate. She gagged. Nothing rose from her belly but a sour slime that burnt her throat. She stumbled from the room, down the stairs and out into the fresh, crisp air.

When her vision cleared, she was astounded to be faced with the quiet harmony of before. How could such tranquility exist next to that house? She swung around to face it, stared hard at it, waited for it to show its true self. It stood there, harmless.

A fresh burst of rage struck her, at once fuelled and dampened by the sheer incongruity of the place. She forced herself to go back inside. She marched upstairs. She crossed the hall, her heart beating the devil inside her chest. Nausea threatened; she shoved it back. She stopped, turned, looked inside.

Nothing remained except the bed frame. After Callum had left that night, she'd stripped the room. The bloody mattress she'd hauled beneath the house where she hacked at it until it was just a mess of stuffing to blaze in the wood stove. She made similar work of the blankets. She scoured the walls and floors, every inch over which the bodies might have passed, and then she cleaned the rest of the house as well. By the time she was finished, two days had passed, forty-eight hours in which she'd worked her fingers past layers of skin, trying to wipe out all memory of that night.

If only it were that easy.

While any physical evidence may have been disposed of seven years before, nothing short of setting the house aflame could match the fire that burned within Mercedes. On her hands and knees on the bedroom floor, she searched each board for signs of blood, a smeared fingerprint, streaks of brown. Surely some stain would remain, some proof of her shattered life. She crawled along, her nose almost touching the floor as her fingertips traced the grain.

Finally, she spotted an irregular darkening in the wood. She analysed this, carefully considering if something else might have caused it, something other than her father's blood beating an arc to the floor, or Paddy's blood, or her own.

Convinced at last, she rose. Raising the window, she stared out at the spot where she imagined he must have spied in on her. Gathering all her saliva in her mouth, she leaned her head out and spat the whole wad in the direction of the woods. Then she shut the window and pulled the shade.

Descending the stairs, her fury mounted again, transcending all rational impulses. The only thing that saved the house from instant incineration was her lack of a match.

In the end she was grateful. Paddy Griffin had taken her innocence, her childhood, and any hope for a normal life. All she had left was this house and the good memories it evoked, time spent with Callum and Joe before they went away, before her life changed forever. More importantly, she had the possibility of dignity as a useful member of St. Jude. She could not allow Paddy Griffin to take that from her too.

Over the next week Mercedes dragged every item in the house either outside to the burn pile or upstairs to her old room. There was nothing worth keeping, in her opinion, but one of her brothers might want something someday. She left that room untouched, except for the padlock she installed. She kept the key on a chain around her neck.

Mercedes moved back into the house a month later, alone except for a large black dog that rarely left her side. The structure was actually solidly built with a good foundation, and she spent the next few years renovating it. The men she hired knocked down some walls and erected new ones. They painted and sanded, they shingled and gutted, they replaced windows and doors.

Except the front screen door. They fixed that up as best they could, but it still had that noisy hinge, even on stormy winter nights. Mercedes wanted to know when someone was on her doorstep.

PART THREE
1993-1994

17

Since their night at Dewey's, Gerry had left a string of messages. Annie had ignored them all. Far from playing hard to get in some coquettish game, she honestly did not want to see him. She felt she'd compromised her standards, which she might have been able to stomach if he hadn't lied to her, even if it was a lie of omission.

So when Gerry stopped by the house the next weekend when she was out in St. Jude, Annie was far from pleased, and even less so when she heard her father inviting him in. She threw her book on her bed and marched downstairs to find Gerry sitting at the table across from Dermot. Lucinda was chopping carrots at the counter.

"And how are you today, Gerry?" Lucinda was saying. She was too polite to ask him what he was doing there but she cast a suspicious glance at Annie standing stiffly in the doorway.

Gerry smiled. "Fine, thanks, Mrs. Byrne." He did not look at Annie.

"Saw your mother down at the church earlier." Lucinda slashed open a bag of potatoes. "She must have a reservation in heaven, the time she spends in there."

"So Gerry," said Dermot, giving his wife a wary eye, "do you run into many from home at the university? Nice to see a familiar face now and then, what?"

"Yes, it sure is. Like yesterday, I ran into Cathy Green."

"Cathy, lovely girl, she is. And quite the looker. Too bad that Cyril Maher got to her first, eh?" Dermot said with a saucy wink.

"Cyril's a lucky one, all right. We had a fine talk, me and

Cathy, so good we were both late for class." He looked straight at Annie. "Some conversations are like that, especially when they're about people you know. Right Annie?"

Ninety-nine times out of a hundred, the Byrne kitchen was so busy with people coming and going and everyday life that Annie's discomfort would likely have gone unnoticed. But now she could feel her mother's eyes studying her.

"Yeah, right. You must be here for that book you wanted," Annie said with as civil a tone as she could muster. "Come on downstairs."

She led them straight to the far corner of the cramped basement room that had served as a high school hangout. Gerry had never been there.

He flashed a sheet of paper in her face. "Read this before you say another word."

"Don't you be telling me what to do, Gerry Griffin!"

"Would you just listen for once?" His mouth tightened, puckering the small scar on his lip.

Never had she seen him so mad, even as a kid being teased about his father, or lack of one. She wasn't sure what to think of this new side of him, but she did shut up.

"You think you know everything," he railed on, "but just for one frigging minute try to pretend you're not the three wise men all rolled up into one." They glared at each other, the musty basement air heavy between them.

She snatched the paper and started to read. In her hand was a financial agreement, including interest, between Gerard Griffin and Mercedes Hann, from the office of Tom Kennedy – a fully legal document. "But Cathy said—"

"I know what Cathy said." He blew out an exasperated breath. "The truth is, your aunt did offer to pay. But I didn't feel right about it so she agreed to lend me the money at the family rate. But I never told Ma. She'd be fit to be tied if she knew."

"Sorry, it's just...after I went and begged and still didn't get a dime, and thinking she was paying everything for you, it was so rotten."

Annie felt humiliated and strangely jealous all at once. Mercedes and Gerry's relationship had always bothered her but she'd never stopped to figure out why she let it matter so much.

"She thinks a lot of you, Annie."

"Yeah, sure, that's why she offered to pay for you and not me," she said, freshly stung. They'd obviously talked about her. "Can we just leave her out of it?"

"Fine by me. There's something else I wanted to ask you anyway."

"What?" Annie only wanted the conversation to end so she could go hide in her bedroom.

But then he moved closer. "It's about that night we went to Dewey's."

She was acutely aware of her heartbeat, and that it, like her breathing, was quicker than before.

"I had a really good time that night, Annie. I thought you did too."

"Yeah," she mumbled. "I guess so."

"That's why I was so confused when you didn't call me back."

"Sorry about that." She looked down at the floor. Her hair fell forward from behind her left ear.

"That's okay now." He reached up and tucked her hair back in place. He did it slowly, his finger seeming to linger an extra second on her ear lobe. "But I was wondering, do you want to do it again sometime?"

A woodsy aroma of aftershave drifted past her nose. "Um, like, how...I mean..." she mumbled, the opposite of the poised woman she dreamed of being.

"You know..." His voice took on a determined tone. "Go out on a real date?"

"Okay...yeah, sure. Back in town though, not here," she said, her own usually firm voice nothing but a throaty mumble.

"Right," he agreed instantly. "Let's wait till we're back at school."

Silence hung about them for several seconds.

"How about Friday night?" he asked, his voice now as low as hers.

Their bodies seemed to be tilting inward, but whether it was to better hear each other or from some libidinal gravitational pull, she wasn't sure.

"I'd like that," she murmured, her eyes focused on the little furrow in his neck, that small, soft-skinned hollow that she could almost taste, could practically feel its warm pulse on her lips. She blinked rapidly. "Friday night then."

Warm hands slid along her arms, up past her bare throat. His left thumb stroked the edge of her mouth as his right hand buried itself in the hair behind her neck, his fingers grazing her scalp ever so lightly. She felt spellbound as he leaned in towards her, certain he could see straight through to her soul. When their lips touched for that very first time, Annie knew she'd never truly been kissed before.

From that moment on they spent all their free time together, although far away from the eyes of St. Jude and their families. Annie had grown up under Lucinda's firm Catholic hand, backed up by Mercedes' strict adherence to the rules of the church. And although they had all sinned occasionally, including Mercedes, or so Annie presumed, certain tenets were beyond discussion. Annie did not remember when she first knew that Pat and Aiden were off limits, but she did know it, as did they. She assumed the same was true for Gerry even if no one acknowledged the family connections.

Yet, even though they shared the same grandmother through their fathers, and they were cousins through their mothers, Annie was confident that, genetically speaking, they were not doing anything terribly wrong. Unfortunately, she knew the church wouldn't see it that way, nor would her mother or Mercedes or any of the biddies down at Burke's. Science would never trump religion.

And so they kept it secret, at least until Cathy Green came into the picture.

It was a blustery day and Annie was rushing to put on her coat after lunch, getting ready for the five-minute walk to the library where Gerry was waiting in a cozy corner behind the stacks.

"Where you going?" Cathy asked.

"Just out for a walk."

"Why? It's freezing out there."

"I thought it'd be good to get a bit of fresh air." Among other things, she thought, smiling.

"Fresh air, eh? Hang on a second, I'll join you."

Annie's smile faded. "Ah…no, that's okay."

Cathy crossed her arms. "Don't you want me to go with you?"

"Sure, it's just…"

"Just what? You got something up your sleeve, Annie Byrne, and you better tell me what before I finds out for myself."

Annie sat back down. "All right, but you can't go blabbing it around."

Cathy nodded expectantly.

"Swear on a stack of bibles?"

"Yeah, yeah, I swear." She leaned forward. "What is it?"

"I'm going out with someone."

"So, why all the mystery?" When Annie stalled, she added, "If you can't tell your best friend, it must be some bad."

"No, no it's not bad. I just think you'll be surprised."

"Fine, I'll be surprised. Now who is it?"

"You promise not to tell anyone?"

"Jeez, I promise."

Annie inhaled deeply. "Gerry Griffin," she said, loving the sound of his name on her tongue.

Cathy sat up straighter. "Give over! You and Gerry?" She thought for a moment. "Wait now. Isn't he a cousin of yours or something?"

"For God's sake, Cath, didn't you learn anything in bio?" Annie said, annoyed. "Besides, that's ancient history. Nobody hardly remembers that."

"If you say so," Cathy shrugged. "So I guess you worked out all that about your aunt and the money?"

"Yeah, he came out to the house after he talked to you."

"Sorry about that, by the way."

"I felt some stupid. That frigging Aunt Mercedes—"

Cathy raised her hand. "Enough about that old battleaxe. Tell me all about you and him. When did it start?" Her eyes widened. "Holy shit, do Aiden and Pat know?"

Annie laughed. "Couple of weeks and, no, the boys don't know. You're the only one and we want to keep it that way. So, what do you think?"

"I don't know, girl. A few years ago it might have been odd, but it's different now. I mean, none of us are the same as we were back in high school, are we?"

Annie smiled, relieved. "No, and it's a good frigging thing, too."

"Especially Gerry. He's after getting some good looking, actually."

"Isn't he, though?" Annie felt herself blush. "But you promised, not a word?"

"My lips are sealed, so long as you tell me all about it."

"Sure, but I got to run now, he's waiting for me."

Annie rushed off, buoyed by the knowledge that someone finally knew. Someone she could trust, and talk to, and tell how wonderful it all was.

Yes, so very wonderful, and in ways she would never have imagined. Annie was surprised to discover a sensuality she'd never dreamed she possessed, experiencing an inexplicable delight in the most unlikely details. Like his hands. Gerry Griffin's hands captivated her. His fingers were long and lean, the nails neatly trimmed. His hands seemed sure, capable, sensuous even. Sometimes she would catch herself watching how he held a fork, or lifted a beer glass, or simply reached toward her. Imagine his gentle touch on her neck, her lips. Barely grazing her skin, yet sending warm currents through her entire body. Before long, she'd find her mouth open, her breath whispering in small flutters. And although she'd have been embarrassed if anyone were to have the slightest inkling what she was thinking, she couldn't keep the sinful grin off her face.

For the rest of that long island winter, they revelled in the minutes, the hours, the days together. Time was insignificant even as it sped by.

Then, suddenly, spring was approaching and, with it, the end of the school year. Their world was in jeopardy.

"Annie?"

It was a Thursday evening. They were stretched, fully clothed, across her mattress, having just enjoyed the first long, sweet, lingering kiss of the day. Gerry's right hand was combing her hair, each pull-through sending a fresh shiver along her skin.

"Yeah?" She snuggled closer on the bed, nuzzling his neck with her nose.

"What are we going to do after exams?" His arms tightened around her.

She felt her body tense. "Go home, I suppose. Try to get a job."

They were quiet then. Annie closed her eyes, concentrating on his hands as they made small circles in the centre of her back.

"Maybe we don't have to," he said, his voice hoarse, his arms pulling her closer.

She didn't answer. She couldn't think beyond his touch. Wrapped up in the raw power they had over each other, she pulled back just enough for her mouth to reach his. Their lips touched tentatively at first, lightly grazing, savouring; then, falling into oblivion, they gave in to this new passion that owned them. Soon, hands and hips joined in as they experienced bodily reactions the Nuns had failed to mention. With the threat of being separated hanging in the air, it was all they could do to remember to breathe.

"What do you mean, we don't have to?" she asked eventually.

"We could take summer courses. It's not too late to apply."

She sat up. "Then we wouldn't be stuck out in St. Jude."

"A couple in spring session, a couple more in summer. What do you think?"

Annie was having trouble concentrating as his finger grazed the inside of her arm just above the elbow. Her body felt as if it might melt away. He pulled her back down.

"Go on and get the diapers." Sadie shooed Debra down the nearest grocery aisle, then stood waiting, her eyes on the steaks laid out on their trays behind the glass.

If I gets that bit of sirloin for Gerard, and some of that blade for the rest of them, shouldn't be too dear.

Luke Ennis passed a package of sausage to Janet Foley, whose close-set eyes gave Sadie a quick once-over before she nodded and proceeded on her way.

Poor thing, looking more like Bessie every day.

Luke turned to Sadie. "Hello Mrs. Griffin, and what can I get for you?" He smiled, his front teeth protruding slightly.

Nice fellow, that Luke. Bit of a rabbit, mind you.

"Afternoon, Luke. How much do that last bit of sirloin there weigh?"

"Six…seven ounces maybe."

"Right, I'll take that, and throw in a pound of that blade there."

"I got more sirloin in the back. Just give me one second—"

"No, don't go to no trouble for me, the blade is fine."

"It's no trouble at all, Mrs. Griffin. I'll—"

"I wouldn't think of it." Sadie's voice was firm. "The blade is fine."

Would've made a fine catch for our Debra. Looks ain't everything. Too bad he got mixed up with that Beth Byrne.

Sadie watched him wrap and tie the parcel. When she got home, she would cut them so all the pieces looked similar. Only she would know which was which.

Lucinda Byrne stepped up to the counter. "Sadie." She nodded curtly and turned to her son-in-law. "You got any nice hamburger there, Luke?"

Some cheap, that one. Poor Derm, stuck with hamburger when he could be having steak.

"Ground some fresh a few minutes ago, good and lean like you likes it."

Sadie sniffed. "I just picked up a fine bit of steak for supper. Our Gerard be here tonight. Poor boy don't get home much, he's studying all the summer at the university. So devoted he is. He wouldn't want to be wasting nobody's money, no, no, not my Gerard." She glanced sideways at Lucinda.

"That's funny." Lucinda looked more puzzled than amused. "Annie's going to summer school too."

"Is she now? Gerard never said nothing about that."

Then again, why would he? Not like he ever hung out with Annie Byrne, thank the good Lord.

"Neither did Annie, about him, I mean. I was surprised when he came by the house—"

Out of nowhere came the shrieks and cries of a child.

"Mark?" Instantly oblivious to Lucinda, Sadie looked about for the source. Before she had a chance to move from her spot Debra appeared in front of them, a crying baby in her arms.

"Debra! What happened?"

"I was reaching for the diapers and bumped his head. Is he okay?"

"What have I told you about a baby's head?" Sadie yelled, her calloused hand already inching its way over the fine downy hair. Satisfied there was no damage, she lit into her daughter. "You got to be more careful. I'm sick of telling you."

"Fine looking boy you got there, Debra." Lucinda was looking intently at Mark. "Lovely head of hair on him. Some dark, isn't it, almost black?"

Sadie's head jerked towards Lucinda. Her mouth tightened.

What's she gawking at? Heard them frigging rumours probably. Frigging lies, more like it.

Sadie carefully placed Mark back in Debra's hands. "You're learning, Debra. You're doing just fine, no matter what anybody thinks."

Debra cooed and shushed the baby, bobbing to and fro until he quieted down.

Sadie took the package of meat from Luke and nudged Debra forward. "Best be getting on. Boy needs his nap. Good day, Lucinda."

Lucinda was still looking at Mark. "Oh...yes...bye now."

Sadie could feel Lucinda staring after them all the way down the aisle.

On the way home, they passed the post office just as Aiden Hann was coming out. From the corner of her eye, Sadie saw him stop and watch them, then turn and go in the opposite direction.

Goddamn son of a bitch.

For Annie and Gerry, St. Jude was a world away. They only went home twice the entire summer, each time for one night, each proclaiming to their parents how busy they were at school. Living in St. John's, they had the time and the space away from all who knew them to get to know each other in almost every way.

Yet somehow they managed to hold back, to not take that final step, through May and June, through July and August and on into September. But Annie was no fool. She had learned from Beth's experience.

Gathering up her courage, she made an appointment to get the pill, far off campus and away from prying eyes. It may have been the nineties, but she was still a good virginal female Catholic Newfoundlander. She'd been born with original sin and the guilt that shrouded it; she did not want to get caught planning for sex to happen.

As she lolled in her seat on her way to the doctor's office, the sounds of the bus exhaust gradually receded, leaving only a welcoming white noise behind her heavy eyes. Soft autumn sunshine, the apple trees along the boulevard, the beauty and serenity of the morning, all combined to ease her fears.

She spent the next three hours in a small, fusty, overcrowded reception area squeezed between two pregnant women who kept up a constant conversation over and around her, talking non-stop about husbands and babies and dirty diapers while they all waited for the doctor to return. Each time the phone rang or someone new arrived, the nurse behind the desk repeated the same litany in clipped tones: "Dr. Spencer was called to a delivery and should be back shortly." As the morning wore on and the noise grew louder, even the nurse started to look flustered. After one particular phone call, the receiver hit the cradle with a bang. "She's going to be at least two more hours," she informed the room. "So you can stay or go as you please."

They all frowned and murmured amongst themselves. No one rose.

"At least two hours," she said, her voice raised. "But don't count on it."

Annie hated to leave empty handed but she was beginning to think that if she'd managed this far without losing her virginity, perhaps she should put it off a little longer. Surrounded by crying children and sick or pregnant women, all of whom had been forced together by some stranger's problematic delivery, she was no longer sure if sex was a good idea. Was it all a sign for her to go home and keep her legs closed? Maybe God was trying to tell her something, give her another chance to do the right thing, or at least not do the wrong one. She grabbed her knapsack and hurried outside.

Annie knew little about sex. She knew where it went and how it got there, but her mother and sisters were not exactly open on the subject, nor was it a topic she discussed casually with friends. Her main source of information was Cathy Green.

Cathy had been having sex with her long-time boyfriend Cyril for close to a year and she complained about it constantly. Things came to a head one October weekend. Fed up with the constant groping and pleading, Cathy sent Cyril home to St. Jude alone on the bus. She stayed in residence, glad to have a few days when she wouldn't have to fend him off. Gerry had to go to St. Jude as well and Cathy convinced Annie to stay in town with her. Knowing she wouldn't see Gerry while out home, Annie agreed.

Seven o'clock that night, Cathy showed up at Annie's room, a case of Blue Star beer cradled in her arms, a bag of nacho chips and a jar of salsa on top. After her second beer, Cathy started in about the sex and didn't shut up until the case was empty.

Annie listened, appalled, while Cathy described in detail how difficult it was to get beyond their first time. Neither she nor Cyril had any previous experience with actual intercourse. To Cathy's surprise, and Cyril's dismay, it was not as easy as they'd always thought it would be. At first, it was so difficult to get it in they thought they must be putting it in the wrong place. Time, and some furtive research, assured them they were right on the mark; it just wasn't going to slide in as smoothly as they'd always expected, especially after Cathy had tried for so long to prevent that very thing.

Annie felt her legs squeeze together as an image of herself and Gerry trying to figure out how to do it flashed before her eyes. As curious as she'd been about sex, now she wished Cathy would just shut up. But Cathy wasn't finished.

Once they'd finally gotten past their first time, Cathy assumed the worst was over. Unfortunately, sex between her and Cyril didn't get much easier. Still, in Cathy's opinion, at least they had each other and, occasionally, they could try to have sex, too.

Cathy's eyes had widened at this point and Annie knew the worst was yet to come. Cyril became obsessed. He wanted sex constantly. He was willing to skip classes and meals on the chance that they might do it, anywhere, anytime.

Annie couldn't imagine Gerry acting like that, but what did she know? Maybe Cyril couldn't help himself. Maybe that was why the church wanted women to wait until they were married before they had sex, so that it was too late to say no.

The more beer they drank, the more Cathy talked - about the pain and the bother, about the frustration of condoms and the mess of pulling out fast, about how she wished they'd never done it in the first place. By the time Cathy stumbled back to her own room, Annie's stomach and the room were both spinning. She threw herself at the toilet, sick with beer and fear.

Come morning, tired and hungover, Annie concluded that it was definitely an omen. Sex was off the agenda.

The next weekend, she and Gerry were in her room sprawled across the bed. One of those groin-weakening kisses sent everything Cathy had said right out the window of Annie's mind. All she could think of was Gerry lying next to her, holding her so tight and kissing her so hard that she didn't care if she ever saw daylight again.

They did it again that same night and the next morning too. She had to wonder if she and Cathy were doing the same thing. How could Cathy not like it? Then, as the realization hit home, Annie offered a silent prayer, apologizing if it was wrong, but at the same time thanking Him for letting her be one of the lucky ones to like sex.

Annie would not have believed she could feel closer to Gerry, but after they made love she could no more imagine a life without him than a life without breathing.

Caught up in the joy of each other, the weeks flew by in a haze of lust and hormones. Each morning Annie awoke waiting to see him, to hear his voice, kiss his lips, to feel his eyes on her face, his fingers in her hair, on her skin.

Then they went home to St. Jude for Christmas.

Gerry was interested in a program at Dalhousie University for the fall, but only if Annie would transfer to Halifax with him. Relishing the prospect of being so far away and on their own, just like a real couple, Annie told him she'd be gone in a heartbeat. This meant the secrecy they'd both tacitly agreed upon would have to end, but they decided that Christmas, with emotions running high and liquor flowing freely, was not the time to break the news. They would wait until January.

In the meantime, they arranged to steal a few minutes together each day by sneaking off into the woods for a pre-set rendezvous, which is where they were a few days before Christmas, frolicking in the bushes, oblivious to the snow and the cold and the rest of the world, when the boys happened upon them.

"What the hell?" Pat's voice sounded behind them.

"Pat?" Annie arched backwards and twisted around. "What are you doing here?"

"What am I doing? What are you is more like it?" He started to reach in towards Annie. He looked confused; Annie was on top.

"Fuck's sake, Annie, you desperate?" Aiden added over his brother's shoulder.

"Watch your mouth, you saucy bastard," she shouted.

Gerry was struggling to get both he and Annie up off the ground. "Now, guys."

"I think you should stay out of this," warned Pat.

"I think he's already in this," Annie retorted, landing on her feet.

Aiden shoved his face in front of her. "Well, you get the fuck out of it, Annie."

"Mind your own business, Aiden," she warned.

"I don't get it," Pat said. "When did this start? Why didn't you say anything?"

Annie rolled her eyes at him, spreading her hands to indicate the four of them standing there in the woods. "Why do you think? Look at the two of you!"

Aiden spat on the ground. "Messing around with a fucking Griffin."

"That's it, I've had it!" Annie glared at Aiden. "How dare you—"

"It's okay, Annie." Gerry's voice was low and soothing as he moved between them. "Listen, guys, sorry we never told you, but we didn't want my mother to find out. You know how she is." With a tentative smile, he extended his hand.

There was an awkward silence. Standing behind Gerry, Annie caught Pat's eye. Silently, she mouthed "please," her hands joined together as if in prayer. That, and Gerry's conciliatory tone, seemed to have some effect, at least on Pat. He gave Gerry a weak handshake. Still, it was better than his brother's reaction.

"Enough of this shit," Aiden muttered. "Let's get the fuck out of here, Pat."

As Annie watched them tromp out of the woods, she knew their secret would be short-lived – Aiden had a pretty loose tongue when he was drinking. She had to stop him before that happened. God knows she'd done him enough favours over the years. He owed her. They both did. Matter of fact, they could help get Gerry into her father's Boxing Day party as well.

That afternoon she went to their house. They were alone, thankfully.

"You can't tell anyone, guys," she said right away. "Just for now, okay?"

"Why the big secret?" Pat looked hurt.

"Oh you know…it's just kind of complicated, what with Sadie and Mom and Dad and everything else."

Aiden snickered. "Maybe you're just ashamed."

"Indeed I'm not."

He stuck his head out at her. "Well, I am. I'm ashamed for you."

"Fine. Just shut up about it, will you."

"Don't worry, I wouldn't admit you had anything to do with that lot."

Pat gave his brother a disgusted look. "And who'd know better than you?" Before Aiden could respond he turned to Annie. "You sure about this?"

"Just give him a chance, would you, Pat."

Pat shrugged. "Okay, if that's what you want."

She smiled at him, happy to have him on her side even if he didn't smile back.

Sadie stood at the front window looking down the snow-covered street, a wet cloth in her hand. Her eyes were narrowed, her lips pursed. "Where's Gerard off to now?"

Debra did not look up from the TV where Bob Barker was trying to get a contestant to give him a price. "Don't know, don't care."

"Every morning the same thing. Just goes off by hisself, not a word to anyone."

Debra watched until the commercial came on, then she folded her arms and leaned back against the couch. "What I'd like to know is why he's so frigging simple lately. Always got that shit-eating grin on his face. Drives me nuts."

Got a point there. Never seen Gerard so happy. And sure why wouldn't he be? Got the world by the tail, he do. Free education, that's the ticket right there. I bet that's it. He's off doing stuff for Herself, bit of payback.

"Who knows, maybe he finally got a woman," Debra added, her tone disgusted.

Sadie wiped the cloth over the remains of a dead bug on the window. "Thanks be to Jesus he's not into that."

"What? You want him to be going after the boys? Like father, like son?"

"Debra!"

Some crotchety, that one. Can't blame her, I suppose. No

boyfriend, no job, no money. Beth Ennis's fault. Wasn't for her, Debra'd have that job at the plant. Boils me. What do that Beth want to be working for anyway with two babies at home? And Luke - God help him, stuck with her - he's on at the meat counter now, regular paycheque and all. Not like Debra with a youngster no one's laying claim to. That really boils me, that do.

Debra turned up the volume on the TV. "You said it, not me," she yelled.

"What I means is Gerard got better things to do than be hanging around with some floozy. He's probably doing stuff for Mercedes. And turn that thing down."

"Sure he is, little Prince Perfect." A wail from down the hall got Debra to her feet. "Whatever floats your frigging boat, Ma," she said, leaving the room.

Sadie went over and flicked off the TV then returned to washing the window. Her arm moved back and forth across the top, into the corners and down the sides. As she cleaned she wondered, as she had so often since Mark was born, who the boy's father was. Debra was saying nothing, and neither was anyone else, at least not when Sadie was around, not even Phyllis or Bessie. Sadie suspected they knew something but she couldn't come out and ask. Then they would know that she didn't know. The only time she'd heard anything was one day when she'd been cleaning the church. Some of Debra's friends had been smoking behind the building and Sadie overheard one of them say that Aiden Hann was the father. Sadie had flung down the mop and marched straight home. Debra had been furious and denied it in the strongest language Sadie had ever heard from her daughter's frequently foul mouth. Sadie had felt better then.

The window squeaked as Sadie, her mouth bunched into a tight, hard grimace, pushed harder and faster on the cold, wet rag.

Our Debra got better sense than mess with that lot. Might be a Griffin but she's not that stupid.

18

Although the guest list to the Byrne's Boxing Day party had always been open to interpretation, Lucinda had never extended it to the Griffins. While anyone could drop in on a funeral, there were certain proprieties when it came to parties – unwritten, unspoken, but understood. However, if Pat and Aiden were to accidentally run into their new friend Gerry on the way over and invite him along, that would be acceptable.

Late in the afternoon they made their entrance. Aiden abandoned Gerry as soon as they were in the house, but Pat got him a beer and hung out with him until Mercedes came along. Annie had been surprised to see her aunt at the party. Mercedes had missed Christmas Mass, which was so out of character that Annie had assumed she must be really sick. But she'd made it to Christmas dinner, and now here she was again, looking perfectly healthy, talking to Gerry.

With her boyfriend firmly entrenched among the partiers, Annie relaxed, happy in the knowledge that anytime she wanted, she could look around and see him, and in her own home with no one the wiser. As the day wore on and everyone got merrier and noisier, they found themselves gravitating towards each other more often. Several times, Pat joined them.

Around seven that evening Annie went upstairs to use the bathroom. When she came out, a flicker of movement in the doorway across the dark hall caught her attention. She assumed it was someone looking for a coat or dropping one off. When her eyes adjusted, she saw Gerry's face smiling at her, his finger pressed to his lips. Stepping silently from the room, his familiar hands settled in around her waist as he steered her backwards into the bedroom.

Although sex in her parents' house was out of the question, an old-fashioned make-out session on a soft bed was irresistible. Slightly drunk, as much on the taste of each other as the liquor they'd consumed, their hungry mouths and searching hands explored temporarily forbidden territory as they necked and nibbled and stole every ounce of pleasure they could from each other.

Out of nowhere, light flooded the room. They lurched to their feet, blinking madly and grasping each other's arms. Mercedes stood in the doorway. She looked stunned, horrified even. Her mouth moved. Nothing came out. Clamping her lips together, she looked from one to the other of them, then grabbed her coat from the bed and rushed past them out the door. Not one word passed her lips.

In the harsh light, the upheaval within the cramped room jumped out at Annie. The musty pong of winter wetness hung in the air. Coats and scarves were strewn over the bed and floor. She and Gerry had probably pushed them aside in their haste to go at each other.

"Annie?" Gerry's hand squeezed hers. "You all right?"

She bent to pick the coats up off the floor. "Yeah...yeah, I'm fine."

"That was weird." He took the coats from her. "Not like her at all, was it?"

Annie shook her head. "I suppose we better get back downstairs."

The mood broken, they rejoined the party. Annie went in one direction, Gerry in another. Mercedes was nowhere to be seen.

Annie was sitting on the sofa talking with her grandfather when she saw her mother come in and motion to Gerry that he had a phone call. Gerry followed Lucinda out but returned within a minute and came over to Annie.

"That was my mother. I need to get going." His eyes widened. "She said I have to stop at your aunt's, too."

"Oh?" Annie's skin prickled. "What does she want?" And why would the message come from Sadie? Had Mercedes told her about the scene in the bedroom?

"She didn't say, just that I had to go there and then straight home."

Annie noticed her grandfather staring at them. "Glad you could drop in and have a beer with us," she said in an offhand voice. "See you later."

"Right. Good night. Merry Christmas, Mr. Hann."

"And a Happy New Year to you, Gerry," Callum answered.

Gerry got his coat and went to the door. There was no chance to talk to him about what had happened in the bedroom, a fact for which Annie was grateful at first. With a smile plastered to her face, she waved goodbye.

But something was wrong. She knew it in her heart, that sudden lead weight inside her chest. As he put on his coat and gloves, making small talk with her father at the door, she waited for him to look her way. She needed to see his eyes again, to lock into one private glance and know that all was well. But just as Gerry moved to look in her direction, Aiden stepped in front of him. Her father opened the door. He left.

As a winter wind swung the door shut behind him, it was all Annie could do to stop herself from chasing after him. If they could have that single second, one tiny kiss or whispered caress, then maybe the knot in her stomach would ease and the peculiar fear that had come to possess her would disappear. One moment, that was all she needed.

Sadie waited. She looked out the window, down the wet, slush-covered street, and she waited. She took another swallow of vodka from the small flask in her apron, and she waited.

What's he doing at that Boxing Day party anyway? Our crowd don't get invited to them shindigs. And what got Mercedes in such a panic? Never heard that schoolmarm voice so shook up. Not like her to lose her cool. Something's up with her lately. Not been to Mass in ages, not even Christmas Day. New priest is cranky and all, but that'd never stop Mercedes Hann, biggest Catholic alive, that one. Why's she missing Mass? And why the hell is Gerard taking so frigging long to get here?

She looked at her watch. A full hour had passed since she'd spoken to him on the phone. If he'd gone straight to Mercedes' house, he should have been home by now.

That's him! At the corner. About goddamn time, too.

Sadie watched as he came closer. His head was down, his hands deep in his pockets. Taking a final sip from the flask, she shoved it beneath the chair cushion. She slipped a mint into her mouth just as he opened the door.

"What did she want?" Sadie asked immediately.

He was staring at her oddly, as if he wasn't really seeing her, as if his mind was somewhere else.

"What did Mercedes want?" she demanded.

He took off his coat and dropped it on a chair. His hand rose to press against his forehead, then moved to massage his eyes and the bridge of his nose.

"Gerard? Is something wrong?"

"I don't... no, nothing." He looked towards the door, his expression confused.

Sadie felt her blood rise. "What did that woman do to you?"

He hesitated.

"What did she say? Out with it!"

"Just that...that it's wrong...and it's... against God and the church..."

Against God? Frigging Mercedes Hann! Thinks she's God herself.

"...and that it's immoral." His voice rose on the last word, as if he no longer knew its meaning.

Sadie stared, dumbfounded. For the life of her she could not imagine what he could have done that was so wrong. But there was something in his tone and in the way he wouldn't meet her eye that was starting to worry her. "What is?"

He stared at the floor.

She went over to him and grabbed his arms. "Gerard! Answer me!"

"Ma, please—"

She slapped one hand on either side of his face and made him look at her. "What the Christ is going on? Do you hear me? The truth! What's she talking about?"

He closed his eyes. "Being with my cousin," he whispered.

"Being with…?" Sadie paused, confused.

What do he mean? What cousin?

She shoved him down into a chair. "Tell me!" she screeched.

And he did, slowly stammering out how Mercedes had caught him and Annie.

Sadie's heart stood still. Smack dead in the middle of her chest. Not for long, just a few seconds, but she had no doubt that it actually stopped beating as the unwelcome image filled her head. She couldn't speak. Could not think past the image and the words, the words and the image, playing over and over in her stupefied mind.

"She said there were things we didn't know, secrets, that we're more related—"

His mouth closed abruptly. He seemed to think for a second before continuing in a fast yet shaky voice. "She said we were too related, that we couldn't be together, that Annie…that she'd be ruined forever."

Sadie found her voice. "You and Annie Byrne?" she growled.

"Yes. Listen, Ma—"

"You been sleeping with Lucinda's daughter?"

Gerry nodded. His shoulders started to shake. Then he started to cry, bawling his eyes out right in front of her.

"Gerard! Stop that nonsense! Now what the fuck are you talking about?"

He told her all about it then, how they'd been going out for almost a year, how they wanted to go away together. And then, tears streaming down his face, he confessed that he was in love with Annie Byrne.

Oh Jesus. Oh God. Mother Mary help me.

Sadie's knees were weak. She could barely stand up. She clutched the chair with both hands. When Gerry reached out to her, however, all she could see was Annie Byrne's face. She smacked his hand away.

Sadie went to the holy water font and dipped her fingers in. She took a deep breath and blessed herself. Then she got her flask and took a large swig.

"But I don't care," he cried. "What does it matter as long as we love each other?"

Sadie almost choked. "What does it matter! You want a bunch of retards for youngsters? Mother of Jesus, Gerard, how thick are you?"

"But Ma—"

"Don't 'but Ma' me, you stupid fool. I could smack the day-lights out of you, getting involved with the likes of that…that no good…" Sadie wanted to scream, to open her mouth and scream her lungs out. She needed to strike out, to hit some-thing, someone. She punched her fist into her palm.

Annie Byrne! Fornicating with Lucinda's daughter. God help me.

"You're no better than the goddamn Griffins!" she railed. "After all I done for you, the sacrifices, the lies, everything to make sure you were better than them, and now look at you, just look at you! It's sinful, disgusting," she screeched into his face. "And yes, you knows what the church says, of course it mat-ters that you're related."

Hang on. More related? Who? Him and Annie? Annie! That witch, that slut…

As Annie's face filled Sadie's mind she completely lost her train of thought. She started back in, ranting and raving, be-rating the Hanns and the Byrnes, the likes of which should not be free to walk the earth with good people like herself.

Out of air, she stopped, though she was far from finished. That's when she saw the alarm on Gerard's face.

"Ma, take it easy, calm down," he said, his hand reaching out to her again. "You're scaring me."

She opened her mouth to continue, but all that came out was a wheezy breath.

I got to calm down. Got to make him listen. He's the only good thing I got. If he goes over to the Hanns everything I'm after working for will be wasted. This whole stupid life will be one big lie. I got to try another angle.

Sadie put her arms around him, cajoling him and telling him that he had not known the evil of Annie Byrne's ways, and thanking the Good Lord that they'd found out in time.

Suddenly inspired, she thought of Father Cunningham, the contrary old priest who had recently been assigned to the parish. She grabbed the phone. Her voice frantic, she begged him to talk to Gerard, now, tonight, before a mortal sin stained his soul forever. They would come right over, she said, dear Father, please don't let him spend his life atoning for the mistakes of his youth, please spare him the pain she'd endured because of that exact same thing, please don't let him break his mother's heart. She could feel Gerard's eyes fast upon her as she pleaded for help. She begged some more.

Head bowed, he went with her to see the priest.

And when that was done, when Father Cunningham was finished with him, she made Gerard swear on her life never to see Annie Byrne again, not even to say goodbye.

Why place himself into temptation, she said? Why tempt the devil? No, he just had to go away, from St. Jude the next day, from St. John's as soon as possible.

Sadie phoned Mercedes and between the two of them they convinced him that they knew best. He would transfer to the mainland immediately. Mercedes would make the necessary calls. It was the only way, they told him, that all of it would be buried forever.

Still he resisted. "Please, Ma," he begged. "I can't just leave."

Sadie leaned in so close that they were practically sharing the same mouthful of air. "If you don't do this I can promise you one thing. Mercedes will pay the price. I knows all about her, Gerard, there's nothing gets past me," she bluffed. "You should know that by now. But her secret's safe with me, long as you does the right thing."

"What do you know?"

"Never you mind what I knows. You just listen up. You owes me, Gerard," she said, "and you owes Mercedes, bless her kind and gentle heart, the only good Hann to walk this earth."

Hah!

"You do what you're told and no one need ever know. If we all vows to keep the secret, it can be done. I knows how to keep a secret, the Lord knows I do. I can keep a secret better than anyone alive, believe you me."

"What are you talking about, Ma?"

"Don't you worry. You does what I says no one will know about any of this."

He hung his head. "Please don't make me do this."

Sadie grabbed his head and lifted it to look at her. "I'm warning you, Gerard. I knows more about Mercedes and the whole lot of them Byrnes and Hanns than you can shake a stick at. There's stuff goes way back, stuff that the Griffins are caught up in too, bad stuff, Gerard. So if you gives two shits about us, and about your precious Mercedes and even that goddamn Annie, you'll do like I says. I'll not be telling you twice. Now get packing."

He stared at her for the longest time. Then he went to his room and took down his suitcase.

Several days later, Sadie's phone rang. She'd calmed down by then, through sheer force of will. Occasionally, however, it all flashed back at her, and she could feel the pressure of her blood raging through her heart.

"Hello?" Sadie's voice was sweet, welcoming even.

"Could I talk to Gerry please?"

Hah! The little slut finally gave in.

"Who is this?" Sadie asked innocently.

"It's Annie Byrne, Mrs. Griffin. Is Gerry there? We found some gloves."

"Oh, Annie, is it? And how is your dear mother?"

Yankee whore.

"Fine. She thought the gloves might be Gerry's."

"Gloves, eh? Hmm, no, no I don't think they'll be his. I'm sure he had them on when he left. Isn't that right, Debra?" She turned to her daughter who was feeding the baby porridge at the kitchen table. Debra shrugged.

"When he left?" said Annie.

"Yes, Gerard went on back into St. John's a few days back."

"Why? I mean, I didn't think he'd be gone back so soon."

"Yes, well neither did he now," Sadie said, somehow managing to stop herself from yelling out that if it wasn't for Annie, he'd be in St. Jude having breakfast with his mother that minute. "But your aunt needed something and he couldn't refuse her now, could he?" Sadie rolled her eyes in disgust. "And just because it's Christmas and I barely seen him all year, for pity's sake, that's no excuse not to do a little favour for Mercedes, good woman that she is. You're lucky to have such a—"

"Aunt Mercedes sent him back to town early?"

"My, yes, she phoned here in a right panic, the night of your father's party it might have been, yes I'm sure it was, said she had to see him right away, and the next thing you know, he's off to St. John's." Sadie was thoroughly enjoying herself now. "And I don't mind you know, he's such a good student and a hard worker too, and now moving to that Dalhousie, didn't Mercedes go there herself, a long time ago of course, isn't that right?" She hadn't meant to give quite so much information but the moment had gotten the better of her. She'd won.

There was only a breathy silence on the other end of the line.

"What colour were they?" Sadie asked.

"Huh? What?"

"The gloves, dear. You said Lucinda found some gloves?"

Hah! Gloves, my arse!

"Oh, right. Never mind, it doesn't matter."

"Well, I'll tell him you called," Sadie lied. "But he got more important things on his mind than gloves." Sadie was beaming as she hung up the phone.

"What are you grinning about?" Debra asked.

"That there was Annie Byrne."

"That witch. What did she want?"

"Something about gloves. Nothing important."

"That crowd pisses me right off."

Sadie looked fondly at her daughter. "And why is that?"

"So full of theirselves, thinks they're better than everybody. Like I was at the store the other day and that Sara and Beth were over by the magazines, and I knows they were talking about me, tittering away when I walked past them."

"That Annie's quite the tart from what I hears."

Debra laughed humourlessly. "Nothing but a stuck-up tomboy."

"Is she now?" Sadie watched her daughter carefully. "I suppose that comes from hanging around with them two cousins all the time."

Debra slid another spoonful of food into Mark's mouth.

"Not much good comes of that, now does it?" Sadie added.

Debra glanced over at her mother, then back to her son to scoop up the excess food from his chin with the side of the baby spoon. "Open wide, Markie." She shoved the spoon back in.

Annie slid the phone into its cradle. She turned to the window. A fresh layer of snow blanketed the ground. Not a single footstep broke the fragile surface. Perfect for making snow angels. You just needed someone to pull you up when you were done. You couldn't make a good snow angel on your own.

What was that devil of a mother of his talking about? Why hadn't he called her to let her know he was going back? And what did Mercedes need him for, anyway? Annie was tempted to confront her aunt, but she was still too embarrassed.

She returned to university before the end of Christmas break. As lost as she felt without Gerry beside her, she was grateful to drop the pretence that all was well. The first thing to catch her eye when she opened her door was the white envelope.

"Dear Annie," he wrote, "I hate to have to tell you this way, but I don't know how else to do it. We can't see each other anymore. It's just the way things have to be. I hope you won't hate me. By the time you get this I'll be in Nova Scotia. I'll never forget us. Goodbye Annie." It was signed, simply, "Gerry."

She sat on her bed in a fog as fragments of memories ran through her head - their first night at Dewey's, the days, and especially the nights, spent together, the Boxing Day party. Her mind kept zeroing in on her aunt's face. What could have been so horrible that it rendered the woman speechless?

Confusion turned to anger. Why would he just up and leave? How could he get on that plane knowing how hurt she would be? It didn't make sense. She read the letter again. "By the time you get this," he'd written. Gerry wouldn't have expected her back on campus this soon. Maybe he hadn't left for Nova Scotia yet. She rushed to the bathroom and scrubbed her face with cold water, then took the stairs two at a time.

As she passed through the front entrance of his residence, the click of the door latch resounded behind her. There was no one around to hear it. On the second floor she slowed her stride. A light shone from an open doorway.

Gerry lay on his bed, his eyes closed. His right hand, long fingers outstretched, rested on the small bear she'd given him for Christmas.

The act of waking up took him mere seconds, but it seemed to happen much slower. His eyelids rose. His eyes settled upon her face. The warmth in his smile sent her heart singing, so that although everything up to that moment had pointed to the end, she was so desperate for hope that she would have accepted the most farfetched explanation. But in the next instant, his eyes shot wide open.

"I got your note." She held it out, let it drift to the floor.

He pushed himself off the bed. "Annie, I'm so sorry."

His room, the place they'd loved and laughed together, now seemed devoid of life. A cluster of mismatched suitcases was stacked against the bare wall.

"What's the hell is going on?" she said.

"I'm transferring up to Dal."

"Why now?" Her voice cracked. "Why not the fall like we planned?"

"I can't explain, Annie. Please just let this be." His eyes were shining, the first tear waiting for the next blink.

Seeing him there, his face in such pain, his voice filled with sadness, and all of it so unexplainable, sent a surge of anger through her - at him, at herself, at whoever or whatever it was that was responsible. "How can I let it be?" she cried out, fear making her desperate. Yet she could tell that there was no point, that something bigger than her or them had insinuated itself into their lives. Still, she couldn't give up. "Talk to me, Gerry. Please."

His gaze fell to the linoleum. "I fly out tonight." It was a cold statement of fact.

Struck with a hurt she'd never known existed, she started to go. But she couldn't do it. She could not walk away. At the risk of any pride she had left she needed to know what had gone wrong.

She turned back, not caring that the tears were running down her cheeks. "Gerry, you have to tell me. What are you doing this for, what happened to us?"

His eyes pleaded with her, but whether it was for understanding or forgiveness she couldn't tell. He took a step towards her then stopped abruptly. A mask came over his face, and his voice was hard and bitter. "I guess you could blame Mercedes. She convinced me, said we're too related to be together."

"But Gerry, we talked about that—"

"Oh, I know. But then she had the nerve to say I wasn't good enough for you anyway. That I was a Griffin and I should know better and just be grateful."

"That's crazy."

"The old bat threatened to call back my loan if I kept seeing you, and when I told her to piss off she had a little chat with my mother, said her son was a fool to wreck his chances on a girl. Then she swore she wouldn't lift a finger to help my brothers and sisters. Now that may not seem like much to you, but to my mother, Mercedes stands out as her only hope to get us out of the poverty that's been the Griffins' lot in life."

He wasn't looking at her, but was instead shifting through some papers on his desk. Annie saw the airline ticket among them.

"Gerry, come on—"

"And the more I thought about it," he persisted, "the more I realized that I'm sick to death of it all - the Byrnes and the Hanns, the holier-than-thou and smarter-than-thee attitudes, sick of trying to fit in. That's why I never wanted anybody to see us. I knew it wasn't right. So I've had it. I'm getting the hell out of here."

He shuffled his suitcases together between himself and Annie. Her entire body yearned to touch him, to let the soft blades of his hair run through her fingers, to hold tight to the fine strands and never let them go, never let him leave her. She made a move towards him.

Taking a step back, he looked directly at her. "It's done, Annie. Let it go." A firm voice. Not a tremble from those lips, lips she'd kissed a million times if dreams could count.

She studied the person before her, this Gerry Griffin she had known for most of her life, and loved for the only part that mattered anymore. This man who she had given every bit of herself to had transformed into an unfeeling bastard.

Somehow she made it back to her own room. Locking the door, she switched off the lights and slept like the dead. No dreams. No nightmares. Nothing.

Until five a.m, when she awoke in an instant. The previous day's events slammed back into her consciousness, sending an odd wavy sensation through her stomach. She stumbled to the bathroom. She would never have believed that love could make you sick, but there she was, puking into the toilet. She might even have laughed if she wasn't so busy throwing up. How corny was that, to actually get sick to your stomach over a guy?

Two days later, she was still sick, her gut a seesaw on a non-stop rollercoaster. Then, as she was trying to get to sleep that night, she sprang bolt upright. She grabbed her calendar from the dresser. Panic rose like fresh vomit in her throat.

Oh sweet Jesus, how could she have been so stupid?

19

The dorm echoed with the lifeless sounds of pipes and floorboards. Annie lay on her bed. She watched the clock and waited - for the weak winter light to filter through her window, for the nearest drugstore to open, for confirmation of a truth she already knew.

Abortion was not an option. Church on Sunday and daily during Lent, prayers every night and confession every month, the Stations of the Cross and the body and blood of Christ - these rituals framed her life. She was a Catholic, clearly fallible, but not a murderer. Annie had never questioned this doctrine before. She didn't now.

Gerry was constantly on her mind. He was always there, hovering in the next thought, the next breath. What if he knew she was pregnant? Surely he'd change his mind. On the other hand, if he cared so little, did she want him in her life? Still, didn't he simply have a right to know? He'd never said if he wanted children, but she suspected he did. As for her, there'd been daydreams of hazy domesticity far off in the future, a presumption of motherhood years away. She'd been more concerned with dreams of a career and an exciting life beyond St. Jude. A life with Gerry Griffin.

Now, here she was, mother-to-be of his first-born child, and she didn't even know his phone number.

Annie sat up abruptly. Of course! Mercedes would know how to reach him. In fact, she might want to have a word with him herself once she knew how things stood. Surely she would expect Gerry to do the proper thing by her niece.

Yes indeed. Mercedes Hann was the answer.

Mercedes did not seem surprised when Annie barged into the kitchen. Except for a hush to Rufus to stop barking, she continued inspecting the four loaves of bread that had been set to rise on the shelf above the stove. The dough was still low in the pans.

"Hello, Annie. I thought you'd gone back to school already."

Annie glanced down the hallway. "Is Granddad here?"

"No, he's gone out."

"Good. Now, could you please explain why you ran Gerry Griffin out of town?"

Mercedes stood still for a moment, then sat at the heavy oak table. "You and that Griffin boy do not belong together, and I told him so."

"'That Griffin boy'? Since when is he that to you?"

"Never mind that. The bottom line is I know more about these things than you do. You'll just have to trust me that you and Gerry could never be in love."

Any last vestiges of respect or fear were gone in a flash of fury. "What the hell do you know about love? You've never loved anybody your whole life."

Mercedes remained eerily calm. "Ann, I have only your best interests at heart."

The situation felt surreal, like she was beating on a soundproof door. "How the Christ could you have my best interests at heart? You don't have a heart."

Mercedes sat in her chair, apparently ready to bear the brunt of Annie's rage.

Annie felt a rush of desperation. Bending down, she looked Mercedes straight in the eye. For just a second, the reflection startled her. Then it was gone. "You have to change all of this back," she said. "You have to phone Gerry and tell him you were wrong. I need him home." The fear in her own voice frightened her. "I'm pregnant."

For the first time the stern old face registered something

other than calm. It was the same look she'd had the night she caught Gerry and Annie in the bedroom.

Mercedes stood up. She began to pace, fast, then slow, then stopping, her hand to her mouth, then pacing again, all while Annie waited for a miracle. She waited in vain.

"Well, you've gotten yourself into a fine pickle. In a family way and unmarried just like your sister." Mercedes walked to the stove and made a show of studying the dough again. "At least Beth had a real boyfriend, not a cousin who left her."

Annie threw her hands in the air. "He left because of you."

"You want to blame me? Think about that for a minute, Ann. If that boy truly loved you, would he have gone away? What kind of love is that?"

"He was thinking about his family and you damn well know it. After all, you said you wouldn't help anymore if he stayed."

The silvered head jerked up but she didn't look at Annie. "I said what?"

"You heard me. Old Sadie read him the riot act because you said you'd take back your loan, and that would be the last red cent any Griffin ever got from you."

"Young *Gerard* surely can exaggerate. The truth is I might have implied I'd pull his funding but I doubt I would have. Besides, Sadie doesn't even know it's a loan. And I certainly didn't say anything about his family." She lowered the oven door and began to arrange the loaves on the middle rack. "Given this fresh glimpse into his character, however, I'll have to reconsider. I'm not sure I want anything to do with a boldfaced liar. Then again, what can you expect from a Griffin?"

"I don't believe you."

She flipped the oven door shut. "Have you ever known me to lie?"

Annie wavered. "Are you telling me Gerry made it all up?"

"Make no mistake about it." She gave Annie a swift disapproving glance up and down, from her chest to her toes, then dismissed her with a wave of her hand. "Now look at you. All the 'A's in the world are useless to you now and there's not one thing you can do about it."

Annie glared at her. "Nothing I can do about it, huh? Just you watch. I won't get stuck in this town and end up like you. No frigging way."

"That's for certain. No education. A baby to raise, and given the circumstances, who knows what it'll be born like. I hear they're looking for people down at the plant. It's seasonal, but you'll be able to get the dole after." Then, her voice cold and spiteful, Mercedes added, "You'll be a nothing in a nothing town, just like the rest of the Griffins."

For one instant, Annie felt a tremendous urge to strike out, to smack the smirk off Mercedes' face. But then she took a hard look at this woman who she had always respected, always looked up to. A numbing chill crept through her.

"Fuck you, Mercedes." She marched out and slammed the door.

For days after, the conversation echoed in Annie's mind. Her own bitterness, her rage and her fear. Mercedes' cold-bloodedness, her heartless honesty. Until finally Annie knew there was another choice. Good Catholic or not, it had to be considered. She was no one's puppet. Not Mercedes'. Not even God's.

Abortion was not a subject much discussed in St. Jude. Annie had assumed all of Newfoundland would be the same. But at the counselling centre she met a young woman a few years older than herself, a graduate psychology student who volunteered her time, who listened and provided information, who kept her opinions to herself.

Given the space and the freedom to think, Annie began to feel again. The panic receded; the pain set in. She was carrying a child from the first and only love of her life. Could she let them tear it from her? What if this was her only chance at motherhood? Even in her desperate state, when the last thing she could imagine was wanting to get pregnant, even then she knew that someday she might feel differently. Whatever she chose to do, her life would never be the same; she did not delude herself that it could be otherwise. At times, she was filled with anger, at herself, at Gerry, at Mercedes. But underlying it all was a vast sadness. Everything she had ever been taught, everything she had ever believed in, told her that what she was about to do was wrong. Still, she made her decision, knowing that in doing so, she was denying an integral part of herself.

The day before the abortion she lay on her bed in tears. Would God ever forgive her? What if some awful thing happened to her during the procedure? How would her parents feel when they found out why? Would they ever forgive her?

Someone knocked on her door. She ignored it. A familiar voice shouted her name. The louder he called, the harder he knocked. When it was obvious that he was not about to give up, she pulled the curtains together to make the room darker, then opened the door.

"Pat, what is it?" she asked, rubbing her eyes as if she'd just woken up. "Keep the noise down. You'll be waking the dead with this racket."

"Sorry. Had to come in town today, and your mother made me promise to check on you. Some dark in here. Where's the light?" His hand skimmed the wall.

"No, don't. Look, I'll call you later. I was up all night studying."

"Sure, no problem." He flicked on the lamp. "I made you some soup."

She tried to turn her head away, to hide her red eyes and blotched face.

"Goddamm it!" Pat's fist hit the desk. "It's that son of a bitch Griffin, isn't it?"

"I don't want to talk about it."

"What the hell were you thinking, getting caught up with him?"

"I mean it, Pat." Her hand was under his elbow moving him towards the door.

“Fine, fine.” Twisting out of her grasp, he opened the curtains and took a good look at her. “Aw, Annie. Come here, girl.” Wrapping her in his arms, he held her like a child. The gesture was so unlike him that she started to cry. He kicked the door shut.

Patting her back, he sat her on the bed. “There’ll be other fellows, lots of them.”

She nodded numbly and tried to smile.

“Tell me about it. I promise I’ll just listen. Honest, I won’t say a thing.”

Annie was afraid if she said one word, she would lose control completely.

“Why don’t I stay for a while, keep you company?”

She forced her voice to remain even. “No, you go on. I’ll be all right now.”

When she insisted, he went to the door, but once there, he waited, his hand on the knob. He stood there for so long that she finally asked, “Something wrong?”

“No…it’s just…you’re not in trouble or anything, are you?”

What? Was it printed on her forehead?

He walked back and squatted down in front of her. “Are you pregnant, Annie?”

“Oh God.” She couldn’t hold it back then. Out it came, the whole story, until finally, her voice shaking uncontrollably, she told him about the abortion.

“Frigging Aunt Mercedes, and that arsehole Griffin. Aiden was right about that bastard all along. If I ever gets my hands on him, I’ll break his neck.” He stopped and looked at her. His eyes softened. “But that’s neither here nor there right now, is it?”

She shook her head.

“You got someone to go with you?”

“Not yet. No one knows. Maybe Cathy—”

“Never mind that goodie-two-shoes. I’ll take you over.”

“Oh Pat, will you?”

"Of course I will, Annie."

"Do you think I'm awful to be doing it?"

"No. I think it's the right thing. I mean, what choice do you have?"

"Pat, no one else knows about this, okay?"

"I'll never tell a soul, I promise."

"What about Aiden?"

"This one's just between you and me, Annie. Forever."

She'd known him her whole life, but she felt she'd never really known him at all. When she needed him most, Pat was the best friend she could have asked for. He stayed with her all the next day, and close by for another two. He made her cookies and soup and endless cups of tea, he brought her ice cream and magazines and Tylenol. He talked to her sometimes and he shut up at others.

On the fourth day, he went home. Aiden was getting curious.

Alone again, an intense sadness locked onto Annie's heart. She felt empty, void of life, unloved, unlovable. She tried not to think about Gerry, about what was, what could have been, but her thoughts were not so easy to control. Neither were her dreams. There was one that kept recurring, the details changing but the crux always the same. She was on the beach, searching frantically, trying to find something she had seen from the kitchen window. She didn't know what it was, only that it was tiny and precious and that if she didn't get to it right away the sea would take it back again. She would be running along the shore, tripping over rocks or dodging driftwood, pushing against the wind or fighting the water and sand around her feet, but, no matter how hard she tried, she could never reach it before the waves washed in and carried it away.

Somehow she managed to keep up with her courses, leaving her room only if she had to, for classes and meals, to fulfill her RA duties. She slept a lot. She did not socialize. She let Cathy and her other university friends believe it was all due to Gerry moving away. They let her be. Her only visitor was Pat, who drove in about twice a week to make sure she was all right.

Citing exams and term papers, she managed to avoid St. Jude until March. When she finally did arrive at her parents' house late one Friday evening, her mother wrapped her in her arms and gave her one of the biggest hugs they'd ever shared.

"Annie! I was starting to worry with your not coming to see us for so long."

"Sorry, Mom, I just got bogged down with school stuff, you know?"

"I know, girl, but it's only a few hours, home and back. Still, you're heading into your third year now and things are harder, I suppose. So how are you?" she asked, uncharacteristically tucking her arm into Annie's as she led her into the kitchen.

"Fine. How's everything here? Where's Dad?"

"Gone to your aunt's with a drop of broth. We're right worried about her. She got a wicked bug, been in and out of bed for weeks now. Never steps outside the door. Keeps asking about you, though, all the same," she added, her eyebrows raised.

Annie shrugged innocently and asked after her sisters.

Her father bounded through the back door. "Annie, my love, you're home."

Smelling of winter and warm, clean sweat, his evening bristles gave a comforting scratch to her cheeks. "Hi Dad, I missed you too. How's things going?"

"I'm right as rain, but Mercedes is looking some poorly. And as usual she won't go to the doctor no matter how much your grandfather pesters her. Says she's just tired and we should mind our own business and quit fussing."

"Oh well, can't imagine there'd be too much wrong with her."

He gave her a hurt look. "That's not very nice, Annie. She keeps asking when are you coming home. I think you should go over there."

"What? Now?" Annie was sorry she'd left the sanctuary of her dorm room. "Look, I'm tired. I just want to go to bed." Grabbing her bag, she escaped to her room where she fell into a deep sleep almost instantly. She'd been doing that a lot lately.

First thing the next morning, her mother started in. "Your grandfather wanted me to wake you up and send you over. I let you sleep in but now you got to go see her." She finished wiping the counter. "What's she so interested in you for all of a sudden?"

"Darned if I know," Annie muttered. "Just let me have a cup of tea first."

The dregs of the tea had grown cold in her cup when the phone rang. When she heard her mother answer and say "Hi, Dad," she knew her time was up.

She walked slowly, working hard to generate some steam, some reserve of anger. All she felt was a barrenness as flat and cold as the ground beneath her feet. As she approached the house, she surveyed the back yard, the flower boxes, trees and bushes all covered with snow or burlap. In summer they sang with perfume and colour. Now they lay dormant. It was hard to believe they would ever come back to life.

Callum met her at the door with a hug. "Some good to see you." He leaned back to look at her. "You okay? You're looking kind of pale there."

"Yeah, yeah, I'm fine. Just tired."

"You and Merce both, it seems. She's resting out in the front porch." He took her coat and hung it on a hook. "I don't think there's anyone she wants to see more than you. I don't know why but I'm guessing you probably do. So go on in, okay?"

Annie nodded. She didn't offer an explanation.

Years ago, Mercedes had renovated Callum's old bedroom into a year-round sunroom overlooking her garden. In the summer it was the prettiest room in the house, the view through the picture window changing gradually throughout the season. On this day, all Annie saw outside was the harsh reflection of the morning sun on the cold, hard snowpack. Inside, she was struck by the contrast of the warm yellow walls against the pallor of her aunt's skin, further highlighted by the colourful afghan that covered her. Annie recalled the last words she'd said to Mercedes. She was surprised that the memory made her sad.

As she stared down at her aunt, so pale, so lifeless, she wondered, is this what she would look like dead? Mercedes was eerily still. A second thought struck her – what if she really is dead? Annie opened her mouth to say her name. Her tongue seemed frozen yet her nerves tingled with a mixture of revulsion and fascination. She touched the arm under the afghan. Mercedes' hand jerked. Annie shrank back.

Milky eyes looked at her. They moved to Annie's stomach then back up to her face. Any sympathy Annie might have felt blew right out the frosted windows.

Annie's mouth slit into a crisp smile. "Dropped a few pounds, didn't I?" Her voice cold and deliberate, she added, "Had a little help, mind you."

The eyes drifted from Annie to the open door.

"No one else noticed," Annie answered the silent question. "Of course, they didn't know how bad I needed to lose the weight, now did they?" Her heart felt like ice, a reprieve from the pain it had grown accustomed to.

Mercedes didn't speak.

"Is there anything else you wanted from me?" Annie asked, the words so saccharin-coated they could have come from Sadie Griffin herself. She waited, stubbornly refusing to look away. "Go ahead and ask. The sky's the limit, obviously."

Mercedes' lips parted. Still she said nothing. But her eyes seemed fuller and sadder than before. Witnessing a mortal sin can do that to a person, Annie figured.

Annie's heart started to hurt again, the ice thawing into a dull throb that wandered in and settled right down, spreading through her body. She gave up then, sick of the game, sick of Mercedes, sick of herself.

She was closing the door when she heard a mumble from the bed. She listened for a minute until she recognized the novena.

The thought that Mercedes might pray for mercy on Annie's hopeless soul made Annie want to just lie down and cry forever, to give in to the futility and the waste and the crushing sense of defeat that she couldn't shake. Because for all her tough words, Annie had lost herself. And she had no idea of where to search, and no conviction that she even wanted to find the person she thought she'd been. The one thing she did know was that a novena would not be near enough to save her.

Annie went to school. She ate her meals. She worked and studied hard. She learned to keep moving, to carry on. She discovered that when the spirit dies, the body doesn't always tag along; a person is simply stuck with living. The world keeps turning. Every morning brings another sunrise. For most people, the drudgery of just being alive eventually starts to pay off and they're rewarded with minute slivers of pleasure, brief glimpses of how they used to live in the world back when they were happy. Life begins again, even though the world and how they view it is permanently altered.

Prior to the fall semester, Annie transferred out west to study geology. Rocks had always fascinated her. Rocks were hard, solid. They took forever to change.

In the years that followed, she saw little of Mercedes, brief unpleasant meetings during her sporadic visits home. Yet whenever Annie spoke with her mother on the phone from Calgary, Lucinda would say that Mercedes had been inquiring about her, asking how was she doing at university, did she have a boyfriend, and always, Mercedes wanted to know, was Annie happy?

Yet each time Annie came home to St. Jude, her mother would wonder aloud why, if Mercedes was so concerned over Annie's well-being, why then did the woman always make herself so scarce during the visit. In fact, Lucinda complained to Annie, Mercedes saw far more of Gerry Griffin during his trips home than she did of her own niece. And each time Lucinda would ask if something had happened between them.

Annie never enlightened her.

PART FOUR
1999

20

The morning barely dawns. It's a miserable day for a funeral.

The procession of vehicles makes its way along the road. In the black hearse at the front, Mercedes leads the way as, one by one, the cars fade into the fog.

At the gravesite, Annie stands next to her mother who, on her other side, is flanked by Dermot, Callum, Pat, Aiden and Joe. They are surrounded by family, friends and neighbours several hundred strong. Annie steals a quick scan of the crowd. She does not see him, yet just as she had in church, she senses his presence.

Father James, the handsome new priest, spends an inordinate amount of time on the virtues of forgiveness. Considering that he didn't have much of an opportunity to get to know Mercedes, Annie thinks he is doing a fine job of sending her off.

On the opposite side of the casket stands Sadie Griffin. Her eyes are intent on the young priest's face. The tip of her tongue darts out to moisten her mouth, which is slightly open; her hand comes up to graze her lower lip, then it slides down past her chin to her neck, where it rests. Annie turns her eyes away.

Father James makes the sign of the cross. The coffin begins its descent; the mourners huddle in. As the first shovel of dirt hits the casket, Annie hears a sharp intake of breath next to her. She offers her arm. Lucinda leans heavily on her until Dermot takes over and leads them all away. They're a jittery crew, a few hungover, all full of the edgy darkness and nervous energy that comes from seeing one of their own off on her final journey.

At the house, Tom Kennedy is waiting for the family. He reads the will.

To everyone's surprise, except perhaps Callum's, Mercedes had sold the house before she died. The proceeds are to be shared among the nieces and nephews. As Pat's name is read, his head shoots up. Annie smiles, then soon realizes her name is not on the list.

Next comes the property in Bay D'Esprits. Mercedes has left the smaller cabin to Callum and the larger one to Lucinda and Dermot, along with a substantial sum of money. Annie is grateful for the peace this will bring her mother. She is hardly paying attention when Tom Kennedy informs them that, except for several small bequests, the remainder of Mercedes' estate is to be divided, one half going to The Meade House for Unwed Mothers, the other half to her niece, Annie Byrne.

Annie is blindsided. Her mind is numb. She knows she should have questions but before she can get her bearings, the meeting is over. On his way out, Kennedy asks her to meet him in an hour. Then everyone rushes to congratulate her, making a great noisy fuss as if she's just caught the prize fish of the day.

When she enters Kennedy's office, she has a sense of the familiar. She wonders briefly if she might have been here before, but then realizes it is the smell she recognizes, an earthy, spicy scent. Before she can identify it, Kennedy rushes in.

"Sorry I'm late. I was seeing one of your aunt's beneficiaries, Gerry Griffin. Had to run by her house to get something she wanted him to have." Without waiting for a response, he hands her a plain white envelope. "Mercedes left this for you, said she hoped it would explain things."

Annie thanks him and slips the envelope into her pocket, preoccupied with the knowledge that Gerry had been in the office before her, that they might have bumped into each other in the waiting room, or in the doorway, or in the hall.

"Annie?" Kennedy is looking at her, waiting for something. "I said I have to witness you read it. She was very specific about that."

"Oh." Annie's fingers fumble to open the letter. There are two pages, written in Mercedes' strong hand.

"Dear Annie, I am so sorry for the pain that I have caused you."

Annie's heart beats faster. After all they've been through, why now is Mercedes sorry?

"You have suffered more than anyone else because of something that happened to me many years ago. I will not rest unless you know the reason why.

"Gerry Griffin's grandfather, Paddy Griffin, was your grandfather too. I am Lucinda's mother. Paddy Griffin was her biological father."

Annie hears herself gasp. She can feel Tom Kennedy looking at her. She stands and walks to an open window before continuing.

"Callum and his late wife adopted Lucinda at birth but we were never allowed to tell anyone. Judith threatened that she would make Callum's life a living hell if he ever breathed a word. She kept the threat alive even after she was dead. The only other person we have ever told is Lucinda. She had a right to know, as do you."

"When I saw you and Gerry together, I panicked. Sharing a grandmother was bad enough, but I assumed you had both come to terms with that as well as with Sadie's connections to the family. But sharing a grandfather too, there could be no getting around that, not in your hearts, not in the eyes of God.

"All these years I have steadfastly kept the past where it belongs, knowing it was the only way to protect Callum and Lucinda. It never occurred to me that by doing so I could cause you such heartache. I could not bring myself to tell you in person. I couldn't bear to see the look in your eyes when you found out the truth.

"So I told Gerry, some of it anyway, and begged him to trust me when I said it could cause you irreparable harm. I traded on our friendship when I made him swear to leave you and to keep my secret. Gerry has always kept that promise. He has been a true friend to an old unhappy woman."

Annie's hand shakes as she moves on to the second page. For so long she's been tormented by the fact that Gerry and Mercedes' friendship survived, flourished even, despite what happened. How was it that they had been able to forgive each other but not her, or her them? Until this moment, she's always felt the blame must lie with her.

"As I have watched you from afar, it has been my greatest fear that you will grow old, alone and bitter, and become the woman that I am. You have a right to know why Gerry left and that it was not your fault. The rest, how it all came to be so long ago, is no longer important. It is best left buried."

A dull ache settles in Annie's throat.

"As for the abortion, it was the only thing you could have done, Annie. It was not a union to produce a healthy child. That was why I goaded you into it. I believe that God has forgiven us. It is time for you to do the same."

The tears come as the truth of the letter hits home. Breathing deeply of the fresh salt air that sweeps in through the window, she glances outside, up the hill to the graveyard where Mercedes lies. Her grandmother.

"The only person who has all the answers is Callum, the man who has always been your grandfather. Believe me when I tell you he has good reason not to share them.

"As for the money, I pray it brings you freedom and happiness.

"Finally, your mother. Be good to her, for me. Let her into your life.

"I have always had the greatest faith in you, Annie. I wish I could have told you that. Perhaps I should have."

It was signed, simply, "Mercedes."

Annie refolds the pages and slips them back into the envelope. There are so many questions, so much unknown. But she decides that today is not the day to look for answers. Today, she will respect Mercedes' wishes.

After finishing with the paperwork, Kennedy sees her to the door. Outside on the sidewalk, she takes a moment to gather her thoughts. Eyes closed, she leans her back against the brick face of the building, trying to absorb all she has learned. So much has changed.

Footsteps approach. Instinctively she knows.

She opens her eyes. He stands before her, hands in his pockets, his gaze steady on her face. She remembers the familiar aroma in Kennedy's office.

She glances away, off to the side, anywhere but at him, wanting only to escape.

Then he says her name. "Annie. Please don't go."

Hearing his voice, it's impossible to leave. So she turns and faces him and gives herself a good long look at the man who has owned her heart for so long. His face is more mature, thinner perhaps, the cheekbones more pronounced. Otherwise he has not changed. As his deep, dark eyes look into hers for the first time in five years, she is suddenly struck with the fear that he might ever discover the truth. She shivers in the warm June breeze.

He reaches out. "Are you cold?"

She shakes her head, doesn't trust herself to speak yet.

His hand hovers in the air. "I've thought of this moment so many times, and hoped for it every time I came home. But you were never here."

Annie has purposely avoided him, coming home at odd times, mid-March, October, except for that one Christmas when she knew he wouldn't be there. "I'm in Calgary," she says. "I have to go. I have to help Mom." She is terrified that if she keeps looking into those eyes, she will let slip something that can only cause them both more pain. "Sorry… I've got to go."

He catches her wrist. "Annie, I have to talk to you, to explain what happened."

His voice again, this time reinforced by the touch of his skin on hers, those warm strong fingers that press into her lonely flesh.

She turns and leads him silently up towards the hill by the graveyard. They sit on the same boulders she played on as a girl, hidden from the world by evergreens, surrounded by the unearthly security of nearby tombstones.

She takes out Mercedes' letter and hands Gerry the first page. "Read this, then we can talk."

She stares off into the sky's fading daylight, his nearness and the warm scent of him opening the door to memories she'd long ago locked away. He is soon finished.

"Yes, finally I know too." She manages to say it with only a tiny tip of bitterness. "I just found out in Kennedy's office."

"So many times I thought of writing to you and explaining everything. But I'd think of your aunt, the fear in her eyes, how hard it was for her to tell me what she did. And I'd remember the promise I made her." He is quiet for a moment. "Then there was my mother. In the end, I had to make her a promise too."

"Oh? What was that?"

"To never see you again." His eyes shine with a film of tears. "But honest to God, I didn't really believe it would be this long before I did."

"Never is a long time," she says.

"Too long." He waits a moment before continuing. "I've never seen my mother so furious as she was that night. It was like she was possessed or something. All she could see was the two of us together, me with Lucinda Byrne's daughter. It sent her over the top. She threatened to ruin us all - you, Mercedes, even her own family, if I didn't do what she said."

"How? Did she know about it all?"

"The truth is, I wasn't sure what she knew, and I certainly wasn't going to tell her. All I knew was that it was possible. With Ma, anything is." He pauses and looks off into the distance, then shakes his head and grins wryly. "It took me a long time to forgive her, but in the end I had to let it go." His voice softens. "She's my mother."

"The things we do for family, eh?"

"Yeah. Like Pat."

"Pat? What about him?" She keeps her eyes down, focused on the ground. Please, dear God, tell me he kept his mouth shut.

"It was the year you moved out west. I was home for Christmas and stopped in at the bar. And there were the Hann boys, feeling no pain. No sooner did Pat set eyes on me than he starts ranting on about what an arsehole I was and how it was all my fault you left. Aiden was right behind him too, with that stupid smirk on his face."

Annie can picture it, Pat fighting mad, Aiden letting his older brother stir things up while he, as usual, stood back and enjoyed the spectacle.

"Then Pat mutters something about promising to break my neck and takes a few swipes at me but he's too drunk to do any damage. Couple of guys hauled him away but I just went on home. Last thing I wanted was to fight with Pat, drunk or sober."

"I really am sorry, Gerry. We always looked out for each other, you know, the three of us, since we were kids. They're more like brothers than cousins." The thought comes immediately - *and you don't sleep with your cousin*. She forces herself to ask the question. "How did you feel about it, our being so closely related, after what we did?" She watches his face, so strong in its new maturity.

"I tell you, I didn't feel ashamed." His voice is defiant. "I know I was supposed to. I tried telling myself that what we did was wrong but I could never convince myself it was wicked or sinful or any of the words my mother used that night."

"She was that mad, eh?"

"Beside herself! You wouldn't believe what came out of that mouth."

"But that's not fair. We didn't know any better. Why was she blaming you?"

Gerry hesitates. "She wasn't blaming me. She was blaming you, plus your whole entire family. She's always had such a grudge, about Paddy and Farley, and about your parents, and that she was a cousin and nobody ever invited her into the fold. She used to rant on about it sometimes, call you all mental cases, especially when she was drinking."

Annie is not sure how to react. For one thing, the Griffins have always been the ones with the reputation for mental instability. For another, Sadie forever proclaimed to be a teetotaller.

"I know what you're thinking." Gerry nudges her. "Them crazy Griffins, queer as three-dollar bills, them are."

She laughs lightly. He takes her hand. Her heart leaps with the gentle pressure, the feel of his skin touching hers.

"Now it's your turn," he says. "How did you feel when you found out?"

His fingers caress the back of her hand. She fights the urge to tuck into him, to bury her face in the warm skin of his neck. When she is slow to respond, he insists. "Come on, Annie. There's been too much time, too many questions. Can we just be honest?"

She moves her hand away. "You want honesty? Fine." She is surprised at the anger in her voice. "Of course it was wrong. It'd be worse than sleeping with Pat or Aiden."

His face tightens but he says nothing.

"But it's not the same, I know that. The thought of doing it with either one of them is just...I can't even think about it." She shudders at the thought. "But I could never feel that way about me and you. I know I'm supposed to, but I don't." Her voice has shrunk to a harsh whisper.

She slides off the rock and walks towards the trees, opening her eyes wide in an attempt to stop the tears. She feels him come up behind her.

His hand touches her hair. She knows she should move away but she is as rooted to the ground as the trees that surround them. His fingers stroke her cheek. He turns her gently and folds her in his arms. Beyond resisting, she inhales the familiar scent of his skin, feels again the safe, strong rhythm of his heart.

Wrapped in a world of sense and touch and earth and trees, they draw apart just enough to find each other for that last kiss, the one they never had, as she allows the years this one forbidden moment on a hidden hillside by the graveyard in St. Jude.

But for Annie, a moment is all it can ever be. The memory of what happened to her, to them, to a baby that still lived in her heart, is too much. A vital part of her will grieve forever over what she did, her belief in its necessity notwithstanding. She steps away from his reach.

"Annie? Isn't there any way?" Tears glisten in his dark eyes. "What if we never had children, then couldn't we be together? Nobody knows, right? We were lucky before, we'll just make sure from here on out."

She feels her body stiffen. He must notice for suddenly he grips her arms so hard it hurts. "Annie? What is it?" His anxious eyes search hers.

The grief strikes so hard it's as if the abortion happened the day before. And suddenly, she knows. This is the intangible something that has been with her since that day, this empty ache, this blank space in her soul. This will always be between them.

"Annie? You were never pregnant, were you? Oh Jesus Almighty, tell me!"

She hears the fever in his voice, the guilt, the regret. It's a story of hurt that is well known to her but not one she wishes on Gerry. In all the daydreams and nightmares that have come unbidden since the night he left her, she has never wished him such pain as that.

They have shared their final moment. She means to keep it, for both of them.

"Good God no, Gerry." For the first time she empathizes

with Mercedes. Some truths should not be shared. Sometimes a lie is necessary. "It's just that all my life I've wanted children. I can't give that up."

His eyes hold hers and won't let go.

She stands her ground.

Annie feels a measure of peace for the first time in years. She has not been wrong about the only man she has ever been able to love, and she will no longer have to go through life constantly trying to hate Gerry Griffin. Reaching up, she lets her fingers trace his face, from his brow to his eyes, down his cheek to his lightly bristled chin, across his mouth to the fading scar on his lip.

Then she walks away.

In need of solitude before facing her family, Annie goes to the church. Choosing a pew near the back, she kneels and bows her head. Her hands find each other, the fingers interlacing. Marble statues and stained glass surround her, familiar, peaceful. In recent years, except for Christmas and the occasional wedding or baptism, she has left the church, and God, to others. She breathes in the aromatic echoes of incense and lemon oil and realizes she has missed it; despite a childhood spent whining about Lent and Easter and having to go to Mass "every frigging day for forty days." Smiling at the memory, she touches her right hand to her forehead, then down to her chest, to her left shoulder then her right. She's ready to go home.

When she arrives at her parents' house, the party is in full progress. The first few drinks have been downed and the crowd has moved on to sombre toasts and overblown memories. The Murphy brothers lead a sing-along of dirges in the kitchen, and her Uncle Frank, well in his cups, is in the middle of a long-winded recital about some other poor soul who had the bad luck to die. All in honour of Mercedes. With the earth still settling around her coffin, Annie thinks she must be doing somersaults in her grave.

Then again, maybe not.

Pat is there of course, surprisingly sober, his enunciation clear as a bell as he asks how she's feeling about it all.

"A little shell-shocked, actually." She glances around. "Quite the send off, eh? Wonder what she'd think."

He laughs. "If she was here, she'd be gone by now."

"Isn't that the truth? Where's Aiden?"

"Him and your father are out back smoking cigars." He takes a small sip of beer.

"Cigars? Tying one on, are they?"

"Three sheets to the wind, the pair of them."

Annie sizes him up. "What's slowing you down?"

He studies his beer bottle. "I got to make a change, Annie."

"Ever think about moving away? Lots of jobs out west."

"Possible, I suppose. But I was thinking more of doing something else, something altogether different." He lowers his voice. "Maybe going back to school."

"Wow, talk about different."

He grins. "Not like I ever excelled at the books."

"Not like you ever tried."

"Probably time I did, eh? I'm twenty-six years old and going nowhere." He plunks the bottle of beer on the table. "I don't want to be doing this in ten years."

"Hey, you don't have to sell me. I think it's a great idea."

"You do? I mean, there's lots would think I couldn't do it."

"Like Aunt Mercedes, you mean?" The name feels different on Annie's tongue, not quite right, but better than before.

Pat's shrug looks like a gesture of surrender. "I think she had a point. About me wasting my life."

"You agreeing with Mercedes Hann? This is a day of surprises."

"Maybe so. But maybe that's why I couldn't stand her. I knew she was right when she called me a no-good Irish Paddy."

"There's nothing wrong with an Irish Paddy, Pat. It was all in her mind. So," she says quickly to change the subject, "what kind of school you talking about?"

He hesitates, then says sheepishly, "Cooking school."

"Sure that's a great idea. But what brought this on suddenly?"

"I hate fishing. I throws up my guts most days, and with Aiden gone, it's no fun at all anymore." He eyes her shyly. "What do you think? Is it too late?"

"Go on, it's never too late, but you better get on it. Like you said, you're not getting any younger."

He grins and picks up his beer. "I'll run it by Aiden, see what he got to say."

"Good luck with that," she says to his back as he walks away.

She goes in search of Lucinda and Callum. They're in the living room putting everything back in its rightful place. With the coffin gone, the room feels empty.

"Need some help?" Annie asks from the doorway.

Her mother looks up. "Where did you get to?"

"Nowhere." She stops. Lucinda stands there looking resigned, as if she knows Annie will only tell her what suits her. "I ran into Gerry," Annie admits.

Her mother puts down the candle she's holding. "Are you okay?"

Annie shrugs. The truth is, her heart is still broken.

"Is there anything we can do?" asks Lucinda.

Annie offers up Mercedes' letter. "I'd like you to read this. Both of you."

Annie walks to the window. She waits patiently. She needs her mother, now more than ever. She needs Lucinda to forgive her so that she can forgive herself.

Lucinda comes up beside her. She tucks her arm into Annie's and squeezes it. Annie squeezes back. They stand quietly together.

"Thank you, Annie," Lucinda says finally.

"What for, Mom?" This was not the reaction she'd expected.

"For trusting me."

Annie leans her head against her mother's. "It took me long enough."

Callum joins them at the window. "Some things in life are better taken to the grave. Other things are best shared with people who love you." He touches Annie's cheek. "I'm just so sorry you had to go through all that, and all alone."

Annie lets out a long sigh. She feels an immense relief. For the first time in what seems like forever, she is free of the weight of anger and betrayal she has dragged around for so long.

The evening is still and clear with a cloudless sky. It is almost too calm, too perfect. Her eye is drawn to the tires in the front yard. Something is growing in the middle tire but Annie can't tell from this distance if it's a weed or a flower. All she can see is a tiny green shoot struggling to poke through the hard Newfoundland clay.

Epilogue

Sadie plants her bum on the stuffed chair that looks directly out the window. She sits patiently, seemingly watching every movement, yet, on this particular occasion, oblivious to all but the far end of the street. There is a throbbing in her temple.

Must be all that tea Gerard poured into me last night. Too much milk in it, gave me nightmares. Up to the bathroom half the night. Ah, no odds. Don't matter now.

Anticipation thrills through her. She smiles and tugs down her skirt to cover her knees and the run in her stocking.

A new dress. Yes, and new stockings too. I deserves it, no doubt about that. Gerard too. Wish he'd get here, find out what she left him. Better be some of that money Bessie was going on about. Least she could do after all he done for her. Not just him, me too, putting up with them stuck-up ways. Make you sick sometimes. Old bitch filling him with high-falutin' notions of what a smartie he was. Hah! Well, he got me to thank, not that old bag.

Sadie reaches into her apron pocket and brings out her flask. She undoes the cap and sniffs at the opening. Smiling, she takes a small sip. She licks her lips, then sips again, savouring the rich taste of the brandy – a special treat for a special day.

Fine-looking man, my Gerard. Them big brown eyes. And so tall, and right smart. Not like what followed on his heels, thick, green-eyed Griffins all. Not the brightest lot, even if they are half mine. Then again, other half's Angus, so what can you expect. Angus! That fucker! Yes, we are so still married, even if he's dead. Just because he took up with that French waiter in Montreal, don't mean nothing. I got the marriage license. Ah, who cares? Got what I wanted in the end. Best thing is, no one got a frigging clue.

Balanced perfectly upright on the chair, Sadie laces her fingers together and rotates her thumbs around and around each other in a continuous circle.

Oh yes, I can keep a secret. No one knows better than me how to hold the truth so far down it'll never see the light of day again. I got to laugh at that. Who'd question me? Goes without saying I'm a God-fearing woman, free and clear of bodily sins. Hah! Stunned as my arse, the lot of them.

Sadie lets her eyes almost close, and her mind sails back to another time, to the young priest she kept house for all those years ago. She moistens her mouth as she pictures him, so tall and handsome, much like young Father James, but better, with those nut-brown eyes that would smile shyly at her when she came in each morning to clean. His bedroom, she always started there, so she could catch the warm, musk smell of him before he'd been gone from the room for too long.

Some good, that.

Then there was the morning she arrived earlier than usual, using the key he gave her for when he had to go out of town. She knew he'd returned early from his trip. Tiptoeing in she found him sleeping in his virgin bed. Damask-curtained windows shut out the morning and the rest of the world. She approached the bed. Her sure hands stole beneath the heavy bedclothes. Before long he rose up, almost as if in protest. The body does not lie, however, and his lay well with hers, melding so they became one under the thick cover of the darkened bedroom.

Locked into her favourite memory, a moan escapes her lips, a tiny guttural sigh. She looks around to make sure she's still alone, then snuggles back into the past and her young priest once more, the frowzy scent of him reborn in her mind. She sees again his room where not a ray of light gained entry into their secret world. After that first time he'd wait every week, eyes shut tight, barely breathing in anticipation beneath the quilted bedclothes. Famished for it, he was always ready.

Seconds after she'd find him, his long sensuous fingers and fine strong hands would pull her onto him, onto his firm, muscled, young flesh.

Sadie sighs deeply, satisfied.

The whole town had missed the nice young priest when he'd up and transferred after only a year in the parish. Rumour had it he left the priesthood soon after.

Fool! Went off to Africa somewhere to join a mission or some such nonsense. Right after I give birth to Gerard, it was. Men! So stupid, every last one of them. Dumb as a sack of hammers. Of course, most women are too. Clueless. Dumb and stupid and clueless. Amazing. After all these years, still my little secret. Hah!

THE END

ACKNOWLEDGEMENTS

This novel has been a long time in the making, and a number of people have given me good advice and constructive criticism over the years, all of which has been greatly appreciated. I specifically want to thank the following: Cecelia Frey, Dixie Baum, Sue Hirst, Joan Beswick, Margo Embury.

A special thank-you to my editor, Ed Kavanagh.

And finally, to Donna Francis, I owe a special debt of gratitude, for her patience, perseverance and good humour, and for always being open to another draft.